# Golden Dunes of Renhala

Book 2 of the Renhala Series

Amy Joy Lutchen

**Golden Dunes of Renhala**

(Book 2 of Renhala Series)

by

Amy Joy Lutchen



ISBN: 978-0-9882815-5-4

Publisher: Amy Joy Lutchen



The characters and events portrayed in this book are fictitious. Thank you for respecting the hard work of this author.

# Dedication

This book is dedicated to the man who called me his own, despite no blood bond. This is dedicated to the man I knew would always be support, despite his own shaky ground full of pitfalls. This is dedicated to the man I knew as Dad.

*To feel sunshine beaming softly on your skin, to only feel it blister the surface;*

*To wallow in the aroma of a garden of roses, to only choke on the congestion;*

*To imagine love wrapped around your heart; to only experience the smother;*

*To know the peace from a loved one's existence; to only shatter at the thought of loss;*

*To know sudo-abominor is to discover hatred wrapped in a lovely package.*

# Chapter 1

## Guilt

His lunges are quick like an agitated cobra, but I match his speed, increasing only slightly with each movement, not revealing my true potential. He's persistent with his swings and I let him continue, hoping to tire him out before he makes any stupid move that he may regret. I pity him in some odd way, with his dull blade and twice as dull excuses. And he just won't give in despite the strong probability of me slicing him in half with the weapon on my back.

His guilt is apparent, and not merely from the fact that he practically high-tailed it in the opposite direction after I approached and mentioned a mere name to him; his guilt is apparent through its simple existence inside of him and the heavy weight of the energy it emits, for I can feel its solidness weighing down his actions, making him just a bit slower with each swing. He's a torn soul and fighting not just me, but also against his own inner demons.

As I ponder the irony of our situation, I repeatedly dodge his advances, becoming bored with the consistency of his method: left swing, right swing, right swing, left swing. I imagine him working in the fields, slicing with his scythe and harvesting his acres of beloved hartflower crops for piddly gold chips. Besides the occasional wrestle with his faithful companion, it's clear he's never had to truly defend himself against bodily harm. He's simply going through the motions his brain is accustomed to.

I've got to stop this before *it* wakes.

"Now how about you stop waving that hunk of metal in your hand before you hurt yourself," I advise, beginning to push back a bit more with each deflection of his blows. His eyes widen at my sudden bursts of energy.

"Why should I?" he spits, sweating driblets of guilt from his pores.

"Because you loved Vanette…once," I reply, giving up one of only a few clues I was given by her father, a current client. I then notice the sudden twinge in his energy field and sense the small hole that has opened at the mention of her name. I immediately send out my feeler to burrow, and just as I enter and notice his eyes widen at the intrusion, the preoccupation of my current task diverts my attention from any *physical* advance. He makes his move. Gathering the last of his strength, he blasts forward with one might last-resort blow.

As I come to my senses a moment too late and avoid the knife burrowing into my jugular, I manage to allow the tip to delicately slice the skin on my neck. He freezes from surprise and watches my face as I withdraw my energy feeler. My hand rises to feel the droplets of blood as they slowly form on the incision. I'm suddenly lost to memories of a painful past—a past that I've tried so hard to forget.

The sight of my blood on my hand awakens that which was sleeping soundly, that which this poor soul before me will soon regret provoking.

My eyes slowly rise to meet his and as I dismount the now-warm pole weapon off my back and hold it firmly in both hands, he takes a step back, perhaps recognizing the spark with which he lit the fire, or merely from being scared shitless at the sight of the two deadly-sharp blades on opposite ends of the pole I hold with authority. He's several feet away now and distances himself still further as the cinders inside me begin burning a bit brighter.

"Stop, please," he pathetically groans as I walk toward him. I continue my approach, ignoring his request. "Stop!" He starts swinging again, but I swat at his arm with my pole, knocking his weapon to the ground. "She deserved what she got! But…but…*I* didn't do it!" he screams.

"Oh. My bad," I respond as I stand still, looking as though I'm pondering a deep thought. "So maybe *you* didn't do the deed. I still need to ask you: How much did you pay to end the pain? One crop's worth? Two? Or everything you had?"

His jaw clenches, knowing I know. "She was a con artist! She was a whore!" *Whore.* The word instantly sets the fire ablaze, and I fight to contain it. "And everyone knew it! Even her father!" he exclaims. "Ask any man in town. Why waste your time!" He drools as he spurts out his useless excuses. "So I paid him to break her heart. As she broke so many…" he sobs as I stand within three feet of him, our proximity not enough to free him from the threat of incineration.

"Whore is such a strong word, you know," I state calmly, letting him collect his thoughts before I complete my contract—not how I intended—but finished, nonetheless. His body shakes as his brain tries configuring a next step. In watching his sore attempts at collecting himself, I decide to allow him one more chance. "Just let me bring you back to town to face her father and you can duke it out, man-to-man." I don't make any hesitation as I approach him and watch as his shoulders slump low, his head bowing even lower. He's broken and it's his time to face the consequences.

*Broken.* I despise this word even more, but sympathy still finds its way to slowly slink forward from the fire, cautiously making its steps across the hot coals. I breathe in deeply, giving it the time needed to reach safety. "Come," I say as I put out my hand to touch his shoulder, allowing sympathy to quench the last flame. Perhaps karma has a soft spot for broken hartflower harvesters that pay for hits.

Unfortunately, karma has different plans for me, for my display of care proves to be my biggest mistake. His right hook connects directly to my cheekbone, forcing me to my knees and refueling sudo-abominor's anger to a fiery magnificence. It's a useless fight against my conscience and I allow myself one tear as I suddenly move with the quickness of a fox. I'm up quicker than a blink of an eye, and with one smooth movement, I jab my spade through his gut in a sad sort of satisfaction.

His eyes widen one last time pleading for mercy, but I simply turn the spade, spilling his blood and demolishing his organs. "An eye for an eye, asshole. Karma's a boastful bitch." As his life energy drains away, but enough is left for him to hear and understand, I whisper, "She was five weeks pregnant."

The last of his energy leaves his body in a single tear which trails down his cheek.

He lies on the grass just as Vanette did, accepting death's open arms. Only *his* heart is still in his chest, and not pinned to the town's bulletin board with a rusty blade—another one of the clues I was privy to before this assignment.

My pregnancy remark briefly brings my thoughts to someone I haven't seen in some time—someone who enters my thoughts repeatedly, and I find myself often trying to switch gears in my rattled brain to avoid the tainted walk down memory lane. I cannot even fathom seeing her stupid face at this point in my life.

Fortunately I hear faint rustling from behind, redirecting my thought pattern to instead comprehend that which comes forth. I do not budge, though, recognizing now what draws near by the simple vacancy of energy. The tall and lean deathman, with all its internal organs hanging inside-out, walks by me as I stand and watch; I'm always ready for the absorbing show of magic. It approaches the dead body and stares a stare void of emotion while moving its hand to settle directly over the body. Then before my eyes, a beautifully shiny, iridescent spectral orb lifts from the lifeless chest and the deathman grabs it with its long bony fingers, caressing it. The orb is then closely examined as it's turned over and over, the deathman's eyes peering into the sinful acts of man. Then with one quick snap it's popped into its mouth.

"I know where *that* one's going. Take it easy." Understanding my words or not, the deathman suddenly waves hello as I turn and instantly travel to collect on this contract—one of my *many* pitiful and maybe-useless contracts. The contracts that usually end up just like this one. I have to do *something* productive with this curse while I can still somewhat control it, because once the control ends, may Neda have mercy on all our souls.

# Chapter 2

## Desperation

"Kailey. Kailey. *Kailey! Wake up!"*

I open one drowsy eye to see her angry little face staring back down at me. Immediately I close it and roll over on my side. "I was having the most wonderful dream, you know."

She climbs over me to get a better view of my face and the small cut on my neck. "I don't care right now. You do realize what appointment you are late for right now, don't you?" She holds on to the collar of my pajamas with enough strength to choke an ox and I can feel her anger like electrical currents tingling down my spine. I notice she smells like my shampoo.

"Jenna, fifteen more minutes." Slowly my body turns to the other side and I pull my covers, forcing her to lose her balance and fall off the bed, hard—all three pounds of her.

She rubs her clothes down gently, adjusts her holly necklace, and fixes her nappy woodsprite hair—which might I add, none of my hair products could ever fix—then screams, *"I am not covering for you this time you stupid girl, no matter what your 'affliction.'"* She storms off and I hear her punching numbers in her little cell phone which I think she has super-glued to her hand. I know damn well who I am making wait for me—and let's just say I know how bad he needs me.

Staring at the urn on my dresser and thinking thoughts of a friend whose ashes are now in a plastic baggie inside that very urn, I can't help but smile as Jenna's voice rises slightly as she talks into her phone. "Yes, I know you have entrusted me, but you know her and her little *problem.* I can't control her, only watch over her. Do you know how many smartphones I'd have to sell if she fails?" She's quiet for a brief moment, then adds, "She'll be there in ten minutes if you send Fidello." My ears catch the noise of my blinds rolling up. "Yeah," she says. "He's here."

"Damn." I mumble as I roll out of bed, knowing that if he is here, I have to get ready. "I'm almost dressed you little runt," I growl as I pull on black stretch pants.

"Don't wear black again, *please*," she yells from my kitchen. I roll my eyes.

"Don't roll your eyes at me," she says from afar.

"I didn't." I stick out my tongue in the direction of the kitchen.

"I saw that."

To my black pants I add an equally black, tight tee-shirt emblazoned with a zombie kitten on the front, and look at myself in the mirror. I look good, in a heroin addict sort of way, with dark circles under my eyes and a bruise on my left cheekbone. If I swish my head just the right way, my long red hair covers the bruise up nicely.

"Black…ah, but I see you dressed it up with a lovely dead cat. Nice." She makes me jump and I blush at her attempt to make me feel better as she stands in the doorway—all six inches of her, giving me her best motherly impression: eyes soft with care as she hands me a toasty, insulated cup of tea. Her eyes then wander to Mortimer's urn. "Can't we do something with that? It still creeps me out."

"No. Don't ask again."

With no retort, she quietly climbs into my shoulder bag, settling in and making herself cozy. I breathe in a deep breath as I take a long sip of tea, letting the warmth and citrusy taste of bergamot prepare me for the day's work. It's funny how a simple thing like tea makes the days livable—well, at least easier—for me. I thank my mother to myself, for she's the very reason I am addicted.

I make sure to give Kioto, my hefty female Akita, a special dog bakery cookie: the kind that smells so good I had to lick it myself…once. Believe me, I'll never do it again. There's a mighty big difference between "Fresh Apple Pie" in the human world versus the same in dog world, and all those dogs are surely missing out.

Along with her treat, Kioto gets her morning kiss on the forehead. Her mouth turned up in a grin, she settles in a corner with her treasure, making sure nobody follows.

I stare as she savors her treat and I feel the bond between us, as tight as the day I found her wandering an alley, scrounging on scraps with her tiny, needle-sharp puppy teeth. She caught me watching her that day and scampered over to me, ears down and tail gently swishing back and forth, feigning submission to a human, only to distract me from her sneaky snatch of the one bite of gourmet peanut butter cookie I had in my coat pocket. After she chomped on my cookie and licked me with her peanut butter-coated tongue, I was immediately lost to her charm, forever in love with a stray.

Since that chance meeting, she's actually saved my life on several occasions, making her more valuable to me every day, and making my love for my baby unmatched by any other mother. I'd do anything to keep her safe and happy.

As I now look down at her, I catch sight of an old faded bloodstain under the dining room table. Instantly a memory of the birth of two adorable creatures under this very table comes to mind. It was a moment of high stress, but as I stand and think back to the outcome of the event, I remember the moment of clarity and respect for the birthing process I felt that day, and suddenly feel a pull at my heartstrings. Despite the blood that was shed upon my carpet, I had experienced the joy of new life as Cheeto, my acquired pet ceetchan, gave birth to two tiny—but dangerous—pups.

Now you won't find ceetchans (large raccoon-like creatures with razor-sharp fangs) at any zoo, or even on a page of National Geographic, because, well, they are native to an entirely different realm than this—a secret realm to most—known as Renhala, the very place where I was born.

As memories have their way of leading the mind to yet other trains of thought, I wallow in the thought of Renhala and the day I had to set my ceetchans free. Just as I learned to appreciate the gift of birth through meeting them, I also learned to respect loss. I had to make the conscious decision to let them live in their native environment for their own safety, and ok, maybe for the safety of my own fingers as well—feeding time was turning into a real risk.

I sigh to myself, and Jenna, noticing my mood, tells me, "They're thriving, Kailey. Don't worry about them. Let's go."

I turn down the lights, lock my door, and walk out my door to the stairs of my six flat. My eyes are drawn to the carpet of the hallway. I notice some sort of reddish-brown stains resembling footsteps on the Berber. I look closely, running my hands over the marks. "What's this?" I notice one directly in front of my door. "Who did this?" Discreetly, I smell my hand.

Jenna sneaks a peek. "You step in something nasty?"

"No."

"Your *boyfriend* step in something nasty?"

"No. These are bigger than my feet, and smaller than his." I continue squatting and begin concentrating as I touch the marks, but get nothing.

Jenna then adds, "Yeah, you'd surely know about the size, alright." She waits…and waits, but I don't even acknowledge her sarcasm as my heart beats a bit fast, my mind running in circles.

"Let's go!" she demands, angrily pulling me from my reckless thoughts and getting my feet moving back down the stairs. I hear my neighbor, Karen, partying it up next door. Ever since her foster child, "Philip," was "turned back over" to the state, she's been keeping loud company and listening to even louder music. Oh, and I hear the occasional flipped cup falling on her kitchen floor which usually results in bursts of cackling laughter. She's becoming increasingly bothersome these days, playing loud music at all hours of the day. Okay, maybe it's part jealousy, but some people actually have adult-like responsibilities around here. I stick my tongue out at her door and continue downstairs.

Intimidatingly burly Fidello is waiting patiently, shimmering in the sun, holding the door open for me as I walk to the limo. On raised tiptoes I kiss him on the cheek as he frowns at me, but I see the corner of his mouth turn up slightly, hinting that he still loves me despite my antics. The door closes firmly, letting me know there is no escaping. Wordless, he climbs in the driver's seat, his head just clearing the ceiling. I see his dark brown eyes watching me through the rearview mirror. His long black hair is pulled back tightly and his presence is one of strength and cool contemplation. He resembles one of Native American heritage, but he was born in Renhala, specifically a region known as Descindo, where they birth special individuals like Fidello: namakons. And Fidello, *as a namakon*, belongs to my friend and confidante: elderly, Asian Gunthreon. Magically they share thoughts, and I can tell by Fidello's glare that Gunthreon is now aware I am under *their* supervision.

Once we begin moving, it's Jenna's clue to jump out of my bag and lighten up a bit. She sits on the limo bar, looking out the window and swallowing several times before we make it past my pothole-riddled block. Her stomach cannot handle driving in vehicles—dragon rides yes, but car rides no. She is doing her best to look at the horizon, but despite Fidello's wonderful ability to create smooth rides, he is not dodging every hole. I give her a small piece of peppermint that Fidello keeps in his limo, especially for her. "Thanks Kailey. I love you," she says without looking at me, and lies down on the seat, closing her eyes and curling up into a fist-sized ball. I pet her hair as we drive to our destination.

I whisper, "I love you, too."

We pull up to an overly audacious, stone-ensconced mansion with three cupolas, a four-car garage, and two carriage houses. The lawn is lush and the landscape is perfectly manicured, down to the very placement of the smallest pieces of cypress mulch. Even the ivy climbs in a pattern. The house screams money.

Jenna wakes, as does my feeler. My heart begins beating a little faster and I say out loud, "Nobody said *he* was gonna be here! This reunion will be the death of me." His energy feels hot and wet, making certain unmentionables of my own feel the same. I gather my courage and think back to our last encounter. It's been nine months since I last saw him, and all the feelings come rushing back full force, no matter how hard I try to convince myself that time heals all wounds. I think it's more like "time inflates all egos," because I see him in the window, a smirk already plastered across his face.

Fidello opens my door and I take a deep breath, attempting to stabilize the chaos running rampant in my chest. My feet moving slowly, I eventually make it to the front porch as Jenna quickly runs inside through the front door which is open a crack—big enough for a fluffmouse. I follow through the doorway and he stands before me, calm and collected. His eyes catch sight of the bruise on my face but do not reveal his thoughts; they do, however, scan my tight shirt and the area where my bra would be if I was wearing one, sending shivers through my body. "Nice…kitty," he says.

Gunthreon walks in from the kitchen, holding his arms out to me and thankfully diverting my attention from *him*. "My little karmelean. I've missed you." His hug is firm and he only flinches slightly as he releases me. He doesn't like the feel of what haunts me: my *problem* as Jenna calls it. He holds my chin in his hands, examining my face. "Poor thing, that's a good one I must say," he fusses, the care in his eyes reflective of his love for me—so parent-like.

"Don't worry about it. How's Russell?" I ask, shaking him off, but still deeply concerned for his grandson. Russell was my ex-best friend Amber's fiancé until she cheated on him with my biological father, breaking Russell's logical frame of mind into smithereens. Russell is also Gunthreon's last living blood relative—the son of his late daughter, Saralle.

Saralle is a mystery to me for she's the only topic that Gunthreon is not willing to talk about, and I know all too well about painful topics. It's best to sometimes let the ill and sleeping dogs *die.*

"Every day in the ward seems an improvement," Gunthreon says, looking forlorn. He then smiles slightly and adds with a bit of hope, "He finally said her name out loud." I return his smile, mine with a bit of sympathy. Then he exclaims, "Oh! He gave me this to give to you. Please forgive him, for he doesn't mean to stir up ugly memories or feelings. He simply wants you to try and remember the good in her." A coiled up necklace with a simple charm is placed in my hand, and as the metal meets my skin, my hand shakes uncontrollably.

Instantly recognizing the silver heart BFF charm, I toss it into my pants pocket and attempt my trick at redirecting my thoughts from *her*, yet again. "Russell will come around in due time," I say. "Please tell him I said hello, will you?" Gunthreon nods as I nonchalantly press the bruise on my face, the puffy tissue underneath moving on its own accord, similar to an anxiety-induced eye twitch.

"Too bad you can't take some ibuprofen for that," Gunthreon remarks, willingly changing the subject back to me. "I'm assuming you closed *that* contract?" I nod. "Good. I'll have Lupa fix you up a compress for your face." He hugs me tightly and the energy shared between us mingles and briefly maintains a togetherness similar to a braided cable, almost like an umbilical cord. As he begins walking away, pulling apart our cord, I hear him say under this breath, "I'll keep praying for a *last* contract." A bit louder, he says, "I'm glad you've come around to letting us join you in your missions."

Mr. Ego-trip himself has to sneak in his own comments: "Why waste Lupa's time? She's busy cooking us some food." His eyes are glued to mine, and his voice resonates annoyance. Gunthreon, his friend before I was in the picture, waves the comment off as though nobody has spoken and leaves the room, heading toward the familiar sound of Lupa humming as she stirs some mouth-watering concoctions on the stovetop.

I stand perfectly still, praying that he'll follow Gunthreon and leave me to my own thoughts, but my prayer is not answered. He walks slowly toward me and stops inches from my feet. His penetrating stare from inches above me feels like he's scanning my brain, looking for a way in that won't be too painful. I can't even look at him without getting all worked up emotionally. His breath is slowly released as his hand rises to my face, brushing against the ugly bruise that graces it. "Oh, Kailey. Why do you continue this?" A mixture of shame and pity stirs around him. I take a small step back to release myself from it.

"I'm doing good for the community—and for all your paypockets," I profess with a bit of snottiness.

"And what are you doing to yourself?" he questions. "This reminds me of that time you shamelessly fought over that unicorn eraser in third grade." He closes the gap between us and his hand moves hair away from my eye, sweeping the skin on my neck, simultaneously. "And you know I don't need the *gold*."

The closeness is too much for me and as I look in his eyes, moving a tad bit closer to his mouth, he suddenly turns his head to look outside the window. I take another step back from him while my heart screams to embrace him—to smother myself in "him," but he made it clear that we were to never be like "that," for whatever reason. He continues to confuse the hell out of me, even after our long hiatus.

"You know what eats me and I have to make the best of it, no matter where it may take me, Ladimer. I would think that you of all people would understand, especially after your own nine-month *retreat*." He doesn't know how to reply and when his mouth finally opens to speak, Jenna conveniently walks into the parlor and hands me an airy popover the size of her head slathered with blueberry butter. She shoves her own treat all in her mouth at once. Both Ladimer and I simply stare at her in awe.

Ladimer turns his attention back to me. "If I could do something for you, you know I would. I tried once and it almost ate me alive, Kailey. And my *retreat* was important for my own well-being. I loved her more than you'll ever know. It was eating me alive." He is alluring with his beautiful big brown eyes and his short silken blond hair and my yearning for his touch increases with every emotion I read in his energy.

Unfortunately, I know what he is referring to about being eaten alive, and it doesn't make the fact any easier to swallow. Long ago, my father, Devoten—once one of Ladimer's best friends—was consumed by my same internal affliction: sudo-abominor, and despite Ladimer's abilities, he couldn't save my father. Sudo-abominor eventually consumed him and the hate generated turned him into an evil and hateful man. Then, by request of my mother, Ladimer swore to secretly protect me throughout my lifetime. It was only a year ago that I discovered their agreement and realized that Ladimer, blessed with the ability to change his outward appearance, had been by my side as various people, keeping a watchful eye on me.

In Renhala, Ladimer is known as a "giver": one who holds the power of life and death in their hands. He can touch you and change your DNA to make you an inch taller, or he can touch you and make your lungs collapse. So basically, don't cross a giver. The fact they are few make him both a rare commodity and a scary-ass foe, coming in any shape or size, depending on his whim at the time.

Now what sudo-abominor truly is, I, as well as others, have no idea. Is it a spirit? Is it organic? Nobody knows the answer. But I do know that as a host, I can now hate with such a passion that it alters my logical decision making, at times turning me into a rampant, unpredictably violent machine, tearing the fabric of my being in half for karma's chains are inescapable. Believe me, I currently have my limits, but death flows from my fingertips with much more of a slinky ease than I would ever want to admit. Sudo-abominor turned my father into a monster—indirectly contributing to the death of my beloved mother—and then as Devoten transformed into an unsuitable host, sudo-abominor thought I'd make a much better home in which to take root and spread its undeniable charm.

Could we call this karma? Do I want to call it karma? It is hard to grasp, but given the fact that I am a karmelean, I have to admit that even I had a small part in Mom's death, also. After all, that's what karmeleans do: invoke karma by reading energies. I am now delivering upon myself each and every day, it seems.

As I look to Ladimer, I realize that sometimes I forget I am not the only one suffering. We are hoping that this reunion of powers may quiet sudo-abominor, if ever-so slightly.

My powers were awakened a little over a year ago, after I suffered a painful and demeaning assault by a stranger, which led to my formal introduction to Renhala by Gunthreon. For you see, while being beaten bloody for no apparent reason as an innumerable amount of unsubstantiated profanities were thrown at me, inside my own head I begged to any higher being listening to help me—to save me—and that was what I got: an extra light in my aura which serves as a beacon for karma. Gunthreon told me that one of the Higher Ones, the two energies which created Renhala: Neda the Kind and Velopa the Stern, reawakened this ability in me after my unspoken plea.

I also have another cool power: I can travel—it's like teleporting—*within* Renhala, which apparently nobody else can do. *And* I can soulsearch, which seems to be Gunthreon's favorite trick of mine. It's where I send a sort of invisible energy feeler outside my body and search for a living creature's energy mapping, or "print," for a better word.

I occasionally try searching for Neda the Kind, but I have had no luck finding it. I think Neda is purposely avoiding me after our last chance meeting, especially after my once-best-friend, Amber—who I found out had a small part in my life-altering assault, and was pregnant with Devoten's child (my half sibling)—disappeared after lunching with Neda, who had taken on the form of a black Louisianian English teacher. I still don't really know what became of Amber after that meeting. I tell myself I hope she got what she deserved, but then shame creeps up on me and I feel pity for the Amber I once loved and trusted—the girl *before* she met my father and infatuation buried its hooks in her soul.

Then there's the child. I really would have loved being Auntie Kailey—you know, the aunt that secretly lets her nieces and nephews stay up late watching scary movies, or the aunt that buys them that way-too-expensive-but-must-have birthday gift. I also admit that once in a while I buy that child I've never met a little gift here and there—things that I would hope might bring a warm smile or giggle. If only I could feel the child's energy and bask in the innocence we adults slowly strip ourselves of, my life might be different now. Maybe. Maybe the monster I've become wouldn't be *as* ugly.

It makes me a bit sad that despite my being a monster, the cool tricks up my sleeve make me quite the popular hire in Renhala, hence, a large influx of new clients at my place of occupation: Chicago-based Helping Hands, Inc. It's here that I deal with the trickiness of accounting for "otherworldly" realm contracts, as well as the possible ethical dilemma of karma-for-hire. But as I tell all my clients: "It's bound to happen at some time." I just possibly speed up the process.

We tend to keep my little *problem* or *secret* to ourselves, because if others outside my small circle found out about sudo-abominor, they'd most likely hunt me down like a Salem witch and curb the spread of evil by distinguishing me. Most clients just think I'm bad-ass tough and know I'll get the job done. They are totally unaware of the vile creature lurking inside of me that's ready to rip the throats out of anyone who looks at me the wrong way.

As my thoughts heat up by simply thinking of my father and Amber, so does the weapon on my back: my rune-etched monk's spade, a centuries-old artifact named for the early monks who carried the long pole weapon with them on their travels. One end has a short shovel-style spade for digging graves to bury the newly departed and the other side consists of an extremely sharp crescent-shaped blade for defense, or offense, however you like to look at it. Most Renhalan travelers have a special weapon on them at all times. In my current realm, unless you are a traveler, or I have my hand on it, you can't see the spade, but it is always there clinging to my back *and* my soul.

Ladimer feels the heat emanating from me, and turning back to his comment, says, "We are going to fix you, somehow, but you need to stop those thoughts before you burn up or explode, Kailey. There's no evidence your father is alive." I can read from his energy that he doubts what he speaks.

"Where's the key then? *He* was the key. And I know that when something disappears, there's a strong possibility it's not gone forever." He shakes his head, admitting he has no idea. "I feel something lingering similar to his energy minus sudo-abominor. His energy is alive, Ladimer." I think back to the moment my mother died, minutes before I turned my father into an inanimate object—a silver key—the very same key that disintegrated before Conner's unbelieving eyes, leaving *him* proof of Devoten's demise and a handful of a dear friend's cremated remains, but leaving *me* with an uneasy feeling of possible escape. This feeling has been somewhat confirmed, as of late, by the sensation of touching an energy very much like his, but too elusive to firmly grasp.

To add yet another tease to my life, the same day the key disappeared, I learned that I had a brother several years older than myself, whom my mother had kept a secret. I know nothing of him: his name, his location, or why he was kept a secret. My only hope, Ladimer, refuses to give me any information, stating that it's not his information to give, but my mother's. The fact she's dead doesn't seem to be relevant to him and it's wearing my patience thin. *And* I don't know my brother's energy, so I can't search for him. It seems a lost cause.

I close my eyes and think of my mother: the single most important person to ever grace my life. She may be gone from this realm, known as Abscondia, but I call to her energy beyond, often. Currently I get nothing. Her energy still tends to visit me at the oddest moments, only leaving me with a void each time she leaves, but at least it's a reminder that once we leave this life we're never *really* gone. Unfortunately, this knowledge doesn't fill the aching gap left by the death of the person I've always loved the most. I miss her every single day.

Concentrating entirely on past happy moments, I force my existing anger to dissipate, but it's only replaced by a deep and painful sorrow. Jenna steps toward me and I hold my hand up, telling her to not come any closer. Both she and Ladimer watch me, not knowing what I might do next—a common occurrence in Jenna's life these days. Their simple act of watching me turns the tides of my thoughts and a brutally loud scream suddenly escapes my mouth. Both of them jump. Seconds before Gunthreon and

Lupa enter the room, I swiftly grab my monk's spade and strike a stray spider on the wall with such force that I blast through the drywall and insulation and hit imported Renhalan stone.

Hacking at where the spider was, I collapse to the ground, dropping my monk's spade at my side. "*I hate spiders!*" I cry.

Ladimer moves to embrace me, but is interrupted as Conner enters the front door, his shaggy brown hair falling around his face. His bright blue eyes tunnel through everything and everyone in the room until falling on my face. He runs to me and strokes my hair as I attempt to breathe in a steady rhythm into his shirt, breathing in his cologne and underneath that, the scent of his skin. A small spark of electricity hits me as he makes contact with my skin—something I have grown accustomed to after many of his caresses, but I don't know exactly why it happens. He holds me tight, his beautifully-muscled physique enveloping me in a cocoon of sanctity and his energy gliding across my own, similar to a warm breeze brushing one's skin. I could stay here forever.

With an accent sounding a bit like an Irish brogue, he coos, "Let it all out, Kailey. You need to cry." He kisses my forehead as I shake my head no. "I am here for you, now." His last words are spoken in a language only souls understand. I know through this last spoken truth that he, my soulspeaker, supports me, giving me a foundation I can stand firmly upon, knowing the ground will not swallow me up whole. Conner and I are currently dating, but something deep inside constantly whispers to me that his constant support may be the only reason he is my boyfriend. I ask myself daily if that hidden voice is sudo-abominor or my conscience, but either way, I know I *need* him.

Short, solid, grey-haired Lupa holds her love, Gunthreon, as I feel the energy of the homeowner, Sir Cuche, come rushing into the room, joining our party. As Lupa tries to hold her embrace on Gunthreon, he brushes her off as Sir Cuche approaches, but unfortunately, he is too slow in his attempt to warn Sir Cuche to keep quiet. "*Look what you did to my house, you tramp!*"

Ladimer is at his throat quicker than I can blink. "Don't you *ever* call her that again, or you will never hear your own words come from your mouth again." Sir Cuche tries to speak but no sounds escape. His eyes widen in fear as Ladimer lets go of him, giving him the okay to start gasping for air through his thick brown beard.

"Ugh. Ehh. I am taking the expenses out of your fees!" He stomps off, returning to the kitchen.

Within a second's time, I shake off Conner, follow Sir Cuche, and pour myself water into one of his expensively thin crystal glasses. The liquid is cool and refreshing with a hint of lime. I then pour him a glass and set it in his hands before he can even reach the refrigerator or open his mouth to reject the offer. This lightning speed of mine is also another gift inherited from my mother who was once known as Quicksilver for her ability to move fluidly with speed and grace unmatched by any other. I only use it occasionally, though. It's too much of a reminder of how much I miss her.

Sir Cuche looks at the wall and slouches as "What?" escapes his mouth.

"Sorry…sir."

This makes him straighten up a bit in his seat and he looks directly at me. "I don't appreciate things like that you know. I am your client after all."

"Yes, well you know what to expect, don't you?" I sass, righteously. "You signed the paperwork…and you called me a *tramp*. What's up with that?"

His face is one of surprise as he responds, "That just jumped out of my mouth." His gaze then turns solemn as he continues to speak. "I beg of you to get this job done…*please*. The not knowing is killing me. I need this to be over. Hopefully your friends will help you find her."

In the months we have been working together, I have never heard the magic word from his mouth, so his desperation is in fact growing. If he's begging, he is indeed serious. Perhaps it's my friends that scare him.

I smile. "I will finished our contract by the time you have that fixed." I point toward the parlor with its torn-up wall.

"Agreed." A sweet smile forms on his lips as we shake hands. He quickly withdraws, however, as everyone else enters the kitchen. Gunthreon catches the exchange and smiles ever so briefly—but long enough for only me to notice.

Sir Cuche stands up, brushing his silk robe, sloughing off the momentary display of weakness. "Lupa," he blurts, cockily, "are you going to feed us, or do I have to have your head cut off? I can pay to have someone do that you know." We immediately all gasp at his comment and turn to look at her face.

Lupa stares at Sir Cuche, her crow's feet deepening as she raises a chef's knife and points it at his crotch. "Well you must know that I can *personally* cut that off, too. Clear?" Despite her grandmotherly appearance, Lupa can kick anyone's ass and then still have enough energy left over to bake them an apology cake.

He clears his throat and whispers, "I need to use the lavatory. Excuse me." We all laugh quietly as he leaves while Lupa furrows her brow at Gunthreon. She then wiggles the knife in the direction of *his* goods.

He immediately stops laughing and turns toward me with an attempt to change the subject. "You ready to go now?"

I know what sort of reply he is expecting and he gets it. When food is around, my mind is usually one track. "Not until I eat some of that mushroom and dill omelet." Lupa rushes to grab some plates then pours me a cup of hot water from the kettle on the stove as Conner drops a tea bag in my cup. He squeezes my shoulder and grabs the honey from the countertop as Ladimer sits across the table and simply smirks at me and sips his hot coffee.

# Chapter 3

## Hallucination

Sir Cuche leads while we all trail ten feet behind him through the Plummet Forest. Gunthreon and Lupa trail furthest, Lupa constantly doing goofy things to make Gunthreon smile, like adding flowers to his hair. He looks happy, but his embarrassment hovers around his head like birds in a cartoon as he pulls the brightly colored wildflowers from his head.

We bask in the beautiful scenery, only whispering to each other when something peculiar is spied. Jenna, the all-knowing nature goddess, introduces me to my first jambleberry. They are large, purple-ish, juicy berries that explode—literally—in your mouth upon contact with saliva; the taste experience is practically orgasmic. Once the berry juice leaves its skin, it warms to the touch and a slight hallucinogenic is released, giving you the brief belief that you are standing before gods and all sorts of mythical creatures.

In my first experience with the berry—also my first experience ever of *anything* hallucinogenic—I witnessed Lord Ganesha: the eight-armed, reproductively-charged, elephant-headed Hindu god who shook its head "no" at me in a very disappointed manner. My emotion began as "scared shitless," worked its way to "awestruck," then ended on "fuming," for who has the right to judge *my* loins? Jenna warned me that you could only eat a few within an hour's time or you might screw up your brain a bit, so I'd only eaten two, the second happening accidentally. I had attempted to pull one off the tall bush to save for later, but handfuls of them fell on me along with a hideously grotesque, prickly bug. One berry just happened to fall in my open mouth, and the bug bounced off my cheek, pricking me during its fall.

This second berry conjured up Jesus. The experience was laughingly entertaining because he just smiled at me and held up his fingers in a peace gesture, then began smoking a joint as he floated away on a rainbow cloud. I told Conner about it and he said I should stop eating the berries before I fall deeper into insanity than I already am. He refused to try a berry, but Ladimer popped one in his own mouth and then asked for my compact mirror. I just rolled my eyes at him and of course neglected his request as we continued onward through the forests of Renhala.

Renhala is basically like a giant puzzle, with many different lands connecting to each other; each piece is just as important as another to complete the big picture. Some lands are exactly like The States back in my realm, and others are entirely dreamlike—even nightmarish.

I've done some serious traveling over the past year and have walked many a territory: some for work, some for pleasure, and some for pure revenge. Our current nomadic travels are related to a job for Sir Cuche—which in my opinion, is never going to come to completion.

Sir Cuche was born about a half decade ago in Renhala, and through succession, became master of a very vast land and ruled with his wife, until one day she disappeared. Once she vanished—turns out she was the one who was *really* ruling the nest—his kingdom fell to pieces and he eventually was pushed off his own land, forced to wander and search for a new kingdom that would accept his unruly superiority complex.

Not finding anything acceptable, he decided to take the biggest risk of his life and come to Abscondia, despite the constant rumor that the realm I reside in is bad for everyone's health. Renhalans believe that advanced technology is killing us in Abscondia and that we are all being ruled by evil forces, such as whomever is "administering" electricity. They rely solely on internal magic, and I often think that maybe they are on to something, considering Renhalans live much longer lives. Ladimer and Gunthreon are both perfect examples, living hundreds of years each.

Many of our items in Abscondia are taboo in Renhala, such as all items electrical and even those battery-operated. Renhala even has their own law agency known as Unapproved Foreign Objects Enforcements, or UFOE for short. However, not all Renhalans abhor our technological goods, Jenna being the perfect example of a convert. She's even set up her own side business, boosting the amount of goods traveling between planes. Woodsprites make the perfect entrepreneurs, for they have to constantly have their hands in some sort of mission, and that's why my boss, Evan, and Jenna are business partners. I'm just the major workhorse and all others are support when I need it.

Evan is a sweet boss and very supportive of me despite his thrust into the world of Renhala, by me, literally. Unfortunately, with newbie powers comes newbie mistakes.

Approximately ten months ago, while sitting at my desk at Helping Hands, I was eating an extremely tasty handful of kalamata olives I had packed in my lunch. Well, the mere thought of olives brought memories of an olive spread I shared with my friends in Renhala, and my boss happened to walk into my office as I moaned a particularly loud moan of satisfaction. His eyes met mine and we instantly traveled (I carried him with me) to The Big Cheese—the very restaurant housing the memorable olive spread.

He immediately fainted, and once he woke, I was forced to feed all my Renhala knowledge to him. After silently listening to my speech, he decided to take a week away from work, but after minutes upon returning, he happened across Jenna, who was peeking from my purse. From that moment forward, he knew he was not insane, but now part of something he never imagined. The right side of Evan's brain immediately set off on hatching a plan for using this new realm for new business.

Meanwhile, after Sir Cuche had moved his residence (and most of his wealth), he continued to travel, looking for his wife, and eventually heard stories of a woman with extraordinary abilities who might help him in his search.

Sir Cuche eventually found me at the office of Helping Hands, and after telling his story to both Evan and I, offered to pay a very large retainer fee for my services. Evan knew this was the needed answer to our business woes, so my first contract was written up on the spot and eagerly signed by Sir Cuche.

That first contract helped make Evan's transition into Renhala smooth, but for me, that first contract continues to be a hellishly rocky road. It seems that whenever I get within a hair's length of Sir Cuche's wife, she vanishes, again and again. I've grown fond of Sir Cuche in an odd way and hope that he'll give up on her, for I fear that she has possibly grown out of her love for him. Perhaps karma is teaching Sir Cuche some lesson or another.

As I ponder the thought of admitting my belief to Sir Cuche, Gunthreon suddenly stops in front of us, forcing me to fall over my own feet as he turns west and yells loudly, "I suggest that whomever is following us step out into plain view." Power flows outward from Gunthreon, creeping silently over all open ears within an audible reach, for he is a master persuader—that is *his* gift; his voice holds the power in itself, forcing anyone to submit to what he "suggests."

I know who has been following us for the past mile and feel that both Jenna and Ladimer know as well, for they stop and stand, rolling their eyes and twiddling their thumbs while Conner quickly grasps his sword hidden underneath his shirt, fearing for an ambush.

Lupa smiles at me and this is my cue to play with Sir Cuche. Some of us know we shouldn't, but it's just so damn hard not to because of how earnestly he tries to hide his vulnerability by always playing the hard-ass role.

I go with it. "Gunthreon, it's approaching and it's *huge*!"

"Kailey," says Gunthreon, but Lupa hits him in the arm.

Sir Cuche's eyes widen as he holds his dinky little pocket knife far out in front of his body. The blade Jenna owns is twice as big. I try hard to contain the laughter welling up inside me.

The footsteps approaching speed up, sounding as though a rhinoceros is about to trample us. I enhance my false fear by twirling around in place, yelling "Oh shit! What are we going to do? There is no place to run!" Conner moves closer to me, shielding me with his body from the oncoming storm, unaware of our prank and willing to risk his life for me. I feel a bit of guilt, but continue with the cruelty, because telling Conner would be the end of the fun.

Ladimer decides to finally join in. "I will not be able to heal us from what is drawing near. We must all fend for ourselves!"

Lupa screams as a giant, brown-furred, seven-foot creature breaks through the forest, trampling the nearest weeds with his three feet and bouncing his long arms off the bark of the surrounding trees. Its head is monstrous and its yellow eyes search the forest in front of it, then stop on Sir Cuche, who is standing as close to Gunthreon as possible. This creature, a greble, weighs at least six hundred pounds and looks as though its hungry, which I know he most likely is, since six-hundred pound grebles eat constantly, and enjoy their sweets, I must say.

Whimpers escape from Sir Cuche's mouth seconds before he falls to the ground in a faint.

I run towards the greble, jumping over Sir Cuche as the large creature reaches out, swooping me up in his arms with a giant's strength. His embrace is loving and he let me kiss him on the cheek. "Bu! I've missed you, buddy."

Jenna comes running over, too, and climbs up his leg, also planting a smooch on Bu. Conner frowns at me, not liking that he was not involved in our little joke. I'm sure I'll get an earful when we are alone, for he hates to feel we are always one step ahead of him; often he's right.

Bu's warmhearted smile makes my day, as it can any day, and my worries of Conner's bruised ego wash away. Bu is one of my best friends and one of only a few souls I would trust with my life.

Grebles are known to be foul, selfish, back-stabbing creatures, but Bu was raised by Gunthreon for a portion of his life and has none of those cruel qualities. He is also the only greble that you will find wearing a fanny pack of tools as he strolls through the forests or streets. Unlike other grebles his size who use brute force to accomplish everything, Bu is extremely dexterous and can operate and repair the smallest of items with his large hands and tools. Instead of opening a locked door with a kick of the foot, Bu would most likely have the perfect gadget with which to pick the lock. He is an extremely underestimated adversary when it comes to battle, because he uses both his strength *and* technical knowledge.

The first words from his mouth are: "Where's Kioto?"

Of course I should expect this, but I am still hoping for a "What hurt Kailey's face," or a "Bu missed you!"

"She's at home where she can be safe."

"Kioto won't stay there long," he says, matter-of-factly.

Kioto and Bu bonded the first time they met, which wasn't over a simple cup of milk and dog biscuits, but a time when they both saved me from having my head bashed in and my brains eaten by a dirty greble named Tartarin who was intent on killing me because I apparently was holding back his boss from demolishing Abscondia in its entirety.

Tartarin worked for my father, and last I saw him my father was slicing him up with a blade, for Tartarin was the one who inflicted the deadly wound upon my mother. Despite the fact that Devoten was once eager to rule all realms, and my mother stood in his way, he still felt a deep connection to her and snapped when Tartarin ripped her transplanted kidney from her body.

I was told Tartarin did not survive my father's attack, but I still have countless nightmares of him, which often morph into dreams of my father. These dreams wake me—sudo-abominor ready to hunt. On these searches for my father, my inner self—the Kailey I used to be—fears what might happen once we come face to face. I try not to even think of him, for sudo-abominor often takes that as a welcome to begin chase, yet again. It's tiring, really. This constant soulsearching either brings me *to* that energy, or grasps and brings *forth* that energy, but my father is proving to be very elusive and I am constantly traveling from one place to the next, even when I don't plan on doing so. I find myself, none too many times, grasping at the last bits of his energy as it dissipates, becoming miniscule particles of the atmosphere. My feeler, pushed forward by sudo-abominor—yet pulled back by my conscience—never really gains enough strength to conquer in this epic game of tug-of-war. As sudo-abominor gains its strength with time, I fear that my conscience may someday fall face first, muddying me and turning me into the ugly monster my father once was.

Soulsearching may be Gunthreon's favorite ability of mine, and it is one of the many reasons why I am successful at what I do, but being able to soulsearch is definitely not my most endearing quality.

Just imagine enjoying the privacy of your bathroom while slathering your face with charcoal mud mask, when you suddenly find yourself standing in front of me in an aisle in the grocery store. It happened, really, when I was only thinking of buying some treats for the office. I'm so lucky that my boss, Evan, didn't fire me on the spot, especially since he was wrapped only in a towel and then I proceeded to ask to see his pores up close. But then again, who else could slice off an enemy's foot, pull forth a healer from another realm, and have him reattach the foot, all before karma has the time to decide what the hell she wants to do about that? Certainly no one else Evan knows.

Sir Cuche is now sitting up, sniffing some smelling salts Lupa carries in her bag—a bag aptly named an everything pack. She carries an innumerable amount of things in this pack—anything she can fit into it—and retrieves many an item, from pots to woodsprites, as long as she remembers they are in the pack. It's some sort of magical abyss that holds *everything*. All you have to do is think of whatever object that you put in it, reach in with your hand, and whallah! You hold it once again.

Sir Cuche comes to his senses and sees Bu hugging Lupa. "What?!" he exclaims.

I am the lucky one that gets to break the news to him. "Sir Cuche, this is Bu. Bu, Sir Cuche. Bu is a special friend of ours." Bu comes over and holds out his gigantic hand to Sir Cuche who hesitates before deciding it must be safe enough and proceeds to hold up his hand as royalty might do, presenting his thickly-banded solid gold and ruby-encrusted wedding ring. Bu spots the ring then speedily dips his own hand in his fanny pack, pulling out a new tool: a bright, rune-etched wrench that looks to be entirely forged of gold. Sir Cuche's mouth drops as Bu places the wrench in Sir Cuche's delicate hands, his muscles clearly straining to keep it off the ground.

"I must say this is very lovely, and *quite* valuable." He turns it over, admiring the craftsmanship. "Hmm. Well made." Sir Cuche hands it back to Bu who places it carefully back in his pack. He's suddenly aware that we are watching him and his face scrunches up in the usual fashion as he displays his unhappiness with the situation. He clears his throat loudly and squawks, "And yes, that joke was not funny." While gathering his composure, he brushes off his extravagantly gold-gilded robe, a task that usually means he has either 1) ended up on the floor due to someone's shenanigans or 2) ended up on the floor because of his own clumsiness. He continues brushing, asking no questions whatsoever, only stewing in his embarrassment, and most likely adding this event to his long mental list of possible reasons for not paying the remainder due on my contract.

Bu simply shrugs and starts chatting with Jenna, who has hitched a ride on his shoulder and is currently holding her nose closed as she lounges comfortably. Grebles stink, but I've noticed recently that I don't even really smell Bu's stench anymore. Most likely because I've just grown used to it, somehow.

As I watch them, I catch brief sentence fragments from Jenna, like "out of control" and "retainer fees shrinking." I smile slightly as I feel their energies playing with each other, almost like a children's game of tag.

We press on, following a clue received anonymously by Ladimer. As we approach the edge of the forest, I suddenly freeze, feeling an energy enrobed in hurried anticipation approaching from the opposite direction. Ladimer sees me and asks, "What is it?"

A single, dirtied young farmhand teen comes up from behind, wheezing as he catches his breath and speaks toward me as he approaches. "Are you the one known as Kailey, the karmelean?"

"Who wants to know?" I reply. Jenna shakes her head at me, telling me this boy has no ill intentions. Woodsprites can usually read whether one's aura harbors good or bad thoughts, which also gives them insight into which sorts of powers an individual may have. I grab my monk's spade off my back just in case, for I know there exist those seasoned individuals who have learned to hide their auras from readers like Jenna.

"I have a message for you." He approaches with an outstretched hand, holding a sealed envelope. Conner steps forth before Ladimer has the chance and attempts to take the envelope, only to force the teen to wield a small pitchfork. "I am only to personally hand this to Kailey, by request of my…Madam Eve."

Conner soulspeaks to him, telling him that we will not harm him if he commits no form of assault.

I step forward and take the envelope from the boy, noticing the slight brush of his hand against mine. "Thank you. What is your name?"

"I am Terro. Nice to meet you. I never get to meet anyone famous. You're awesome!" Knowledge of my powers has traveled fast and I redden with embarrassment at the comment.

Gunthreon speaks to Terro, thanking him, and asking him to return home.

The boy turns and as he runs back from where he came, he waves goodbye and blows me a kiss as he disappears behind a tree. Ladimer laughs. "Wow, Kailey. You've grown to have quite the fan base, haven't you?"

My hands eagerly open the envelope and I read the letter out loud:

*Dear Kailey, please excuse me for my eagerness, but I request your services as soon as possible. I fear something terrible has become of my darling daughter, Flora, and need immediate help in finding her. I can pay beyond your wildest dreams if you were to prove successful.*

*I will be the woman dressed in snakes, seated in the rear of* THE PERFECT PLACE *located in Golden Dunes.*

*Desperate,*

*Madam Eve*

"Dressed in *snakes*? Madam *Eve*?" I laugh. Jokingly I add, "Where's Adam?" I look up and apparently Bu is the only one that heard my hilarious joke as he stands motionless, staring at me. Everyone else is fretting over Sir Cuche, who looks riled as usual.

"Bu don't know Adam."

Sir Cuche struggles to make his voice heard. "No way. You are working for me now." He doesn't stand a chance.

Ladimer adds to the conversation, helping us make the decision to meet Madam Eve. "Golden Dunes is actually on the way to where your wife has last been spotted. I must also meet a contact of mine nearby who may prove to be quite the asset in the search for your wife, Sir Cuche. I'm as eager to find your wife as you." We all know how eager Ladimer is already to get rid of the nuisance known as Sir Cuche.

"Fine, as long as you remember that I come first," spouts Sir Cuche, standing as straight as his back allows him, "and I might as well watch that you don't spend all my retainer fee on expenses not related to my contract."

"Of course," I say as I stare at Ladimer. "Onward to Golden Dunes then?"

Bu says, "Bu likes snakes. They tickle," and rushes forward with Jenna bouncing on his shoulder.

I follow, scratching the itchy bug prick on my cheek, and wonder what kinds of trouble may await with *this* contract.

# Chapter 4

## Thirst

Golden Dunes proves to be just that: endless mountains of tiny golden silica, expanding for as far as the eye can see underneath two hot and unforgiving suns, one small and yellow, and one large and orange and riddled with canyons of what looks like molten lava. Off in the distance, skimming over the dunes, are a few small sand vortexes whirling in fury, but seemingly harmless as they die down within seconds.

I walk, dragging my feet up the nearest dune, sweating from the heat, casting my feeler out to reach for the nearest energies. An odd burst of energy ricochets back to me, making me slightly dizzy and forcing me to stumble just as sudden bursts of swirling sand sprout up, twirling in anticipation, only to expire quickly.

Ladimer comes up beside me. "It's the sand."

"What?"

"It's reflecting your feeler's reach right back at you—grain by amazing grain." He bends down and lets the dry sand run through his long fingers. "We're gonna have to do this *my* way." Appearing pompous, and sticking his hand deep in the sand, he searches for something—anything to give clue to where someone may be, here in Golden Dunes. "Damn," he says, withdrawing. With no life energy via plant roots within what seems miles, Ladimer's own powers mean nothing. "Only small, miniscule bacteria normally found on nitrogen-rich sand."

Lupa then walks up next to us. "You guys are useless. See how it's done." She stands firmly and cups her hand near her mouth, then screams at a voice loud enough to reach Abscondia, "*HELLO? WHERE THE HELL ARE YOU?*" We stand and wait as the remainder of our friends join us at the top of the dune.

A figure appears at the top of a nearby dune and we scrunch our eyes, attempting to see it more clearly.

My eyes widen as I realize what it is. "It's a deathman."

Lupa screams again. "*NO, NOT YOU, BUT THANKS!*" It waves at us and disappears back down the hill. "I don't want to see what's on the other side of that hill, please."

Jenna and Bu nod, simultaneously.

Deathmen gravitate to dead—or dying—beings, collecting the soul orbs of the creatures that pass, and acting as some sort of scorekeepers for Neda and Velopa. It seems that us lower creatures are not the only ones drawn to competition.

The only way to avoid a deathman's grabby hands is to be buried in the ground, beneath dirt, and from the looks of the area, there is no escaping one here, unless sand also counts. As we stand, motionless, another creature appears even further away and yells back to us: "*COME! YOU'RE WELCOME HERE!*"

We all look to each other and continue onward toward the figure, dragging our bodies like dead weight through the sand, Bu seemingly having the hardest time because of his massiveness. All the while Sir Cuche is having no problem whatsoever since he's on Conner's back.

Arriving at our destination, Conner dumps Sir Cuche in the sand, and not very gracefully. I blow Conner a kiss as he rolls his eyes, licks his lips, and wipes sweat from his brow.

Sir Cuche jumps up quicker than lightning, brushes off his robe and proceeds to shake and blow the sand from his beard. Conner looks at me with the evil eye, hissing, "You're lucky I love you." I kiss him on the cheek as I look over his shoulder and catch Ladimer's eyes before he turns to Gunthreon so they may approach the figure that beckoned us.

"Can I assume one of you is Kailey?" queries the human-like creature. He looks straight at me, clearly knowing who I am. He stands about six and a half feet tall, with dry, scaly, limp skin, and his eyes full of life and exuberance. He is ashen in color and appears to be hairless—at least everywhere covered by his long khaki shorts. "So nice to meet you. I'm Elivon." He shakes my hand firmly and holds it for a moment. "You're sweating, hard. How absolutely lovely." I try to pull my hand from his brace and he doesn't lessen his grip, even after I swiftly grab my monk's spade off my back and hold it to his throat with more pressure than I would normally. I also instinctively grab a hold of his energy.

"If you don't let go of my hand, this sand will be soaking up your blood." Unfortunately he makes a slight movement toward a blade at his side, and without thinking, I am suddenly slicing off his hand with one clean swipe as I rip off a chunk of energy from his field. *This is new*, I think. I quickly release the energy, not really knowing what I should do with it. It dissipates as Jenna, looking mortified, stares at me.

Lupa yells "Kailey!"

I mount my spade with no sympathy for the creature and brush off the sandy feeling left in my suddenly dry hand. A feeling of lifelessness in my grasp disintegrates as quickly as it appeared, and as I rub my hand I curse to myself, then notice a sand vortex that has lifted to life and is approaching us, and pretty quickly.

Elivon apparently doesn't bleed, but does indeed feel pain, apparent from his hellish screams. Conner is suddenly standing over Elivon with his own blade exposed, but Ladimer gestures for him to put the weapon away. Conner does, but not until Gunthreon speaks, asking him to please do so.

Ladimer picks the hand up and magically reattaches it as his power swells around his aura. "Sir, respect our life and we'll respect yours," Ladimer warns him diplomatically, then gives *me* a warning glare as he notices the swiftly-approaching vortex, which seems to be getting larger by the second.

Elivon recovers quickly and seemingly isn't worried about the vortex. "I should have expected that," he says, meeting my eyes. "I am sorry for forcing that situation upon you. It's just the draw." He massages his wrist, thankful that he once again possesses both hands.

Gunthreon explains out loud, but looks toward me, "Those of Golden Dunes are deprived of water, as you can see, and it's just that the likes of us are…full of it." His anxiety bubbles as the approaching vortex gains more speed.

Conner speaks an opinion, favoring Ladimer's direction. "Some more than others are…full of it." Ladimer only grunts.

"Can you bring us to The Perfect Place? And maybe before that sand attacks us?" I ask, wiping the sweat from my brow as Elivon actually licks his lips. My hand is then drawn to the infamous bug prick which feels as though it's on fire. After touching it, I inhale sharply, both from the pain and from the obvious ugliness of the damn thing as both Jenna and Bu cringe with scrunched faces.

Ladimer suddenly, and loudly, clears his throat as he looks to Elivon, pulling the scaly gentleman to his senses. "Of course!" responds Elivon. "Actually, you're standing on it."

I look down and stomp on the hardened sand beneath my feet. I then jump up and down. Bu suddenly seems interested in the sport and starts his own jumping. Elivon runs forward in an attempt to refrain him, but is a fraction of a moment too late as we all fall through the thick layer of sand, landing on a smooth polished surface inside the hill. The vortex quickly brushes over the gaping hole in the ceiling. Several deformed creatures resembling Elivon, seated at rows of tavern-esque tables, stare with widened eyes. They hint of a hidden thirst with elongated tongues or uneven eyeballs. A bartender passes a drink to a patron who has a gaping hole in his arm. The patron nods at Elivon.

"All these energies were right beneath me," I whisper in shock, "and I didn't even know it. Hmm."

Elivon speaks to the patrons in a strange language and they continue with their games and conversing as he leads us to the doorway of another room. In passing a particularly crowded table, he suggests rather than asks: "Gurgl, can you fix that?" as he points to the new entrance we made in the ceiling. A creature, much like himself, but much shorter and stockier, and with one arm much longer than the other, grabs a bucket of a clear, thick substance and disappears through a hole in the wall, but not without scoping me out and smiling at me, creepily, and for too long.

It's considerably cooler here, inside the dune, and I thank Neda for the break from the suns as I examine the area, including the impressive bar made of a long, single piece of rich, dark wood. Bu also notices the bar as I see his eyes wander to the brackets holding it in place. However, his interest is really sparked by a knocking sound coming from behind and beneath the bar. Most likely contemplating what tool will fix the problem, Bu opens his fanny pack and slowly turns and heads in the direction of the bartender. The fellow cringes a bit and reaches below our sight for a concealed weapon. I watch, hand on my monk's spade, until Bu is allowed behind the bar and is engaged in conversation. The bartender smiles, scrunching up his nose at the sudden stink in his vicinity, but giving me the okay to release my weapon.

Standing in the entrance of the doorway, away from the expanse of dry sand and angry swirly cyclones, I sense a presence somewhere here different than all the others. I look across the room and lock eyes with a beautiful woman, surely not the same race as Elivon, seated against the far wall. Her skin is supple and her locks of luscious blond hair fall around her body like a cascading waterfall of fluid gold. Adding to the mesmerizing effect of her beauty, dozens of snakes of different shapes and sizes slither over and around her, never leaving her body, which is also adorned with diamond-and-emerald-studded, silver jewelry; bracelets, necklaces, and arm cuffs twinkle with every sconce's gift of light.

Glancing at her entirety, I notice not a single hair on her head is out of place. I pat down my own head of unruliness, suddenly feeling a bit hobo-ish. *I need a shower.* She's definitely a high maintenance kind of gal, but the gleam in her eyes says she's definitely one who'd put up a worthwhile fight to keep what's rightfully hers.

I hear Jenna take in a deep breath as she watches the many snakes writhing across Madam Eve's body, intertwining in her hair, and moving gracefully along her skin. Bu, now finished with whatever he was doing behind the bar, is the first to move forward and Madam Eve smiles lovingly at him as she slyly reaches in a hidden pocket. I can't seem to feel her energy, and the sight of Bu frightens most, so I understand her possible fear. "It's okay," I tell her and her hand moves back to her lap. "I must say your jewelry is beautiful."

She nods at me with a smile. "Feel free to touch, my dear," she offers Bu, who reaches forward slowly and allows a snake to move along his arm and across his body. He giggles and picks up another. In my direction she says, "I've worked very hard for this jewelry." She moves in to whisper to me. "Let's keep it our secret that it's imported. Platinum, I think you Abscondians call it?"

"Yes. Very nice." I smile pleasantly, but inwardly I'm coveting every single piece she wears.

"Madam Eve, it's my pleasure." Intervening, Gunthreon reaches out his hand and she daintily shakes it, her form-fitting, flesh-colored gown slightly twinkling under the active snakes. I stare, not quite understanding how the snakes are possible, and how the hell she takes off the dress. A smiles appears on my face, for Renhala always seems to enthrall me with a new trick almost every day.

"All mine," Madam Eve hums. "I've heard great things of Ms. Kailey, and of course all those who travel with her." She looks to Ladimer who bows slightly. He then proceeds to walk toward me after my incessant touching of my face. He lays his hand on the bug prick and a coolness spreads from his fingertips, instantly making the site feel better. Madam Eve releases a slight moan of pleasure and I realize Ladimer just showed off for her; he healed me not for my sake, but for her attention.

Under my breath, "Nice," escapes my mouth. "Thanks for letting me suffer so long."

He whispers back to me, "Karma had to be fulfilled, my darling." I give him a bit of elbow to the stomach which makes him gasp, but he finishes with a laugh.

Sir Cuche, thankfully diverting attention from us, pushes his way forward, making his presence known. "I am the one known as Sir Cuche."

"Oh. Yes, of course, the great Sir Cuche." Madam Eve winks at me as Sir Cuche straightens his shoulders with regality. "You all must forgive me for my desperation and hurriedness. If you feel comfortable talking here, we can safely." She nods to Elivon who immediately sends all the other patrons out of the room, but remains, moving to sit next to Madam Eve.

I speak to her directly. "Don't you fear for yourself, here? You are evidently *unlike* all the others." I turn to Elivon. "Please forgive me Elivon, but I did witness your hunger."

A flash of anger from Madam Eve disappears as fast as it appears as she looks to Elivon who adjusts his seating. "Sorry, Eve," he whimpers as he examines his wrist.

Her attention turns back to us. "No worries. The people of Golden Dunes and I have an agreement that spans decades. I live on the neighboring land of Luvia. Maybe you've heard of it?"

Ladimer nods and replies, "Absolutely the lushest farmland of Renhala."

Madam Eve smiles widely. "Well, we live harmoniously next to one another to keep the exchange of goods flowing smoothly, as well as for a few other reasons...but that's for an informal conversation," she says, the corner of her mouth rising slightly as she looks to Elivon.

"What could *they* possibly give *you*?" I say, blatantly speaking my thoughts. A slight ripple of warmth suddenly emanates from Madam Eve.

Suddenly, I fell Jenna pulling at my pant leg and as I look down at where she's pointing, I notice matching clay-beaded anklets on both Elivon and Eve. My eyes wander from Lupa to Gunthreon and settle on their matching rings. *I just insulted Madam Eve's mate.* "I am so sorry," I apologize. "You're a couple."

Madam Eve continues her story as Elivon gently takes her hand in his. "We have a rather large number of crops of a starchy grain which is highly nutritional, as well as delicious, that we grow in Luvia. Perhaps you've had starcka?" She looks at me as though she expects me to start drooling immediately at the word spoken. I shrug my shoulders in ignorance and she actually frowns. "Well, you wouldn't *believe* how much we export." I can almost see the dollar signs in her eyes. "But anyway, the people of Golden Dunes produce a sifted nutrient that seems to be the only food our crops truly enjoy, and we in turn give them the starch byproduct produced by our refinement process. They use it to make a sort of cement from their sand and use it to mold all their homes, stores, etc." Elivon kisses Madam Eve's hand as I notice one of her snakes avoiding any possible contact with him—the same reaction I got after sending my feeler toward her for a second round, except I got hisses, too.

Lupa's interest is suddenly sparked. "I would *love* to see your crops if I could. I have a certain way with plant life, myself." Lupa smiles and Madam Eve's eyebrows rise at the possibility of yet another business deal as she realizes that Lupa must have a plant-related gift. One look at Lupa's garden in Meadow's Edge would have Madam Eve foaming at the mouth.

"The woman grows frangles the size of pumpkins and asparagus you could mistake for trees," I say of Lupa to test Madam Eve's reaction. I look to Jenna since my feeler may evoke something chaotic if I attempt to feel up Madam Eve. Jenna's confused expression is not encouraging as she squints at Madam Eve.

Turning the subject, Madam Eve says, "Well enough of me. I need to get down to business. Kailey, I have requested you here in hopes that you may be able to find my missing daughter, Flora. We had an argument and she's been missing for about three days now. I was hoping that maybe she ran off to a girlfriend's or forbidden boyfriend's house—Elivon won't allow her to date yet since he believes her studies are more important right now." She casts me a glance that states their opinions clearly differ on the subject. "I am now fearing the worst. You *need* to find her for me—for us."

Sir Cuche answers, "We are already on a mission for one missing woman. We can't possibly try to find another." Madam Eve reaches under the table and pulls out a huge velvet bag and begins pouring an endless stream of gold coins and jewels at our feet. Sir Cuche humphs, but eyes a particularly large ruby-red gem.

"We will need you to sign some paperwork," Jenna remarks, already holding a contract in her hands.

"Where did you pull that from?" I say. But I'm not sure I want to know. Gunthreon lifts and shakes Lupa's everything pack at me. "Oh."

Gunthreon turns to speak to Elivon which makes Madam Eve uncomfortable as she leans forward toward them, not wanting to be left out of any conversation. "Elivon, my dear sir, is Flora your biological daughter?"

"No," he snaps, Gunthreon evidently hitting a sore spot. I ask myself why Gunthreon went directly for the blow, but keep the thought to myself.

"I just need to know who we can and cannot speak to regarding any information we find," says Gunthreon. "It states in our missing children contracts that we speak first to the biological parents involved." This clause is new to me.

Madam Eve interjects. "Residents here…have mating issues—well at least in regards to the results. They have a diminishing population due to most babies being stillborn, or…deformed. *My* offspring had a different father, for both health and beauty's sake." Elivon's face muscles tighten as he manages to hold back a comment as Madam Eve continues to talk. "But I give you permission to provide Elivon with any information that arises. He is as much a parent as I, maybe even moreso at times. Elivon is truly great with the kids. Did he tell you he works at the school as a teacher? He's got much more patience and intelligence for all that scientific mumbo-jumbo." She squeezes his hand.

Elivon adds, "We are a formidable team, I must say."

"I see. So it shall be," states Gunthreon. "I suggest we move as swiftly as possible." As Gunthreon finishes his sentence we all notice a change in the snakes writhing across Madam Eve. They speed up, slithering "swiftly" around and around at breakneck speed—just as suggested.

Madam Eve locks eyes with Gunthreon. "My, my, Gunthreon. What a great gift. Hope it comes in handy." She smiles at him and a look of greed passes quickly across her face.

Elivon stands and stares at the snakes and a flash of repulsion resembling a spark of electricity strikes out from his body as one very long snake reaches out to him. He then turns and smiles at us as though he's not a walking lightning storm, but sitting on cloud nine. "Thank you all so very much. My Eve, as well as Flora's brother, Terro, have been out of sorts since Flora disappeared. Our life has been without true sunshine since she disappeared."

I think of Terro and the cute dimple I noticed in his cheek as I speak to Elivon. I now see the resemblance between mother and son. "We'll need lots of information and cooperation. You prepared for that?"

"Yes, Kailey." He extends his hand and I hesitate, then raise my own to his. His smile is innocent as he releases my hand after one quick, but tight squeeze. I feel sudo-abominor stirring inside.

"Good. Got any decent tea here?" I ask.

# Chapter 5

## Birth

My mouth instantly waters at bite number two of Madam Eve's pride and joy: starcka croquettes, and I have to say they are definitely one of the most delicious things I have ever tasted; they're all crispy on the outside, moist and flavorful on the inside. Madam Eve makes it known to us that the batch of starcka used was a batch she had been reserving for a special occasion. We are all seated in Elivon's dune around his table and seated in various-sized piles of a thick-stalked and squishy straw. His abode is most humble, with no items of luxury or wealth that the eye can see, only books, books, and more books. I notice that his "decorative touches" are mostly scientific books that I will never understand, and only one lonely book is different: an encyclopedia of flowers. He repeatedly walks around the room grabbing the tomes and putting them in a pile away from us, giving us more room for our legs.

Apparently starcka can be cooked in anything from appetizers to desserts, for it simply enhances whatever you cook with it, bringing out the truly enjoyable aspects of each ingredient. Surprisingly, I find myself questioning the calorie content after no decrease in my desire to keep eating after two hours of mouth-shoveling. Jenna herself eats a seven course meal, then follows it up with three desserts.

Bu, I think, eats a whole crop alone. Madam Eve finally whispers something in his ear while she holds her nose, and Bu, with a sudden drop of starcka dumplings and a strong sense of guilt spewing from his body, apologizes to her. I refrain from speaking to her about it, for the dumpling *I* just shoved in my mouth would most likely just sputter all over as I talked. Then I shove another in my mouth to follow it as I watch Madam Eve and her movements.

Jenna appears next to me and, seemingly reading my mind but still chewing on an extremely large and salted starcka breadstick, mumbles, "I can't make her out…and I saw what you did to Elivon, Kailey." I was hoping to avoid this conversation. I still don't know how I ripped off his energy.

"Yeah? Well…" I say, still chewing as I think about how I couldn't read Madam Eve's energy, either. I hand Jenna a starcka-breaded tomato slice. We both sit and chew and stare at Madam Eve as she openly flirts with the men of our group, getting all close, giving them shoulder hugs, and letting her snakes occasionally rub against them. I tell myself I should probably do something about it…once I finish my food of course.

"Those snakes totally throw off her field. It's all jumbly. I can't tell what her power is, or even if she has one," Jenna admits.

"I think she's seduction. Look at her," I say, accidentally spitting out a piece of food in Jenna's hair. I pick it out, and deciding it's still edible, put it back in my mouth. She ignores the gesture as I wonder why the hell I just ate it. "Are all the people of Luvia covered with reptiles?"

"Never been to Luvia. Don't know," she slobbers.

After I finish my last cup of peach-and-hartflower-infused starcka tea, Elivon directs all of us by the light of the Golden Dunes moon—an unbelievably tiny but bright moon—to his marketplace, which to my surprise is entirely inside the dunes. As we follow Elivon through endless tunnels and approach noises which resemble the noise of a hustling-and-bustling community, we finally reach a large doorway. Walking through the doorway and peering below us, we all "ooh," especially Lupa.

Below us is an expanse of a "room" in which several merchants and vendors peddle their goods, while children run from shop to shop, chased about by shop owners and fussing mothers. It's a fun place with many goods and plenty of bartering.

Elivon and Madam Eve lead us down a stairway, and as we enter and all marketplace dwellers catch sight of us, I notice there is a sudden hush that falls over the inhabitants. Bu, being the last to walk in, has many a woman gasping and grabbing her children as they flail to escape mom's clutches. Elivon waves his hands and speaks a word that eventually has them moving again, albeit slower than before.

As the children escape their parents and congregate, they all freeze in their group and stare as we approach, some mouths opening, others hidden by their tiny hands. I walk by them, but upon giving them small smiles and winks, they suddenly laugh and continue with their play, dodging between adults and stealing an occasional fruit or candy, but still keeping a watchful eye on the big fellow, Bu.

I notice Bu feeling a bit self-conscious; he walks behind us as he tries avoiding any frightened expressions by looking down at the path as he walks. Feeling bad for him, I straggle behind, matching my step with his and striking up random conversation.

Suddenly as he gains the courage to look up ahead, he begins slowing his steps as one small child steps directly in his path. She's a small scaly thing with a long mane of hair held back by a chain of beautiful green flowers, and her bright eyes are full of life—like Elivon's. As she slowly raises her hand, Bu brings his large hand down to her and in it she drops a fruit of some sort. He eyes it as she then motions to her own mouth, advising him to eat it. After he pops it into his mouth and chews, the folds of skin above his eyes rise in surprised satisfaction. He gives her a large thumb's up as a smile worthy of melting an iceberg forms on his face. Walking by the child, he lays a gentle hand on her head. Giggling, she runs off to her mother who then hugs her tightly, sneaking me a small smile of pride.

We see all sorts of new and exciting goodies and contraptions as we walk along the small concrete paths that are lit up by intricate metal lampposts that burn sweet-scented oils. Inhaling deeply, Lupa suddenly steps off the path toward a fruit dealer and engages him in conversation as she picks up two large melons, positioning them close to her chest, attempting to catch Gunthreon's attention. She does as he suddenly chokes on something unseen. I can't help but laugh with Gunthreon as Lupa pretends she has no idea what she's doing.

Ladimer is drawn to a jewelry vendor as he veers off and waves us on as he examines a copper metal cuff. Conner and Sir Cuche stay alongside us as we continue on, following our hosts.

Elivon is especially interested in one large place of business as he pulls us all quickly inside and hushes us. There are several workers who are seated toward the back of the shop making an extremely loud ruckus as they pound a substance into a fine powder—there's no need for hushing since we'd most likely not hear each other anyway.

Working quickly, the workers mix the powder with various other powders, and those wearing protective gloves drop an occasional droplet of brown oil into the mixture. I notice that the oil is stored in a barrel marked with a big red X.

Stirring the concoction and then beginning the pounding process all over again, the staff work diligently, almost enough to be totally unaware of us watching their work. Elivon watches with a gleeful eye as he pats them each on the back. "They are making the nutrient that Eve uses on her starcka plants," he shouts. He then marches us all out and follows Madam Eve as she directs us forward.

Pulling us all toward a doorway with a large rainbow lollipop hanging above, Madam Eve opens her eyes wide as she suddenly eyes an empty bucket inside the shop. "Vic! Where are the new fruity starcka drops?" she yells as Jenna jumps from bucket to bucket, looking at all the colorful sweets and grabbing a free sample here and there.

The one I am assuming is Vic suddenly appears from behind a small sand counter. He seems totally thrown off guard as his eyes are drawn first to Madam Eve, then Elivon. "Must be those damn kids again!" he replies, quickly. "I swear, Madam Eve, your starcka drops are like drugs to them. Their grimy, stealing little hands are always in that bucket!" He smiles at her and her face suddenly beams back. "I'll make sure to refill it when I can. Forgive me for I'm super busy now," he says as he grabs a bucket of sand, a large sanding pad, and the same goo we saw earlier, then begins filling a dimple in the floor.

"Thank you, Vic." Madam Eve replies. "Remember, if you double your order next month, I'm giving a twenty percent discount!"

Without looking up, Vic says, "On your way out, grab a handful of our new goodies in the orange bucket near the door. We call them Willow's Wafers. My wife makes them." As we proceed out, we each grab one—Jenna four—of the wafers which very much resemble the communion wafers served in Catholic churches. Melting in my mouth and fizzing a bit, it leaves a small layer of something deliciously sweet and honey-like on my tongue.

After our purchases are made and bellies are filled, we leave the marketplace and travel back through the never-ending tunnels, following Elivon to the final exit. Once outside and dragging our heavy feet through the sand that is still hot to the touch, Elivon leads us to the dunes that will house us until my contract is completed. We each enter, reveling in the cool floor, but soon realize that as Bu gets stuck in the doorway, he's much too large to enter. Elivon soon lets out a high-pitched and whiny sort of whistle which summons Gurgl with his pickaxe in hand. I stare as Gurgl suddenly moves with a quickness much like Quicksilver as he widens the doorway. He catches me watching him and flexes his muscles.

"Please let me know if you need *anything*," Elivon requests as he looks at me, and me only. I squint my eyes at him and he quickly turns and leaves. Madam Eve follows him, but sneaks me a sly smile as they totally disappear through the door. *Weird bunch.*

As we make our makeshift beds from straw, Bu pulls me aside, away from all other ears. "Kailey, when Bu was fixing that cooler behind bar, Bu saw *stuff*."

I think of Renhala's aversion to electrical appliances and wonder what kind of cooler here actually knocks. "Their *cooler* was making that noise?"

"Yes! Pressurized water. So cool, Kailey! Bu fixed evaporator." His particular realm of knowledge always baffles me. "But Bu see weird things—" he whispers at a lower octave, "—things Bu don't see anywhere here."

"Like?"

"Special things from Abscondia—equipment, like stuff Bu wants here."

"Where?" I ask, concerned. "By the bar? Maybe they're just getting with the program. They have a cooler after all."

He looks at me as though I spoke French, then replies, "Bu got confused which door you went through and ended up by a room with a guard. It's stuff that's special—stuff maybe Kailey don't understand. Maybe stuff UFOE would break." I can tell I'm not going to get far with my stupidity on all things technical.

"Is it dangerous stuff, Bu?"

He stares at me for a moment. "Bu could make it dangerous. But only if Kailey asked."

"I would not ask that of you. We'll have to investigate later." He nods and continues fixing his bed of straw, paying meticulous attention to the specific positioning of his handfuls of straw.

As I stand, admiring Bu's skills, I ponder what the people of Golden Dunes may be harboring. At one point in my painful past, I was on the verge of death because of advanced technology developed by Renhalans and I won't allow it to happen again. Indeed I got to meet the awe-inspiring Higher One, Velopa, from the experience, but the only reason I'm alive after that encounter is karma. I don't want to test my luck now, especially while cursed with sudo-abominor. Through that experience I also learned how easily persuaded the UFOE is to turn the other cheek.

My mind is suddenly sidetracked when I realize we may not be back home to Abscondia for a bit, so I decide to travel home and check on Kioto. Jenna decides to go for a ride, and in a blink, we are back in my apartment. Kioto gives me the typical "Where the hell have you gone without me?" attitude as I snuggle up to her on the floor and try rubbing noses with her. I scratch behind her ears and she decides she can spare a single lick to my cheek.

"One would think you were raised by wolves," proclaims Jenna as she switches through the home shopping channels, stopping on Elena's Electronics Hour. Over the year, many goods have been purchased via the shopping networks and delivered to my apartment to be sold in Renhala. I'm even of gold member status now.

After three purchases, and a "Yahoo, I'm gonna make us rich, baby!" from Jenna's mouth after hanging up the phone, she decides that she should meet up with Evan at Helping Hands to tell him about our possible new contract with Madam Eve.

Suddenly, the loudest scream I've ever heard from any neighbor resonates from Karen's apartment next door. Both Jenna and I jump to our feet, as well as Kioto, and just as we make it to the hallway and I'm about to break down her definitely-not-soundproof door, I hear others laughing inside and yelling something about a Jell-O shot stuck in their hair. I raise my hand to pound on the door, but refrain and decide that I'm not an old maid—just yet.

"I'm outta here," Jenna shouts over the hullabaloo.

"See you later, Jenna," I say. "Oh, wait! Think you can indiscreetly check out The Perfect Place and their storage of some kind of equipment? Bu found something of interest there. It may be right up your alley."

Her eyebrows rise. "What kind of equipment?"

"That's what I need you to find out."

"Oooh! Sure I will." She waves goodbye and leaves my apartment building, beginning her mission to Helping Hands, unseen.

Suddenly, Karen's head is peeking out her door. "Hey, Kailey!"

"Oh, hey Karen."

"We're having a little shindig here. Why don't you join us? We've got an extra yummy batch of brownies," she slurs with a huge grin as some random male shows up next to her, shoving a small piece of said brownie in her mouth. Smiling, he holds one up for me. A bit of white wine sploshes out of Karen's glass and ends up dripping down her leg. She ignores it.

"No thanks. Maybe next time. They sure do smell good, though."

She laughs and mumbles, "Smell good! Ha, you're so funny, Kailey." Giving me a "Bummer," she then proceeds to stare at me as I wave goodbye and walk back into my apartment.

Looking through the peekhole, I see her look down at the footprints imprinted on the hallway carpet and begin emptying her wine glass on them. She then rubs the wine in with her shoe. She shrugs and walks back into her apartment.

After I leash up Kioto, we go for a nice long walk as I watch her nose sniff greedily at the air and her ears turn to sounds I will never hear. It's an enjoyable walk, and as we return home, I notice a small change in her demeanor. As I tug on the leash, directing her to the door, she refuses to enter. "What are you doing?" I say toward her, as though I expect her to answer. She keeps an alert stance with her ears pointed to the sky as she scans the area. I notice nothing after sending out an obligatory feel of the area, and eventually pull her into our vestibule. After repeated whimpers, and once inside my building, we trudge upstairs. I pull off the smiley face stickers which have appeared across my door and stick them on Karen's.

I stick my key in the keyhole and as I turn, I notice it was never locked. "Hmm," I mumble to myself.

Deciding that my still-spastic dog needs to go out on the balcony, I close the sliding door behind me. I take a quick shower, heat up my kettle, then make a delicious cup of Gunthreon's almost-extinct tea. As the familiar scent resembling roses and crème brulee dances in the air and settles in my nose, its effect is almost instantaneous as I drift into a state of total relaxation. I roll into my couch, being careful not to spill my treasure and take turns watching Kioto through the glass door and watching the end of Elena's Electronic Hour. Their newest shiny product: the customizable color and scent humidifier has my finger on the phone, but I pull myself together and instead give in to the entirely-persuasive sandman.

The dream begins with my mother—which they almost always do. She's dancing before me, swaying her hips back and forth as her anklet tinkles. Her white gown shimmers and floats on an unfelt breeze. As she looks forward, I realize she's not looking at me, but beyond me. I slowly turn around as a sense of worry wakes and that's when I see Elivon standing, smiling at my mother.

My mouth opens to yell, but not one iota of sound escapes. Frustrated I turn back to my mother, but instead of seeing her, it's Devoten before me, hooded in his godforsaken cloak which I have grown to despise. I gasp, which wakes me from the dream and conjures a sense of anxiety that immediately has my feeler scanning the area. Then I feel it: an uneasy energy that should not be in my apartment. My eyes finally beginning to focus, I see down the hallway near my bedroom a cloaked figure, staring in my direction.

Jumping up and grabbing my monk's spade off my back despite the overwhelming fear hatching inside me, sudo-abominor has my legs racing toward the figure. The phantom quickly disappears around the corner but not without smearing some red liquid and gook on the wall with its hand and sending the single word "Kailey" through my head. I smile though, because it did not leave without a brief examination by my feeler. Sensing a matching anxiety to my own, I close my eyes and follow, appearing in Gernwood, Bu's homeland of pus-filled puddles and hauntingly horrible acts of torture. In the distance I see several single-taloned white rabbits: a colony of meeples, which are perhaps the most dangerous creatures in Renhala.

The figure I hunt darts behind a castle wall as I see the tail-end of the cloak and I run to follow. Once again it vanishes and I close my eyes, only to be brought back to my apartment. Not satisfied, I instantly travel back to Gernwood. Unfortunately, I find myself in a particularly dangerous situation: face-to-face with a large meeple. "How stupid you humans are," it announces, its talon fresh with blood and its voice resembling a heavy load of weights against my body. "What's a pathetically fragile creature like yourself doing here?" My thoughts are suddenly ones of weakness as my body fills with fatigue—for that's a meeple's power. My now-heavy monk's spade falls to the ground as my arms slump at my sides.

The meeple moves ever-so-slowly as it lays its front paw and talon against me, forcing me to fall to the ground. Laughing as it watches my attempts at movement, its mouth moves near my face and its heavily-capillaried eyes scream of the hate bubbling behind them. "Any last words before I end your meaningless existence? You're taking up too much space."

Then without warning, and with extraordinary strength, sudo-abominor trudges forth with large and mighty steps, giving me the ability to smile—and widely—as my feelings of self-loathing wash away. The astonishment in the meeple's eyes warrants a loud and triumphant laugh from my mouth. "Surprise!" I shout, sarcastically, and the meeple releases a small bit of pressure from its hold on me.

"How?" It says, startled and confused. My hand fishes near my body for my spade, but the meeple, suddenly having the strength of three men, pushes harder against me and my searching arm, allowing me no room to grasp the weapon. "You're cursed," it snickers as its knife-sharp talon comes in contact with my temple, slowly marring my soft skin, "with sudo-abominor." It smiles as best a dangerously evil giant rabbit might, still pushing harder against my temple, forcing a large expanse of my emotions to come surging forth. Images of my mother and Gunthreon and Bu reel quickly through my mind, and as one lonely, but bright tear breaks free from the true me, it reflects off the meeple's eyes back at me. "You know I haven't seen sudo-abominor since Devot—" Its speech is suddenly interrupted as its body is suddenly lifted off of me, flying backwards as though from an unseen kick to the chest.

As I gain the strength to sit up and look forward, there before me is the back of my cloaked intruder, hunched over the meeple, blocking my view. With brutal thrashing noises and gurgling death sounds, the meeple's body—now a bloody mess of fur—falls to the ground with a loud thump and a bright red splash of blood.

A brief shiver races up my spine from the anticipation of looking into the eyes of my bloodied savior. My hand moves swiftly to grab my monk's spade as I pull myself up and brace for battle. "*Face me!*" I yell, just as my feeler embraces the edge of its energy—but I'm too slow as the being disappears. I search, then reappear in my apartment to find Kioto frantically jumping and barking outside on the balcony. I let her in and as her ears perk up at precisely the same moment the same tickling "Kailey" resonates through my head, she immediately darts down the hallway, fully disappearing on her own quest to Renhala.

In my anguish, and as I travel back and forth between realms almost instantaneously, I realize I lost the figure, *as well as Kioto.* With such a brief touch of my visitor's energy, I wasn't able to hold onto the true feel of it, and for some reason I've never been able to grasp, let alone *feel,* Kioto's. It's almost as though hers simply does not exist, when in fact I know other animals have faint pulses.

Frustration overtakes me and I slash at a lamp on the table then fall to the floor. Screaming loudly into my hands, I imagine what it may feel like to wrap my hands around my father's throat and squeeze with all my might.

I return to Golden Dunes, tell my story, then nuzzle up with Conner and wallow in Kioto's disappearance as I notice Ladimer's change in his body language as I wrap Conner's arms around me.

Conner soulspeaks in my ear and I breathe in the truth of his words, bathing in the simpleness of them as his hands then encompass my cheeks and he kisses me delicately on the lips. I close my eyes and imagine a world devoid of meeples, bloody handprints, and sudo-abominor as I grip onto the solidness of his energy and wrap it over my own like a baby snuggling into the security of its favorite blanket.

Gunthreon proceeds to make me repeat the story three times in graphic detail, each time resulting in exchanged glances between him and Ladimer, with no divulging of information in my direction whatsoever, only a suggestion that perhaps I should keep my distance from Abscondia.

Lupa offers to prepare me some starcka dumplings and I accept, hoping that food will help settle my nerves, but as Bu helps her prepare sweet cream sauce with ingredients from her no-bottomed purse, I see a few of his tears drip into it, creating a temporarily-shining sauce. Lupa waves her hand quickly in front of her face to fan away Bu's stink as he continues stirring. Surely he doesn't smell *that* bad.

My eyes rise to see Ladimer sitting on the simple straw bed he made—just enough to keep him off the ground, but high enough for him to stand quickly if needed. He silently calls me over with a quick jerk of his head, and as I concede, Conner frowns as I leave the warmth of his chest. I ignore both males' energies as they come within an inch of each other, almost daring the other to make a move. I'm too tired to separate them, so instead, continue concentrating on my sadness for my missing dog. "Why can't I ever feel her energy? Why is she so different?" I cry as I sit next to Ladimer.

He tries to console me by placing his hand on my shoulder and I instantly feel his care for me, for his energy pulses a bit faster at the touch. My chest heaves a bit a bit deeper and Conner notices as he pretends to not keep a watch on us. Ladimer ignores him.

"Kioto is everything to you," Ladimer says, looking into my eyes, knowing the love I have for such a stubborn animal (perhaps more than just one). "Think about it, her energy is with you every day. Kailey, it's part of you. It's special. You have melded together in your lives so intimately that she's not that much different than your own energy." He pauses as my energy reaches slowly to touch his—an almost secret caress for I can't seem to help myself. His eyes reveal nothing as I make contact. "You've created a 'third' energy—a resultant energy," he says, "which cloaks both of your and Kioto's. It's known as novus navitas, or navi as we Renhalans call it. Do you ever *feel* your own energy? I know you *use* it, but can you actually feel your own as a physical presence?"

I shake my head as he continues ignoring my energy mingling with his. "So what's so special about this 'third' energy, *navi*?" I question the pronunciation.

"Kailey, it's birth." Ladimer declares. I notice a small squeak from Lupa who has evidently been eavesdropping on our conversation. I look to her and she quickly looks away. "I'm sure Gunthreon has given you the speech at one point in time?" he continues. The questioning look on my face warns him I don't follow. "You know, the Neda-Velopa creation myth?" I must look absolutely dumbfounded for his eyebrows rise in disbelief at my stupidity. "Two hands clapping?"

Conner joins us, forcing Ladimer's hand to lift and my energy feeler to instantly retreat. Sudo-abominor stirs at the interruption, upset with a disruption of some plan only it knows. Conner then places his hand in mine, sending an electric shock through my body, pumping my heart a bit faster.

My mouth opens and my head tilts back as I suddenly realize where he's going. "Sound is created…as hands clap," I say. "And yes, of course, the same theory applies to the birth of Renhala." Gunthreon indeed told me that the Higher Ones—Neda and Velopa—were once simple atoms which, as they collided over time, evolved into physical matter. *Colliding atoms. Electrical shocks.*

"As well as the birth *of a powerful love*," Ladimer says as he looks slyly at mine and Conner's intertwined hands, "which can arise from anything from physical attraction to emotional attachment." My eyes widen with the sudden realization of why Conner and I have such a "static," relationship. "Or from constant friction from running against a brick wall." Ladimer can never leave well enough alone. I clench my jaw as he walks away to speak to Gunthreon, both hating and loving Ladimer at the same time.

Conner's energy feels like a volcano itching to erupt. "What's that supposed to mean?" he whines, squeezing my hand a bit too hard as I pull away to escape from further pain.

"Nothing," I bite back. "He's just trying to make me feel better, but he's no good at it." I wriggle my fingers and fight back the anger developing since the death squeeze on my hand.

Conner moves closer to hug me and rubs my hands lovingly. "Sorry." He sits and pulls me to his lap.

Bu looks absolutely forlorn as he see the exchange and possibly senses my unstoppable anger. "Don't get mad, Kailey. Bu will find Kioto." He disappears without an attempt from me at stopping him, only because I know he's the best chance in Gernwood to get Kioto back to me. It's a totally selfish act that I am perfectly aware of, but don't feel as bad as I should.

Gunthreon fortunately agrees, for as he and Ladimer approach, he states, "If anyone can find her, it's Bu. Kailey, are you sure the figure in your apartment was your father?" Ladimer says nothing as his eyes burn a hole through me.

"Yes. It had to be. The energy was familiar."

Conner stands up, almost dropping me, drawing a snicker from Ladimer. "It can't be possible."

Ladimer remarks, "Renhalan magic is strong, and not everything is absolute. When you saw the key disappear, his essence could have *possibly* transported itself elsewhere. Maybe Neda and Velopa didn't think his death was worth the effort. Perhaps karma has her hand in the matter." Ladimer's eyes meet mine. "But that's not to say I wouldn't attempt to choke the life from him if I found him." Conner soulspeaks in answer and I cower at the savageness in what *he'd* attempt to do to my father.

Gunthreon pulls us from our hatefest and reminds us that my father is not on our "To Do" list. "We have other matters at hand that we can solve, so please focus. This new contract is achievable and will reconnect a mother and daughter—something worthwhile and meaningful. Right, Kailey?" He's always hoping that these sorts of contracts might help to fix me, but I recently feel that the contract acceptance is simply satisfying his savior complex. I nod. "Tomorrow we will travel to Luvia and find out the details on Flora, so until then, please get a good night's sleep. Kailey, don't worry about Kioto. She can take care of herself and Bu will be by her side in no time."

I look over at Sir Cuche who is sitting on his uneven straw bed (since we all got our kicks watching him attempt to do something for himself), huffing and puffing. "What's up, Sir Cuche?" I ask, glad to change the subject, for Sir Cuche is always a fun subject.

"We need to do something for me starting at sunrise."

"Don't worry. We will devote some time to finding your wife tomorrow, too," I say, my glare at both Gunthreon and Ladimer forcing eye rolls.

"Yes, Sir Cuche," Gunthreon adds, "we will see what we can do for you. Ladimer has to meet his contact anyway." Patting Ladimer on the shoulder, Gunthreon gives him a huge grin. "Isn't that right?"

"Whoopie," Ladimer groans as he steps out of our dune and into the silence of Golden Dunes. I realize that the silence is actually creepier than the occasional howl of an unseen beast.

I lie next to Conner and try to calm my anxiety as his hands wander to my hair. Falling into a state of relaxation, my eyes close as sudo-abominor fights to get me riled up again. A soft female whisper—a sound that often lulled me to sleep with gentle lullabies—enters my ear. "Sleep." A smile graces my face as sudo-abominor is subdued, for the voice of my mother is pure comfort. Her energy then pinches my butt and as I swat at nothing, Conner makes it clear he didn't touch me. I giggle to myself and drift off to a better place.

# Chapter 6

## Possession

As we wake to the warmth of Golden Dunes, we notice Sir Cuche is already up and dressed in one of his fancy robes, daintily sitting on the edge of his bed, twiddling his thumbs, anxiously waiting for us to start our duties. "Ladimer left already," he says, hastily. "He went to meet his contact. Time is wasting, so let's get going!" Quickly he stands as though we will move at the snap of his fingers.

Lupa throws a muffin at him, hitting him square in the face. "Eat first! And don't you have something lighter to wear besides your big 'ole robes?" Sir Cuche folds his arms. "Haven't you noticed that nobody wears those anymore?" She passes the remaining muffins to Gunthreon and Conner, and also Jenna, who I see has returned.

"Jenna, how's the boss?" I ask. Thinking of my boss and his exorbitant amount of good energy sparks memories of kindness and I suddenly miss him.

Once again, with no embarrassment whatsoever, Jenna shoves her whole muffin in her little woodsprite mouth. Muffling her speech with chews, she says, "Evan said you gotta visit soon. There are tons of new contracts and you are a little behind in the bookkeeping." Swallowing everything, she then moves closer and whispers, "Oh, and no luck with the *equipment* you spoke of."

Just when I thought I may have a decent start to the day, I brace myself as sudo-abominor slashes out meaninglessly at her comment. "Why is it that I am expected to do *everything*!" I throw down the last bit of my muffin, fighting with myself once again, for I was saving the best part of that damn muffin for last.

Jenna responds as she picks the piece up, clearly recognizing the heavily sugar-crusted top and tosses it in her mouth, too. "Geez, Kailey. Come on, you agreed to all this. Hey, where's Kioto?" she says, looking around the dune. "She wasn't at your apartment, so I thought she was here."

I scream and Lupa and Jenna both jump. Leaving our hut by stomping my feet, I stare at the openness of Golden Dunes, stretching for what seems an eternity. It's peaceful now, when the suns are out, in a barren way, settling my nerves somewhat, for the void of emotion and energy lets me quiet my brain. It seems the vortexes are sleeping in late this morning, for there are none within my sight as I continue exploring with my eyes over the glistening landscape.

Suddenly, movement from a ways off near the foot of another dune catches my eyes. Scrunching them to see better, I see two individuals in what seems a very heated and emotionally-charged conversation, as one eventually storms off after being roughly shoved by the other. The remaining figure stops and stands quietly, also looking to soak up the serenity when it then looks in my direction. I see the slither of movement along skin and know that Madam Eve has seen me and knows I witnessed the display. She waves and quickly moves in my direction, practically gliding across the sand.

"Good morning, Kailey!"

"Everything okay over there?"

"Yeah, just a little lover's tiff," she purrs. "You know how that is. I'm sure you and Conner have had your own, right?" Her heavy-lidded, deep eyes reach into my brain as one snake stretches out slightly and hisses with its tongue. "Or perhaps you and *Ladimer*? I see how you two look at each other." She waits for a reaction and unfortunately spots the movement of my clenching jaw, for she nods her head. "It's only about the making up, anyway, isn't it?" She smiles devilishly.

"You're a big girl and have a right to your opinions," I say. "But just know *my* 'tiffs' are morally purposeful and not for the sole purpose of sexual satisfaction afterwards."

"Who said anything about sex? Those were certainly your own words, Kailey." She suddenly makes me want to smack her face, with her snide lift of the corner of her mouth. "Anyways, I signed your contract. Here." She hands me the paper and I examine her signature written in gold ink. "You are now being paid by me, so I expect you to provide…in any way I need," she says as she moves closer.

I open my mouth to respond angrily and she places her finger on my lips. "Shhh. I won't ask for anything that hurts. I just really need my daughter back." Her soft lips then meet mine as I stand, dumbfounded, as her snakes slide about, hissing at me and watching as though I may attack Madam Eve. "Hmmm," she groans as she pulls back, slowly, just as the sand around our feet begins moving about quickly. "Slightly sadistic," she says, more to herself as she watches the nearby sand, looking confused. "My, Kailey what are *you* made of?" she mentions as she touches her lip. Something inside me stirs and it's not sudo-abominor. I blush, almost feeling that sudo-abominor is as thrown off as I am.

Sir Cuche suddenly appears near us and clears his throat before he speaks. "I'm quite sure you're accustomed to being number one all too many times, but right now you are *second* in line, Madam Eve, so please keep that in mind before you make any foolish requests."

Madam Eve furrows her brow at Sir Cuche, then turns to me and says, "There's so much at stake here. I just want my little girl found and safely returned home." Sir Cuche stares defiantly at her as she decides to return from where she came.

I shudder a bit, shaking off the strange feeling left in the aftermath as she walks away, but I hold tightly to the need to suddenly see Conner. "Thanks, I owe you one. She totally caught me off guard with that one."

"That woman is not to be trusted, I tell you."

"She's just a strong and persistent woman who most likely gets whatever she wants," I say. "I can deal with her. I should've cut off her lips, though."

"Yeah, right. You sure showed her after she planted that smooch, didn't you?"

I hold my monk's spade in his direction. "If you tell anyone about this I'll…"

"Kill our contract?"

"Yeah, our *contract.*" I put my spade on my back. "Let's just go find your wife. I'll gladly pass you off."

"Sure, Kissy Kailey," he sasses, causing my building anxiety to fizzle out as I discreetly touch my lips where a tingling sensation remains. I laugh at Sir Cuche, as well as myself, and feel a welcomed warmth that has nothing to do with the blazing sun.

"Let's go find Conner," I say, prompting Sir Cuche to laugh at my sudden needs.

# Chapter 7

## Admiration

We leave Golden Dunes and try to brush off the sand, but it's useless. Jenna repeatedly shakes her head and sticks her fingers in her ears, once plucking an unusually large sand beetle from within. Being closest to the ground surface in Golden Dunes deserves some recognition so Conner picks her up, allowing her to try and comb her hair while sitting on his shoulder.

"Sir Cuche, where are we heading?" I ask as we all follow him, our pompous Pied Piper.

"I had received a message that my wife was spotted at an animal refuge."

Gunthreon asks, "How recently?"

"Within the past week."

"Lead us on," Gunthreon insists as Lupa slips her hand from his and wanders over to stand next to me.

She slows her steps, allowing us two to trail.

"What's up, Lupa?"

"Time for a girl-to-girl."

"Okay…"

"I'm sorry," she says, quietly, "but I have to admit I was eavesdropping when you and Ladimer were speaking earlier and I heard him mention navi. I've always been very interested in that subject." She drops her head and looks to the ground as we walk, hinting to me that the subject awakens a bit of emotion for her.

"And you want me to tell you if I feel it between you and Gunthreon," I comment. I try to carefully establish my words before they escape my mouth for fear of hurting Lupa during a vulnerable moment. "Lupa, I—" she stops me with a shake of her head.

"I'm not looking for it, dear Kailey. I am going to simply request that you never mention the absence of what we speak of in front of Gunthreon, please. I do love him, but Gunthreon lacks that certain…I don't know how to say it…spontaneity, or 'fun' that I crave. He *thinks* too damn much." A certain look of exhaustion passes over her face and then she marches off and returns to Gunthreon, placing her hand in his and sneaking me a glance over her shoulder. I stand for minutes, simply trying to absorb what Lupa just said as everyone else continues walking.

"What the fuck," I moan to myself as I realize that I really know less than I think sometimes. Spotting a jambleberry plant near me, I pick off a berry and toss it into my mouth in defiance.

"What a bad girl you can be. What language," says a whisper from somewhere around me. My hand instinctively grabs my monk's spade as I realize it must be the effects of the jambleberry. As I stand, frozen in mid-chew, I send out my feeler and instantly feel his light and playful energy.

"Come on out, Terro."

"How did you know?" he asks, as he steps from behind a tree, shuffling his feet and kicking the pebbles before him. "I was almost certain I had you! But I guess I'll never be that good."

"Good enough for what?"

"Good enough to stealthily sneak up on someone like Kailey, the karmelean. You are so cool. I kinda follow your stories. You're like a superhero. A hot superhero."

"Me?" I squeak, my cheeks starting to spot red. "You must have me mixed up with someone else."

"Ha. Don't sell yourself short. I heard you do that sometimes."

"How old are you, Terro?"

"Old enough," he says with a mischievous air, and winks at me.

I laugh at the knowledge of this youngster, who apparently knows more about me than I do. I look at him and realize that he has Madam Eve's eyes—beautiful and engulfing eyes. I swallow the spit that has begun accumulating in my throat as my lips tingle and then place my arms around his shoulders and pull him forward as we begin walking. "Hey, I'm really sorry about your sister. It must be really hard without her and all. Any obvious clues left behind? Anything strange?"

"Absolutely nothing," he mutters. His energy emanates a deep, continually-burrowing sadness, reigniting my own grief for Kioto's disappearance. "I miss her," he confides. "She's my best friend, so you'd think if she left on her own, she would have told me *something*. We're twins you know."

"No, I didn't. Your mom didn't mention it."

"Well, I think by even now you might realize my mother's *priorities*," he states, his energy suddenly beginning to speedily dance around, occasional kernels popping like popcorn. I instantly know that this is a delicate subject that he is trying to stay calm about, but it's difficult for him. He sees me watching him, and then adds, "It's okay. She's a good mom. We just have our moments. She's had a rough past, so just keep that in mind and give her the benefit of the doubt when needed."

"Can I ask what kind of rough past?" I think of my own life and the wells of depression that I fell into when blindly fumbling through the darkness.

He looks at me, saying nothing as he falls into contemplation about sharing information on his dear mother. "My mom was abandoned when she was a teen." Amber invades my thoughts as I remember the hell she had to endure growing up after her own mother figuratively left her life, and hope that that very hell will be the reason why she will overcompensate in her own mother-child relationship with my half-sibling. "She had to do a lot to survive—things she's not very proud of." His wet eyes plead with me to give his mom a chance. "Mom has worked so hard to get to this stage in her life. That's why she's got her snakes, you know… After being left for dead by some goons she says she was visited by Velopa."

I quickly inhale and hold my breath, recalling the sensation an unyielding power flowed over my body and fear shook my brain the moment I stood before Velopa the Stern—the very god which struck me and almost left *me* for dead.

"Velopa renewed her strength and left her forever endowed with those…creatures." Opening my mouth to talk, I end up quickly shutting it, for after all, Madam Eve is still his mother and I will not willingly allow any "un"-pleasantries to invade his young ears. He laughs to himself. "Yeah. Well, I'm not gonna keep you from whatever you're doing this morning. I have to go help Elivon irrigate the fields, anyways. There's been a bit of a…drought lately. I'll see you tomorrow when you come by our house."

Before he leaves I grab his hand and squeeze it gently. "We'll do whatever we can to find her, know that." The air around him turns warm and gooey like caramel as my feeler dips itself in it, but with the allure of its sweetness, comes the difficulties of pulling away from the stickiness.

He steps away to begin his journey onward, but stops and turns back. "Oh, I almost forgot." His hand then drops a mini pocket satchel into my hand. "I bought you a gift. And to answer your question, I'm eighteen." His hand lingers in mine, still holding the satchel. "See you later!" Running off quickly, he leaves me stunned. I open the bag and peek inside to see small black dried leaves. Fluid forms in my eyes as the smell of imported Meadow's Edge lilac flowers drifts to my nose and brings me a brief moment of comfort. This young soul has bought me tea from my birthplace: the place where my shining star of a mother introduced me, as well as my brother, to life outside the safety of the womb.

My emotions then do a whiplashing one-eighty as my father, Devoten, enters my mind and I unknowingly force a seam to rip in the bag of comfort, forcing the tea leaves to drop. As I eventually notice them lying at my feet, I curse the heavens, ignoring jackal-headed Anubis—Egyptian god of the afterlife—who has appeared in the very place that Terro was just standing, and then storm off to find my friends.

# Chapter 8

# Curiosity

After a long but peaceful walk with Sir Cuche always a block ahead, we arrive at the animal refuge. Sir Cuche quickly enters and within seconds arguing ensues inside the establishment.

"It's against my policy to give out information about prior visitors!"

"But you don't understand! I am looking for my wife you mangy maggot!" Sir Cuche has already made another friend.

We enter a room which can only be a main office as Gunthreon interrupts seconds before the owner, a plump and balding man in thick leather boots, sucker punches Sir Cuche as he's trying to rifle through the visitor's log. "I suggest we all calm down and discuss the issue in a friendly manner," says Gunthreon in his oh-so-persuasive way.

The owner's mood suddenly changes into one of relaxation as Sir Cuche pulls out several gold bullion—the preferred Renhalan form of currency—from a small pouch. "How's this for friendly?"

"Well, welcome to Hoolie Acres! I'm known as Hoolie Hall. What can I do you for?" he rambles as he slides over the visitor log and kindly takes the gold bullion from Sir Cuche. It's then that I notice all the rather precious and expensive knick-knacks lining the office walls. Several gold and silver pendants, marble vessels, and rough precious stones sparkle in response to the afternoon sunlight creeping through the windows.

Hoolie Hal then leads us to his store beyond the office. Conner and I approach a wall lined with hundreds of pictures of—I'm guessing—hoolies. "Wow, I haven't seen one…in years," he says, the latter as a whisper. An expression of solemnity flashes across his face, but as quick as it forms, it disappears and is replaced with a look of eagerness and child-like excitement, something which I rarely see from him. "I can't wait to see one!" he suddenly exclaims.

My eyes scanning all the pictures, they all look similar: bearlike, but much smaller than the average housepet, with a patch of brightly colored leather-like skin that makes it appear as though each is wearing a different colored hood covering their head and ears, ending at their necks. They're definitely cute, but nothing worth exclamation.

Questioningly, Hoolie Hal says, "You've seen one? Where? I know you are not in my visitor log and I personally care for each and every hoolie alive—to my knowledge—here at my refuge. They are all my children."

Conner doesn't answer, but only scavenges through a pile of handmade hoolie postcards.

Feeling something strange in Hoolie Hal's energy, I respond to his statement. "So, if this is a refuge, why does every single hoolie live here, with you? Are they endangered? Are you the only one that knows how to take care of them? Are they free to travel as they want?" I say, expressing my doubts as rhetorical questions.

He squints his eyes at me. "What are you implying, Miss?" You evidently know nothing about hoolies and how their undying curiosity constantly puts them in danger."

"Kailey, clam it, please," snaps Conner, while eagerly examining dried hoolie dungpies, then moving on to the next table. "The man obviously knows what he's doing."

"I will not *clam* it." My gaze threatens to burn through Conner's eyeballs. "Why are you acting like a moron? Put down those stupid ears!" I snap as my Quicksilver speed allows me to flash toward him and rip off a headband with fake hoolie ears. He continues to stroll around the storefront, examining each and every good.

"He obviously has a thing for hoolies, Kailey," says Lupa as she giggles to herself. Conner blows a whistle which supposedly sounds like a hoolie, but to me, sounds like death by eardrum implosion. Jenna is staring at Conner, too, clearly surprised by this grown man's behavior. She eventually works her way over to Hoolie Hal and I hear whispers about cell phone rates and electronic tablet inventory capacities. She then slips him a small business card which he immediately shoves in his pocket.

Lupa then puts on a hoolie nose and dances around Gunthreon, but reserved Gunthreon shoos her, indirectly telling her he's not up for the sport. She removes the nose as we make eye contact. "Savor that," she advises as she points to Conner, who is brushing a stuffed hoolie against his face. Lupa says, "Passion. Don't knock it." I roll my eyes.

Sir Cuche starts yelling, "She was here! My wife was here!" He then spies Conner and observes him fondling the plush hoolie. "I know that look. Poor guy." He then turns his attention back to us.

Hoolie Hal looks in the log. "Ah, yes. I remember Brenda. She was *so* smitten."

Confusion splashes across Sir Cuche's face. "Not with your hoolies."

"Oh no, not with the hoolies," he mischievously smiles while staring at Sir Cuche.

"Take me to it, immediately!" Sir Cuche shouts.

All I get out is, "Take you to—" before Hoolie Hal, Sir Cuche, and Conner all go running out the door. Lupa shrugs her shoulders as she follows.

Gunthreon stays back with me. "You know, you shouldn't be so hard on Conner. We all have our infatuations. Yours is tea. His is hoolies." He and Jenna start laughing and my anger swells, bringing life to my monk's spade. "Take some breaths, Kailey. Calm down," he says as the smile disappears from his face.

"This is idiotic. Let's go before Conner gets naked and decides to live the remainder of his life amongst the damn creatures." I walk out through the door shaped like a giant hoolie.

As I step out, the noise I encounter is enough to drive me mad as I fall to the ground, covering my ears. Hoolie Hal comes running to me and I allow him to reach near my ears and plug them with pieces of foam. "What is that noise?" I yell as I stand up, the amount of energy around me enough to make me wobble.

"That's the hoolies. They cry like that when they're scared. And for some reason, they are all horrified of something here." He leads me by the hand to a giant caged pen covering a few acres where hundreds of hoolies' energies swirl and overpower my ability to focus on any *one* hoolie. Looking up, I see them all in the topmost of the trees, staring down at us. Conner is standing, foam-eared, bright-eyed, and enthralled by the sight. It is then, as I watch him, that I recognize it: the face of love—love for an amazing animal, just as I love Kioto.

Hoolie Hal is trying to coax a larger, brown, thick-furred hoolie down, but it refuses as it continually points at me. He shouts, "Sir Cuche, head down that path and you will find what you seek. You ma'am, must leave." Staring at me with beady—accusing—eyes, he doesn't break. Sir Cuche practically flies down the path which Hoolie Hal pointed him toward. Hoolie Hal is still staring.

"Why me? I didn't do anything."

"They were fine until you walked out that door," snivels Hoolie Hal. "Did you come with ill intentions?"

"Of course not! It must be something else," I say, even though I damn well know what they see in me.

He looks around, then back at me. "Nah, I really doubt it. It's you."

I inhale deeply, concerned that I am causing these poor creatures some sort of pain by being in their vicinity. "Please give me a chance. I can make them calm down." He continues staring as I walk slowly over to a tree and stare up, hoping I won't end up covered in hoolie poop. Criss-crossing my legs, I sit, not really knowing what the hell I'm gonna do, but willing to try for Conner who is scrunching his eyes at me in the same manner as Hoolie Hal. I close my eyes, recall Gunthreon's meditation lessons, and hope that sudo-abominor can resist the urge to further rile up the hoolies. My energy feeler comes alive once I'm relaxed, and with a gentle push it reaches out to the mass of the creatures, and in finding them, gently caresses them and quiets them. I continue, willing them to be comfortable in my presence as I push back sudo-abominor and its whispers encouraging me to rip off the hoods of all the hoolies.

A gentle smile graces Conner's face as the creatures begin breaking from their huddles and start climbing down the trees. I continue sitting, still caressing the hoolies as they continue to climb nearer and nearer. A sense of innocent curiosity and gentleness reverberates back to me, and as one hoolie reaches out to me, and I am about to bask in the warmth of its animalistic energy, it pulls a hair from my head. "Ow!" I yelp as I quickly swat it away, my monk's spade suddenly heating up on my back. The yelping begins again as I attempt to bury sudo-abominor deeper by focusing on an adorably precious baby hoolie, thinking to myself that Bu would surely adore these maybe-a-little-cute creatures.

Gunthreon steps in, making sure my head is not injured and requests that Hoolie Hal get his "children" to behave or there might be trouble. Hoolie Hal grumbles deep in his throat, then walks to a container to grab a pile of thick, yellowish worms. I'm praying they are for the hoolies.

"It's okay, Gunthreon," I remark as I rub my head. The hoolie who has acquired the hair prize goes running off and then surprisingly ties the hair around another hoolie's finger. They all start sweetly yipping as the two hoolies hug each other. They then all turn to me and stare as I shake my head, covering my hair. Hoolie Hal whistles, calling them over to grab some handfuls of the disgustingly squirmy worms. Jenna also runs over and pops one in her mouth, provoking a simultaneous gag from Lupa and I.

Conner comes near and hugs me. "You handled that wonderfully, Kailey. There's hope for you yet."

"Yes, I think you're right." I smile with pride as I watch the hoolies finish their treats before they climb on Lupa.

"Stop it! *Down*!" she yells. They all stop and stare at her, then sit nicely. I see that one hoolie actually grabbed a hair tie from her pocket and has begun passing it around. It travels from hoolie to hoolie behind their backs. Conner sees it too and laughs.

Jenna seems to be preoccupied with one particularly fat hoolie who keeps playing with her holly necklace. She hugs the hoolie and it gently wraps its arms around her, laying its head on her shoulder, then secretly attempting to undo the clasp.

"They are so sweet," I say to Conner, sneaking my hand in his.

"Yes, they are, and curiously sneaky, but innocent nonetheless," he says, admiringly.

"How do you know so much about them?"

"Well, when I was small—about eight years old—I found one in a forest adjacent to our property in Renhala. The creature was still young and very tiny, and evidently separated from its family. We two grew close quickly after the first day when it stole my clay udoa from me."

"Your clay what?" I say, not knowing the word he spoke.

"Oh," he chirps, "they're little figurines that Renhalan children make. Usually, after you earn your first gold bullion, the clay is molded around the gold, encapsulating it inside the figurine. I modeled my udoa after a grizzly bear I spied on a travel to an Abscondian zoo."

"So your parents introduced you to both realms early," I say, partly to myself.

He nods his head then changes the subject, knowing that the path of that conversation will only fire up my nerves. "My new creature friend was very fond of my udoa, so I let him—at least I imagined it was a *him*—keep it. He kept good care of it, washing it and pretending to groom it like it was part of his family.

"Every day before bedtime, I would sneak off to feed my friend pieces of food from my lunch I saved and he would feed me nuts and fruits from the forest and vegetables he would sneak from neighboring gardens. We would sit for hours, with my udoa next to him as though it was listening and eating too, and the hoolie would nod his head in agreement at all the right times during all my childish stories. He was my one and only friend at that time—my best friend. But, as all good stories come to an end, I learned of loss at an early age."

"What happened? Did someone take it?"

"In a way. A hunter decided to plant a very cruel animal trap near our meeting spot, and I…found my dear friend with his head in the trap, dead." Conner's pain begins creeping out from within and I take his hand in mine, wanting to yank the horrible image from his memory. "Kailey, he was holding a handful of nuts that he was saving for our next encounter—fatty nuts he could have swallowed up himself, for he was such a skinny thing, but instead, he held fast to those berries, hoping to share with me, his foolishly innocent human companion." Conner's mouth turns down, but he continues on. "And in his other hand was…a crudely-formed human-shaped mud figurine that he had made for me. This." Out of his pocket he pulls a small black figure resembling a young boy, with small bluish stones where the eyes should be. I cradle it in my hand as he passes it to me to share, his energy still holding fast to the figurine, not wanting to be separated.

I don't attempt to pull the treasure from the host, but simply admire it, shaking it to hear the trinket rattling inside, and respect it, this rough curio of love. Passing it back to him, I touch his hand and transfer a bit of my own energy with it, hoping that he will know how much I care for him. "I am so sorry." My arms close around him and he wipes his right eye as the hoolies begin approaching. "Let go of that pain, Conner. It'll eat you up alive. Be happy for the moments you shared with him, for those days were the best of his life."

"Thanks for listening." In soulspeak, he recites a small poem of losses replaced by joyful new finds, and the flow of his words are beautiful as they swim to my ears and through to my brain, blanketing my own feelings of loss.

Suddenly, I sense sudo-abominor's fight to break free of the ancient magic of his words and am surprised by a hasty, but strong feeling of malice. "You know Hoolie Hal is using them, don't you? Want me to do something about it? I could easily make him disappear, as well as the pain you hold." Part of me feels embarrassed by the acrimony, but I continue to clench my jaw in frustration as I grip a handful of the pain in the field around Conner.

He separates himself from me and I feel the quick tear; once again I hold someone else's energy in my grasp. We meet eyes and he sighs, most likely feeling my short-lived sympathy was nice while it lasted, but not knowing I just stole a part of him. "No, please," he replies. "Look at the hoolies. They are well fed, clean, and for the most party happy. Just drop it." I then drop his energy.

Gunthreon begins leading everyone to the path that Sir Cuche disappeared down. "Kailey, come on. Let's take a relaxing walk," he says with his hand extended. I take it and revel in the warm energy that is Gunthreon, his gift still having a bit of power over me. I also relax and relish in the inactivity within myself as my brain chatter quiets. "I love you, my dear," he whispers to me, "like a daughter." His smile toward me warms my heart and I hug his arm as we walk.

As we come upon a fork in the path, Hoolie Hal leads us left, when suddenly the path gets very narrow, forcing us to walk single file as I drop Gunthreon's hand and take the rear behind Lupa.

Thick-trunked, oozing trees reach out to us as we continue walking silently, my monk's spade warming as a low-octave grunting noise suddenly reaches our ears from far up the path. Sudo-abominor likes the immediate sense of everyone's fear, making me brave enough to shout ahead to Hoolie Hal. "Are we almost there?" I peek through the slits in the trees ahead, but only spy the oncoming darkness as the sun fades quickly behind the trees. Lupa jumps as I speak and then tightens her grip on Gunthreon's shirt tail.

Hoolie Hal yells back to us all. "Yes, almost there! I only have one warning for you all, so *PLEASE* listen to my *EXACT* directions. Up ahead you will see a red bullseye on the right. *AS SOON AS* you spot it, jump to the left, off of the stone path and continue your way forward *OFF* the path, in the grass, until it veers to the left."

"What?" I say to myself, wondering why the hell Hoolie Hal is asking me to jump around like a frickin' ballerina. As everyone disappears into a small opening between two trees, I stay put, for a noise behind signals something is following us. I sneak out my energy feeler, but it returns with absolutely nothing. The sound approaches and I grab my monk's spade in both hands, expecting a possible deathman to emerge, but as my ears home in on the movement, I realize it's much too fast for a deathman. My feet root as firmly as possible as I position myself for a decent swing of my weapon.

At the same moment my heart beats its fastest, a creature jumps out from the nearest turn and runs at me full speed. I drop my weapon as it jumps at me and then proceeds to lick my face off.

"Kioto!" I cry. As she moans with happiness and slobbers all over me, I pet her fur and nuzzle into her neck, noticing several clumps of matted fur on her underbelly and near her neck. "Where have you been, girl? Mommy missed you." Continuing to squeeze her and rub her tummy and ears, I am overwhelmed with a sense of relief as I deep the deepest of breaths.

At the sound of a loud screech—sounding an awful lot like Lupa—we both freeze. Kioto then growls, but higher than usual. Picking up my weapon, Kioto at my heels, I move quickly down the path, ready for an ambush. My feeler senses a mixture of horror and disbelief from my friends ahead, causing me to rush as fast as the grabbing branches will allow me. As mumbling, then more screaming reaches my ears, I turn a path rather quickly and see legs lying on the ground ahead of me—the torso and head concealed by more trees—with a bloodstain trailing from halfway down the path to the body. Lupa is also partially concealed, crouching near the ground and it's then I realize the legs belong to Gunthreon.

"*Noooo*!" she screams, bending toward him. As I run with Quicksilver speed down the remainder of the long path, with only his safety in mind, I see Lupa look up, then open her mouth to scream something at me. Time seems to slow down as the red bullseye I missed suddenly catches my attention, and as my eyes open widely, my body is suddenly shoved hard left, from nowhere and nobody I can see, forcing me to fall into a patch of brown toadstool-type growths below a nearby tree. My eyes working frantically to assess what is happening, I look back to the bullseye and then see a large spiked log riddled with old blood stains being pulled back up a tree by a gray-haired hoolie. Shivers run down my spine as I realize that the log was meant to gouge me, and as the hairs on my arms salute, a gentle kiss is laid upon my cheek.

Touching the spot where the coldness lingers, I give a small thanks to my mother, for she is still protecting me from beyond.

Once I come back to my senses and hear the sobs clearly, I reach my feeler out towards my friends and feel each unique, vibrational energy fingerprint and gasp at the violent trembling that has overcome them all, as a unit. Each one is still subtly different, but then I realize there's one missing: Gunthreon's.

I reach his body on foot and then gasp at the sight of a thick puddle of blood spreading from Gunthreon's head where the spike impaled him, creating a hole big enough to see his deepest thoughts. His eyes are closed, but his face is contorted into a horribly exaggerated look of surprise.

"Oh my god. *Gunthreon*!" I scream as I pick his head up off the path and lay it in my lap, memories of my mother dying before me instantly flooding my brain. Kioto stands next to me and licks Gunthreon once, then begins whimpering at my side. "No, I can't lose another one…"

Lupa is staring at the blood trail with cloudy eyes, seemingly retreating to a dark place deep inside herself, for she is refusing to acknowledge Conner or Jenna as they try speaking to her. Even soulspeak has no effect.

Hoolie Hal is nowhere to be seen, and in hoping that he may be some sort of assistance, I yell at Conner and Jenna to find him and Sir Cuche.

As I look at Gunthreon's head, I search every millimeter of his body with my feeler, hoping for a small pulse—anything—but the emptiness found smothers my heart. "Gunthreon," I murmur, my hands working back his hair trying to cover up the gaping hole.

"Do you feel him? At all?" Lupa sobs, emerging from her darkness, coming to kneel next to me.

My empty face is answer enough. "No. No, he can't be gone!" Her voice becomes louder as she stares at his face and begins talking directly to him. "Why did you have to save me? I should be lying here, not you!"

"Lupa, what happened?"

"Stupid me and my stupid ways." Her mouth quivers as she continues watching his face. "I saw this mushroom—a mushroom I haven't seen in years…" She buries her face in her hands. "I bent over to get it, forgetting about what Hoolie Hal said."

"And he pushed you out of the way."

"*Yes*!" She spits out, suddenly grabbing Gunthreon's shirt and shaking him. "*Wake up you stupid idiot*!" She begins pounding on his chest and slaps him once across the face.

I quickly grab her hands and hold them. "Lupa, his energy is gone," I whisper, holding her firmly, gazing into her denying eyes. "He made a split-second decision to save your life…"

She painfully pulls away from my grip and then leans near him, whispering soft words into his ear, then kisses him long on the lips as tears drip onto his face. Lying down next to him, she wraps her arm over him, spooning him one more time. "Sunshine, you are my sunshine… You make me happy…" Her sobbing begins drowning out her words, but she continues. "When skies are gray…" Her hand moves to his as she carefully intertwines each of their fingers.

The pain is so great in my heart, and the moment so solemn, that sudo-abominor peeks out, hoping for an opportunity to hate something, anything. My eyes focus on the tops of the trees and I see the gray hoolie sitting on a branch, looking inanimate while waiting for its next unsuspecting victim to emerge from further down the path. Then, suddenly against my will, sudo-abominor is able to hurl out my feeler with its own desire to tear apart the creature sitting so silently in wait. Attempting to pull it back as a burning sensation runs through my veins, I scream in agony; the pain is excruciating.

The hoolie grunts as it suddenly feels the strange presence and attempts to crawl away, but the feeler follows, then latches on with a solid hold and burrows itself deep. Writhing in pain, the hoolie retaliates with scratches, but ends up hurting only itself, for its attacker has no actual physical form.

My heart aches as I watch, not knowing how to help, and it makes me sick that I house such an evil abomination. Sudo-abominor continues to feed on the pain it inflicts, making it stronger as I grow weaker with each empathetic thought my mind struggles to embrace. Kioto begins nipping at my heels—just enough to be annoying, so I swing at her, but she continues persistently until she bites me once, a bit too hard.

In the quickest of reactions, a shot of my energy—hot as fire—launches at her and makes contact, forcing a yelp from her mouth. She backs away from me and the pain reflected in her eyes is enough for me to welcome an invitation from hell.

My body falls on its hands as Lupa pleads for me to stop, probably fearing that I may kill the hoolie which was most simply trained to guard his territory. She's probably also fearing that I might do something far worse to Kioto.

"*I can't!*" I scream as the hoolie whimpers and grunts, then finally stops its fight against what it cannot see, instead focusing all its energy on simply clinging to the branch from which it is hanging, attempting to stay at post.

As sudo-abominor wreaks havoc on the poor creature, and the hoolie cannot take the pummeling any longer, its arms finally let go and I watch as it falls from thirty feet above. Sudo-abominor, guessing the likely outcome, withdraws fully, reveling in the winning situation and anticipating the pain that will surely follow as the hoolie meets solid ground.

Taking this one and only opportunity to make a move that matters, I pull myself up and with Quicksilver speed run underneath the falling creature and prepare to catch it. I do, but with the catch, comes consequences.

Furious enough to almost kill its host without thought, the devil inside begins thrashing about, stirring up an intense objection at my actions to help the hoolie escape from its supposed demise. Lashing out even harder at the creature, it repeatedly hits me with its blows as I swaddle the hoolie with my arms and I fall to the ground. I scream at each laceration, and with each scream, sudo-abominor pulls back in my feeler, undoubtedly feeling the pain which it is inflicting upon the very body in which it is hiding. The attacks become slower and with less force as the realization sets in that if it continues, its current home may crumble to the ground, becoming a useless heap.

As I flinch at the thought of receiving one last blow as sudo-abominor tires, I sense a pulse elsewhere—a pulse I thought was gone forever. Standing up quickly and placing the hoolie gently on the ground, I momentarily forget my pain and swim in the possibility that I must have been mistaken. Lupa's eyes widen as I turn my head toward Gunthreon's body. "Kailey?" she says, a bit of hope hanging from that single word.

Closing my eyes and shutting up sudo-abominor's moaning within, with all the power I can muster, I thrust out for a search as far as possible, praying for a savior. Lupas stirs and stands up as she watches me closely. I concentrate and attempt to pull every resource from my brain. My feeler travels far and quick, racing the wind, when suddenly, I realize I can see—as with my own eyes—where the feeler is traveling, something I have never witnessed before.

I'm in awe as it continues, exhaustion threatening to thwart my journey, but I push it away, reaching and scouring everywhere: over mud-capped mountains, through green rivers, and into poorly-made makeshift huts, places I've never seen with my body's eyes. It's the most exhilarating experience of my life—a cross between my ability to travel *within* Renhala and soulsearching.

*I have to find him.* As I run on empty, feeling as though I may not be able to search any longer, I unintentionally fall upon an unbelievably strong energy which stops me in my tracks: Neda.

It's not the gray-haired English teacher I once knew, but is now a beautiful white unicorn, prancing inside a small circular patch of grass graced with delicately thin, spindly-branched trees. The trees hang low, sweeping their dry and withered arms to Neda as it continues to dance with quick steps and bellow its short neighs. A low, ominous noise resonates from the trees, sounding like a mournful humming.

Entering into the circle with Neda and turning to observe each tree, I notice they possess actual faces in the bark, each different, but all weeping thick and sticky tears. Neda's energy swirls beautifully with the unicorn's performance and I sense its attempt at quieting the trees by dissolving their maladies.

My undying need to help—no matter how strong sudo-abominor is becoming—has my feeler reaching to the trees and massaging the sadness like knots; I'm massaging the aches of broken spirits with an energy full of goodness and hope. Neda is fully cognizant of my presence, and the unicorn watches me cautiously as it continues lifting its hooves, one by one, and creating a sound similar to Native American spirit drumming.

Despite my loss of energy, I continue kneading until I can barely do so any longer. Feeling faint but determined, I attempt to hold on to the moment as a beautiful sound reaches my ears as the trees' expressions begin changing and sprouts of green moss begin rapidly growing on the branches, an occasional pink bulb growing out from each moss patch. Smiles appear around us, and the once sad song slowly morphs into a joyous, heraldic melody of triumphant victory.

A particularly tall tree sings the loudest, and as it reaches a beautiful note of harmony, it leans over me, passing my energy a small pink fruit spotted with yellow nobs. As I grasp the fruit, and look to the trees, a sense of completeness engulfs me and I once again feel like myself. Like my old self. Like the human before sudo-abominor—the human who believed in the golden rule of kindness and unselfishness. Retracting my feeler slowly, for my physical body barely has energy left to breathe, I see the unicorn stand on its hind legs and shoot out of its horn a powerful and magnificent white light point-blank at me. My body holds its breath, bracing for the blow, and as I protect the special gift in my hands, the light reaches my feeler and I know that Neda has just transferred a small amount of its energy—strong and wild—straight into me.

I return to my body and gasp loudly as Lupa rushes at me. Inhaling oxygen and trying to supply my brain with enough to register what I am exactly supposed to do with Neda's energy now that I'm filled to the brim with strength, I meet Lupa's eyes and watch as she steps away from the enormous amount of energy pulsing in, and through me. My feeler immediately shoots off with hopes that Ladimer might know what to do, especially with this gift of special fruit. Within nanoseconds, I reach my target. He's not a single energy unit, which puzzles me, but almost feels intimately connected to another. I have no time to separate the two, so I pull with all my strength and bring both energies back to me.

I am so relieved, that an overwhelming amount of excitement has me jumping toward him, but as my eyes register exactly what that second energy is I pulled back along with him, I stop, my excitement quickly turning into something else entirely different, entirely dangerous. Ladimer's eyes grow wide and his jaws clench as I feel his energy, a medley of surprise and frustration.

My old self cowers once again as sudo-abominor pushes forward with enough force to make my head spin as well as crush the fruit in my hands. "Is she your *contact*? Or are you just *making* contact?" I say through sudo-abominor as the female attempts to cover her naked body with a loose, silky garment that was wrapped around them both. Ladimer's surprise soon turns to anger as he steps toward me in only a pair of drawstring linen pants, fists at his sides.

Sudo-abominor reacts immediately and sends a tendril out to the female's throat. The snake of energy constricts as the gorgeous, black-haired beauty thrashes about as her supply of oxygen is slowly cut off. Ladimer hears her choking, and while continuing to stare at me, reaches me quickly.

"*Stop! Kailey, stop!*" It's not Ladimer, but Lupa screaming at me.

Her voice returns me to my senses as Ladimer grabs my arms, his hands sending a painful sensation through every vein and artery branching out inside me. Through the pain, and wavering resistance to fainting and still holding the girl, I see Gunthreon's body once again in my line of vision. Ladimer continues sending venom through me and as my skin begins turning an ugly shade of gray, I force out the only words I can. "Gunth…reon…dead." His eyes widen and he immediately releases me and turns around to find Gunthreon's body lying still on the ground, his pulse gone again.

Ladimer turns back to me with such anger that I jump back several feet and yell, "*I didn't do it!*" He quickly dismisses me and runs to lay his hands on Gunthreon's body, then begins rhythmically pushing on his chest.

My feeler releases the delicate throat it was strangling and with one rough shove, I reverse the act of soulsearching and send the woman back from where she came, feeling a sense of satisfaction despite knowing that my acts are irrevocable. I then kneel next to Ladimer.

"Come on my friend," pleads Ladimer, "please." Stopping the pushing, he moves his hands to Gunthreon's skull and Ladimer's fluid energy cascades over his patient and rushes into Gunthreon's mouth and ears, and into each and every pore. Bone and skin begin to fill in where they were no longer existent, making Gunthreon's form whole again but still devoid of any living force that I can sense.

Already Ladimer's face reflects a massive energy drain, so in my desire to help fix Gunthreon, I shake off the rest of the fruit pulp and juice from my hand and place my warm hand on Ladimer' arm, knowing that our energy together is an aphrodisiac to him, able to replenish energy. Disappointingly, he shakes me off as his eyebrows rise as he looks in the direction of the fruit. He then scrambles to grab a small chunk of it that lies on the ground, never once looking into my face. After grasping it, and with a small amount of hope in his eyes, he places the fruit in Gunthreon's mouth. Nothing happens and Ladimer begins crawling around, looking for more. "*No*!" he shouts, and as I look to Lupa, she frowns at me, and I instantly feel both of their energies' disgust. I take steps away from them and simply observe Ladimer as he works his way back to Gunthreon. Lupa begins crying as Ladimer's shoulders slump and the hate I feel for myself increases exponentially.

In an effort to continue, Ladimer puts his weight on Gunthreon's shoulders, supporting himself. "This can't be happening. I have to do this." Wanting to wrap my arms around him and handle his energy, I refrain, knowing that I would only make matters worse. Lupa hugs him instead, and as he begins sobbing heavily into her shoulder, her glossy eyes look to mine as I sink deeper into myself. All I can do is look down at the mess of squished pink fruit juice dripping from my hand and think how karma has royally screwed me.

# Chapter 9

## Slumber

Conner and Jenna come running back with Hoolie Hal on their heels, but Hoolie Hal slows as Gunthreon's body comes into view. "Oh no. *I told everyone! I will not be liable!*" he wails as he looks up into the tree at the gray hoolie which is licking the cuts littering its body. "What did *you do to Bringling*?! *Why is he covered in* blood?!" He screams the words, the last quieter and with a great sadness.

Watching Conner's eyes move to Bringling makes me want to jump off the nearest cliff. His energy begins to throb and quickens with each pulse as he speaks under his breath, "Not again," generating in me an overwhelming need to run, but I stay where I am, not giving in to the wanton act of cowardice. Conner's pain constricts my throat and I say nothing as Hoolie Hal's energy field whips up a vicious storm which surrounds his head. I wait for sudo-abominor to work up its own frenzy, but apparently it has retreated and has decided to nap after its earlier attack.

My shoulders droop as Hoolie Hal opens his mouth to yell what I am sure would be profanities, but Lupa interrupts him. "You leave her alone or I have your reserve shut down for negligence. You'll have to explain the dead body and why no wavers were signed." Her calm demeanor doesn't match her eyes as I give thanks with my own expression of remorse, and admire her for her strength in such a dark moment.

Hoolie Hal walks to Bringling's tree and tries coercing him down.

There's a brief moment of discomfort as everyone stands, staring at me. Suddenly a loud noises approaches. I'm too tired to send out my feeler, and feel worthless, so I resolve to stand directly in the path of whatever approaches with an exorbitant amount of speed and force. With everyone else armed, and my hapless stance, it's apparent I will not be of much warrior assistance once the force reaches us. Let karma have me.

Then through the trees emerges Fidello and Bu. Hoolie Hal gasps at the sight of Bu and backs away to hide behind Bringling's tree.

Fidello runs straight toward Gunthreon as Bu slowly registers that something is awry, for his body loses momentum and he searches our faces one by one, stopping on mine. Immediately, his eyes fill with giant tears, and he turns to look in Gunthreon's direction.

As Bu slowly walks toward him, Bu's massive body begins vibrating. To the average eye, he would appear as normal, but as Jenna turns her head toward me and looks with a sadness too big for her small body, I know she *sees* what I *feel*, and it's breaking both our hearts.

Fidello, leaning down and touching his forehead to Gunthreon's, whispers something only he can hear. He then kisses Gunthreon softly on the forehead and stands up, stepping away from the body as Bu approaches, cautiously. The body is lifeless in front of him as he bends down and scoops up Gunthreon's upper body, then sits on the ground. A moaning so sickened with grief escapes Bu's throat and all we can understand is, "Daddy," as he shakes and mumbles while gripping Gunthreon with the strength of ten men.

With no end in sight to Bu's wretched cries, I decide I cannot just stand and watch, so I work my way over to Bu as everyone besides Hoolie Hal decides to follow me. Lowering our bodies to Gunthreon and Bu, we sit closely to each other and listen as Conner begins speaking words to our souls. "He was a great man who accomplished even greater feats. He's truly worthy of Neda's attention."

Bu's crying lessens as he rocks Gunthreon ever so slowly. Pain reaches my heart, forcing me to slump slightly forward for their hurt is too heavy. "Please let me touch each of you." I plead with saddened eyes as I whisper, "Please." I know I can help a bit with the pain and hope that my friends are willing to let me ease their anguish.

Lupa, Conner, Bu, and Jenna all nod, once.

Fidello says with heartfelt emotion, "Sure, little karmelean."

Ladimer sits, both motion and emotion-less, not even shivering as the temperature starts dropping with the approaching night. He takes one more look at Gunthreon and without looking at me, coughs, "If you must." His gaze then turns to me and for a brief moment, I feel the worst sense of loss possible, one great enough to break someone's soul—the very same emotion that plagued me after my mother was killed.

Then, building itself up quickly, his energy wall blockades me from prying any further, letting me know that he, secretly, is not accepting my offer, thus hurting me beyond words. I decide to focus on everyone else.

The last of Neda's energy flows beneath the surface of my own and I will it forward, quietly, purposefully focusing on Neda, and nothing else that may awaken sudo-abominor from its slumber. As everyone wallows in their loss, I think of the wonderful time I was able to share with Gunthreon: all the conversations we had over tea, all the secrets we shared, and his never-ending compassion for a girl he considered his adopted daughter.

Thanks to Gunthreon and his faith in a broken woman, I was able to recover from the worst times of my life. It then hits me that I will never see him standing over the stove, lovingly preparing a meal worth crying over; I will never again see him secretly admiring Lupa's backside as she pulls weeds from her garden; I will never again be able to thank him for saving me, in more ways than one.

Then the deathman appears. Down the path, and approaching at a snail's pace, the deathman walks toward Gunthreon.

Bringing my heavy hands up and laying them on Gunthreon, I watch as everyone does the same, and then I release my feeler. It slinks over each individual, and as I feel it may start its caressing, it continues to slowly slide over and actually examine each person, without any movement to comfort. Letting it continue on its own accord, it then begins pulling small tendrils, like strands of yarn, from each source. Wrapping them together—weaving them—my feeler works continuously, pulling and weaving, pulling and weaving, working to create an impenetrable textile. As the feeler reaches to Ladimer, however, the field around him creates small sparks with each failed attempt at grasping a tendril. He stares directly into me, and with a newfound determination to succeed, I hold my ground, continuing to search for something loose within him. My jaw clenches as I return the stare, not backing down and not giving in to his childishness.

As my feeler suddenly finds the smallest loose string of energy, it pulls, forcing Ladimer's eyebrows to rise. Fighting against his stubbornness, I gather all my strength and with an unstoppable determination, I pull with all my might. He lifts both hands in a gesture of surrender, for perhaps he realized that this is not about fighting *me*, but helping all our friends heal. The string of energy is then interwoven in the intangible fabric hovering between us. With our energies bonded, we are family, enveloped by a strong sense of togetherness and companionship, with no room for hard feelings (even if I attempt to choke people).

Lupa's eyes wander to the deathman which is now feet away from us but has stopped its forward movement toward Gunthreon's shell-of-a-body. She then begins crying and working herself up to uncontrollable sobbing as she closes her eyes and lets her emotions run wild.

Once the textile is finished, it continues floating in the air for a few seconds, then settles over Gunthreon and conforms to his body. My soul mourns for him as I feel all the others, and as I look to Jenna, I notice her eyes squinting. Quickly she covers them as an apparent light only visible to her begins shining, and brightly. Her face turns to me as her mouth opens slightly. Suddenly, and as a shock, I feel it—a small, barely noticeable, warm, but weak pulse. My mouth opens to match Jenna's as I concentrate on the energy—the *new* energy—and know instantly it's the very subject that Ladimer spoke to me of: navi, the byproduct of true love.

"*Wait!*" I scream at the deathman as it raises its arm to point at Gunthreon, its designated target. It freezes, arm up, and tilts its creepy head a bit to the side.

With my increased heartbeat and sudden strength, I call on the last of Neda's energy, pulling every last miniscule piece I can find, and begin knitting it into Gunthreon's cocoon, incorporating a small bit of Neda's life source into the holes of the fabric. Once complete, the third energy begins beating with such intensity that each of my friends feel it. Lupa stops sobbing as the thumping gets stronger. Then, with one giant *BOOM* as navi serves as a jump-start to the heart, I begin feeling the familiar oscillation I thought I had lost forever, the one I've grown to adore, the very pulse that forced me to open my eyes and heart to new beginnings—new beginnings like this very moment.

Suddenly, Gunthreon's eyes open wide. As Bu notices our faces, he looks down to see Gunthreon alive and breathing normally. Bu squeezes with a little too much force as Gunthreon starts laughing, weakly, but *laughing*, and I think it the sweetest sound I have ever heard.

Hoolie Hal steps forward from his tree and yaps, "It was Neda. I know it!" He then gags as he nears Bu.

Ladimer looks to me out of the corner of his eyes, then says, "Neda indeed. Only someone worthy of Neda's blessing would receive such a precious gift—someone unselfish and self-sacrificing, no matter what their afflictions."

We all watch as the deathman shrugs its shoulders, then while continually pointing at me, grunts as though it's asking me if I would rather go. I shake my head and it turns and walks away, leaving no wake of energy behind.

Bu eventually lets go of Gunthreon after helping him sit up on his own. As he finds his balance, we all stare…quietly…waiting. His eyes focus and he looks at us as we hold our breath.

"Well that was interesting," he comments.

Furrowing our brows as we continue to stare at him, we all jump as he starts laughing again.

"Maybe he's brain damaged," says Jenna as Gunthreon's laugh rings loudly through the trees.

"If this is brain damage, dear Jenna, hit me in the head again, because it's one of the sweetest feelings I have ever experienced—well, besides a few unmentionable moments with the love of my life," he says, winking at Lupa. "I love you guys so much!" His cheerfulness scares us as we all look to each other, not knowing how to react.

"Lighten up!" Gunthreon twitters as he suddenly pulls Lupa up on her feet and kisses her with such ferocity I blush. Lupa stands breathless and flabbergasted as her cheeks actually redden.

Jenna slips by me and whispers, "Definitely brain damage."

Ladimer, mouth wide open, is motionless. Gunthreon says to him with a playfulness I've never heard from his mouth, "Close it, Ladimer, or you'll let the broofwings in!" Ladimer instantly shuts his mouth.

"Kailey, I need to speak to you," the newly undead states. "Oh, and thanks for calling me back. There is obviously unfinished business."

"Okay…" I reply, frightened.

Everyone stands and brushes off their clothes, not speaking to each other—most likely running what just happened through their head. Watching Gunthreon's every move, nobody is able to bring themselves to ask him any questions. Bu stands still, simply watching as Gunthreon grabs my arm and pulls me away from everyone. "Kailey, I have a message for you." He also has to separate himself from Lupa's embrace as she tries to hang on to him. "Oh, I'll come back for you, my luscious Lupa," he says with a hint of sexy in his voice, making Lupa swoon slightly as she sweeps her hair back over her shoulder and fans herself with her hand, her energy feeling on fire. My quizzical expression sends Lupa into a giggling fit.

"Yes?" I say to Gunthreon, pondering if he has received a special message from Neda, meant for me.

He then whispers, "I am to tell you…" His long pause is extremely aggravating.

"Yes? What?!" I say, anxious.

Grabbing my shoulders, he then says, "I am meant to tell you that you must tell Ladimer these exact words: 'Speak of blood, for the chains are loose.'" His hands release me and he walks toward our friends.

"Huh? What the hell is that? What happened to you?" I sputter, confused.

"Oh, and," Gunthreon adds as he turns around and gives me the sign for "I love you." Almost fainting at the instant image of my mother flashing across my eyes, I suddenly feel her energy whip by me, quickly tousling my hair. I can't help but jump, making Gunthreon laugh as I attempt to put my hair neatly back in place. My face turns into a smile and I laugh a laugh full of healing power.

"What's so funny?" speaks a voice approaching from beyond, further down the path. It's Sir Cuche and he's holding in his hands one of the ugliest creatures I have ever seen. It resembles a pig, gray in color, but has a ring of mangy fur around its head and a furry tail even mangier than its mane. Its skin is covered in random-sized perfectly-circular bumps, except for its face. As Sir Cuche approaches us, it lets out a grunt, also similar to a pig, but at the end of the grunt is a nasty, wet-sounding hiccup.

"Well besides Gunthreon's death, not much," I say, staring at the monstrosity in Sir Cuche's arms.

Sir Cuche's head turns to Gunthreon, and right when I think he may question what went on, he shrugs his shoulders and caresses his pet.

"That thing is *so* not cute," I say with a bit of snark. Hoolie Hal, hearing my comment, turns his head slowly in my direction as the energy around him begins heating up. "I'm entitled to my opinion," I say, quieter. "Don't worry, I won't hurt it."

Jenna runs toward Sir Cuche and begins jumping, trying to pet the ugly pig-thing.

Gunthreon joins them and begins stroking the pig's mane. "Wow, a grumblepig. Hoolie Hal, I'm not even going to ask you."

As we look to Hoolie Hal, he looks down to the ground and starts kicking dirt at his feet.

"What's so special about this 'grumblepig'?" I choose not to approach it as everyone fawns over it as it slobbers and grunts disgustingly.

Ladimer answers my question as he scratches behind its ears as it grunts loudly, hiccupping and beginning to squeal. "Grumblepigs are special." Conner is smiling, but not like a hoolie-induced smile, but rather a secret-knowing smile. The pig starts sniffing in his direction, squeaking and grumbling as it extends its neck, trying to reach Conner.

Ladimer playfully scratches until it seems that the grumblepig might die from hiccupping. Just as the creature begins violently shaking from the hiccups, it belches, and out of its mouth shoots a chunk of something slimy which lands at my feet.

"Gross!" I exclaim as I take one big jump backwards.

Sir Cuche giggles excitedly, then stops and clears his throat when we all look to him. "Go ahead and pick it up, Kailey. You can keep it."

"But that doesn't—" Hoolie Hal begins to step forward, but Lupa gives him the evil eye, stopping him in his tracks. "Go ahead, Kailey. Take it. I have enough…for now."

"No thanks!" I yip as Jenna walks over and struggles to pick it up. She wipes the slobber off and reveals something shiny underneath.

"I'll keep it!" she shouts.

Walking closer, and as the moon begins reflecting off of the object, I shout, "No way!" and rip the object out of her hands, turning it over and over in mine.

"Hey, you didn't want it!" barks Jenna as she tries jumping to grab the object back.

"How the hell can it do that? This has to be worth thousands." The chunk of gold in my hand is undoubtedly over ten ounces, at least.

Sir Cuche informs me, "Grumblepigs have the uncanny ability to sniff out gold, anywhere. After finding some, they like to eat it." He kisses the ugly thing on its head and the creature snorts in his face. Sir Cuche wipes off the mucus, but smiles. "This is what my wife came here to see. She has—had—an obsession with these creatures." He looks over to Conner, who turns to look in the opposite direction.

Bu approaches and as he reaches out his long arm to pet the grumblepig, it begins thrashing about in Sir Cuche's arms, attempting to get at Bu. Its efforts are successful and it falls to the ground, then lunges and bites Bu's fanny pack. Bu bops it on it heads and scowls as he walks backward, but the creature keeps following him.

Lupa, pulling out a canister of powder, shakes some inside Bu's fanny pack. The powder floats in the air and as the pig approaches, it begins sneezing. It stops chasing Bu as sneeze after sneeze racks its body in fits of trembling.

Suddenly, a loud howl comes from somewhere distant and Hoolie Hal asks us all to return to his office. "It's dark now, so let's head back," he says, leading the way.

Sir Cuche picks up the grumblepig, cuddling it closely to his chest and I trail behind Lupa and Gunthreon who are now arm-in-arm, acting all cozy and new in love. Lupa catches me staring and as we meet eyes, our conversation on the lack of resultant energy between the two of them replays in my mind, so I turn my attention to the gold in my hand.

As we all walk past Bringling's tree, I look up, searching for the fuzzy creature that I unwillingly ravished. Spotting him, I stop walking, allowing everyone else to venture far forward. "I'm so sorry," I say upward, feeling absolutely awful. "I just can't help it. I keep hurting everyone." My want now is to reach out my energy, but I realize that's the last thing Bringling may want to experience, so I keep it to myself. "What can I do to make it up to you?"

Bringling's eyes do not look away, and to my surprise, he starts climbing down toward me. For fear of scaring him, I freeze in place and simply follow him with my eyes until he reaches the ground. He walks toward me on his hind legs, and stops once while he looks me over, carefully. I slowly move to squat and hold my breath as he continues moving closer. When he's within a foot of me, sudo-abominor begins stirring and my feeler suddenly reaches out, but as I think soothing thoughts, it doesn't attack, but caresses his cheek. He moans a pleasurable purr and I hold my hand out. He quickly walks to me, greedily grabs the gold, and begins running back to his tree. Stopping before ascending, he looks back at me and puts his hand up in a goodbye gesture. I do the same and he climbs back up to position.

Bringling starts chipping off pieces of dried blood from the impaling log and I sense sudo-abominor. I run as fast as I can after my friends, hoping to keep the demon at bay.

Finally reaching Hoolie-Hal's office, huffing and puffing but happy, I notice that sudo-abominor relished in my increased pulse, most likely swallowing up my adrenaline like candy. Never knowing what will settle the monster inside, I feel thankful knowing a few weapons in the arsenal.

As I hear another howl from the lands beyond, I quickly enter inside, feeling instant comfort from the sight of my friends, as well as the warmth of the small building. I smile as Bu stands next to Gunthreon with his hand on Gunthreon's head and a huge smile plastered across his face while Lupa and Jenna help Conner pick out a goodbye souvenir. Standing near a small box of miniature stuffed hoolies, I shove one in my pocket for my secret stash of baby goodies.

Looking up after my act of theft, I notice that Sir Cuche and Hoolie Hal are talking very secretively near the log book, with Hoolie Hal's voice getting louder by the second. "—and I don't care *who she is*!"

Approaching carefully, I fear that Sir Cuche is trying to persuade Hoolie Hal to give him the log page that his wife autographed, but instead they pull the log book to the side, out of my view after I reach them. "What's up?" I ask, trying to take a peek. Sir Cuche then calls Ladimer over with a swift gesture of the head. "What's going on?" I say, sudo-abominor turning up the burner under my energy and evidently in the mood for more adrenaline-snacking. "Let me see the…fucking…book," I groan, with sudo-abominor's usual demeanor.

Hoolie Hal says, “I think this has been too much excitement for the evening, and you must all leave. I don’t want trouble. Keep the damn book.” He begins locking his doors and snuffing out lamps.

Ladimer, looking indifferent, has his nose in the book. After he decides to run a finger over an entry, the field around him shakes as he stares at whatever is in the book; he is somehow processing the minute data found in a signature. I can’t take it any longer, so with Quicksilver speed I reach over and grab the book from him and notice the small current of energy lingering on the book as it quickly dissipates. The familiarity of the pulse increases the blood flow through my body as memories of my family—mainly my father—play like a movie reel through my head. One distinct memory, feeling as though it was buried fathoms deep, comes bursting forth, leaving a now permanent impression as I remember the look of total despair transforming my mother’s beautiful face into something hideous.

As my ears once again hear her screams, my small child eyes look up as my father, Devoten, runs out a large wooden door with a seemingly unconscious child, slightly older than myself, in his arms. Pulling myself from the memory of my mother moving with unnatural speed after them, and the screams of pure torture resounding through my head as she beats on the door my father slammed shut, my eyes finally look down to the log book and its latest entry, which clearly happened as recently as the last few minutes. My legs wobble a bit as I see that the signature is still fresh and wet with blood, signed: “Stephen.”

# Chapter 10

## Explosion

"You can keep your book, Hoolie Hal. Nobody wants it," bites Sir Cuche as he wraps his arm around me, attempting to keep me standing straight. Hoolie Hal has practically pushed us all out the door before we register that he's kicking us out. "But I'm keeping this," says Sir Cuche, separating himself from me and sweeping up the grumblepig in his arms, "for this." Slowly he places his ruby wedding band in Hoolie Hal's hand.

"Sir Cuche, you might regret that later. I think you aren't thinking straight," I say, trying to verbalize my genuine concern while still trying to process the meaning of the signature in the book and the swirly mess that is my train of thought.

"Kailey, I see how you and your friends love each other, and how you stick together. My wife was here, and voluntarily at that. She's not looking for me. Our love is…broken. I don't need the constant reminder," he says as his energy droops in a very dramatic fashion. Then straightening his shoulders, he says, "We, as a group of friends, now have a much more important task at hand: to find you help. Your contract with me is finished. I will pay you when we are back in Abscondia." I attempt to talk, but he puts his hands up and shakes his head. "It's okay, really. Thanks for being my friend and understanding." When he looks to me and smiles a faint smile, I can tell he may be downtrodden, but is releasing a burden he has held too closely for too long. The lingering memories of my family make me realize that perhaps I should follow suit.

Hoolie Hal appears perplexed as he calculates fair market values of ruby wedding bands in his head. "Umm, fine. Good deal and good riddence."

The door moves to slam behind us, but Conner catches it before it does. In the beautiful melody that is soulspeak, Conner announces to Hoolie Hal, "Please remember that the ability to come and go is a freedom far more important than what gold may buy. If they are truly happy, they will return." Hoolie Hal says nothing as they share a moment, but then he slams the door and fastidiously locks it. *Slammed door…like the one my father walked through.*

As my attention turns back to Ladimer who is still examining the blood on his finger, I start putting two-and-two together when suddenly I know my next step. My body moves to stand directly in front of him as he looks at me with softened eyes and inhales, waiting for me to speak. "Speak of blood, for the chains are loose," I say as his surprise splashes like cold water over my body. His gaze quickly turns to Gunthreon and the silent exchange between them clearly defines the apparent conversation Gunthreon had with my mom's spirit.

"What did you say?"

"You heard me, Ladimer. Speak of blood, for the chains are loose." He only blinks once, slowly. "Who is Stephen, Ladimer?" I say without any hint of emotion.

His hands reach out to embrace me, but I don't move in, for sudo-abominor pushes back my need for any empathy. My energy rumbles as I stare into his eyes, sudo-abominor waiting in the darkest of caves inside me, waiting to pounce…waiting for his answer, which I now already know. "*Who is Stephen, Ladimer*?!"

Conner steps forth hearing the anxiety in my voice, the anxiety that my friends have learned to fear. In soulspeak—normally sexy and calming to my temper, but now extremely annoying—he says, "Kailey, *we* have brought you no harm." His attempt at diverting my anger away from those before me hits a brick wall as I hold my hand up to stop him from stepping closer, the clear blue eyes that I usually adore now appearing sickeningly pathetic.

Ladimer sighs. "You know the answer, but you apparently need me to say it out loud. It's your brother, Kailey. Stephen is your brother," he says, spitting the words out in all their bitterness.

"Where is he?" I spin around, sending out my feeler, but I come back with nothing. "Why did he sign that in blood? *What's wrong with him*?" Confusion clouds my mind as I begin spewing questions that I feel everyone knows except me as I look to each face around me. "Why won't he just *come to me*!" I say, my voice shaking. "*Tell me*!" I scream in Ladimer's face in a voice unlike my own. A pain much like a vice to the head forces me to wince as anger bubbles and brews inside me, increasing exponentially with each second. When the pain becomes so intense that I feel as though I may break apart into pieces, the pain stops, and something dangerously dark and sinister surges forth.

With weak energies surrounding those around me, I roughly begin searching each soul for hidden secrets—feelings of buried secrecy. Jenna cowers as she swats at my unseen feeler and runs behind the nearest rock. My friends begin shouting at me and I barely hear them as sudo-abominor rips at their auras, particularly Ladimer's. It grabs and tears bits and pieces of everyone's energy, but appears to pull his in large chunks. He falls to his knees with his head down and Gunthreon is the one to rush forward and attempt to stop me from the madness.

Grabbing my monk's spade and using my unmatchable speed as the weapon practically burns my back, I bring it forward. Gunthreon's surprised by my movement as he opens his mouth to speak, causing him to stumble slightly and giving me the perfect opportunity to slice his shoulder open, forcing him to the ground, and forcing his suggestive words to be replaced by a scream.

I can see through my eyes, but cannot control my movement as I step into a madness that buries my sanity. I simply observe from within as I step toward Bu, the huge creature which is suddenly sudo-abominor's biggest challenge. Lupa is scrambling to get at me, but he's easily holding her back. I size him up and despite the weakness I sense in him with his eyes full of hurt, he skillfully jumps toward me after shoving Lupa to the side. I adjust my stance and dodge his large arms as they reach out to grab me. He turns quickly and just as he begins running back toward me, Kioto suddenly leaps between us, growling at Bu. His forward movement stops, and as Kioto continues to growl, she slowly turns toward me. Then suddenly leaping, she knocks me to the ground. My hand releases my hot monk's spade as my chest loses all air, forcing me to groan in both pain and frustration. I sit up, trying to pull in air to fill my lungs.

"*Kailey*! Stay down. Look at what you're doing!" It's Gunthreon, and the fire which has suddenly ignited in his bones drowns out most of the remaining Neda energy that lingered in his field. I feel his sadness at the loss as he most definitely feels different.

Ladimer, with much effort, steps toward Gunthreon and heals the cut on his shoulder with a mere touch of his fingertip. I stay down and his persuasion flows over me, moving into my ears and directly affecting my brain as he says, "Bury that damn affliction. You have *got* to take control!" He moves closer and I observe the look of fear in my friends, the surface of their aura trembling with both contempt and disbelief. "If you don't, you may just kill us all. You need to bury it, *now*! Switch back to the Kailey I once knew."

A sickness suddenly erupts in my stomach and I bend forward, spewing bile on the ground. I sense sudo-abominor pull in deep, repulsed with the act of weakness, and as large brown hands begin pulling me up, I can't help but notice nobody else approaches as Bu holds me tightly. I also realize that navi is most likely the very reason that Bu's scent is masked from me. *For he loves me, and I love him, truly.*

"Bu still love Kailey," he says, softly caressing my hair. It is then that I realize that as time goes on, the more sudo-abominor dominates the true me, turning the clock hands closer to detonation on the ticking time-bomb I have sadly become.

# Chapter 11

## Influence

"I can't control it anymore, Gunthreon. I can only be me when it's resting," I say, sitting on the ground with only him next to me. Everyone else is occupying their own time by throwing rocks, nervously rifling through their everything pack, picking dead leaves out of their nappy head, and polishing their fanny pack tools. Ladimer is scanning the area as though he's looking for something, or perhaps *someone*. "You know, when I started taking the contracts, it was a great asset, but now I'm finally coming to the conclusion it's bound to take over me, entirely."

Gunthreon speaks quietly. "It's important I stay near you. At least I can still influence you, somewhat."

"Everything sets me off. But I need to know more about my brother, please. Please." My eyes beg him to quench my thirst.

"It's best if you talk to Ladimer." The look I give him speaks volumes. "Yes, I know that Ladimer seems to increase your…anxiety. It's just that, well, he is the one closest to the *situation*."

"Why does there have to be a fucking '*situation*!' Why can't he just be like 'Hey Kailey, your brother, Stephen, is alive and well and is working as a graphic designer in Toledo.' Not 'Hey Kailey, your family is a fucking joke and your brother is a maniacal serial killer, but I'm gonna keep that to myself for eternity.'" My skin suddenly tingles as though a window has been opened to a Chicago's winter night, a small warning from my mother that she's listening and is not happy with my mouth. I sigh to myself.

Gunthreon stifles a slight grunt and then says, "That doesn't make sense." I give him a nasty look, warning him to not get close to pushing any buttons. "I can at least tell you that your brother is not a *maniacal* serial killer…but not any less dangerous."

"*See*!"

Ladimer has evidently heard his queue to enter the conversation and wanders on over, a rock still in his hand, possibly for protection from me. Gunthreon stands up and they exchange a look which leaves Ladimer nodding. Gunthreon kisses me once on the forehead, causing sudo-abominor to moan slightly from within, for this one small gesture which has always provided me with a sense of protection, now signifies fragility. I hold his hand before he leaves, eating up the comfort from his grasp and trying to hold firmly to *me*, the girl who once fought for the safety of thousands but is slowly becoming something that may very well destroy all that's dear to her. "Gunth?"

"Yes?"

"Thank you for…never leaving me." His smile is brief, and before he walks away, I say, "But *she*," my head nods in Lupa's direction, "deserves whatever Neda has left in you—that which I have not drained entirely from you, yet. Hold on to the love that disarms you and leaves you open for her arrow to your heart."

Conflicting energies braid around his body, and I know that the love we share has him worried about what future actions may have to be made because of me. He heads toward Lupa and accepts an apple which she instantly enlarges with her abilities as she pulls it out of her everything pack, then sits down closely next to her, giving me one last glance before he bites into the fruit. He puts his arm around her shoulders and pulls her close.

# Chapter 12

# Truth

"Kailey, let's go for a little walk," Ladimer suggests quietly, tossing the rock at a nearby tree, which then ricochets toward Conner. His hand finds its way to mine and he begins leading me away from our group. I catch a glimpse of Conner watching our moves and then try my best at a smile, but suddenly feel that I may be sending the wrong message, so I immediately look to the ground as Ladimer squeezes my hand, once. I hold on tightly.

"Were you looking for *him*?" I ask. "Is he following us?" I say quietly, moving my body closer to Ladimer. I then notice Kioto beginning to follow as we separate ourselves from the others. Thankfully Lupa bribes her with some doggie treats she keeps in her pack. Lupa then shoos us along with her hand.

Ladimer doesn't answer my questions and we walk in silence as I begin involuntarily feeding on his energy, all fluid and hot, and feel as though I could possibly live comfortably on it for the rest of my life—no need for food. I gorge on the warmth and solidness of it, the power of it. Sudo-abominor watches and waits, allowing me to feed and fill my body, but knowing that this energy still poses a strong threat.

The conflict inside me is suddenly so drowning I wobble a bit on my feet, stumbling and moaning as my vision becomes cloudy. Ladimer catches me and then sets me gently on the ground as he kneels directly in front of me. "I can feel that *disease* in your touch," he confides, "and it's getting strong, much stronger. If anyone finds out you house it, you'll be hunted like prey throughout this realm. Nobody can find out before we find how to help you, and stop it." I nod my head, still looking down, focusing on the dizziness, knowing this is what forces sudo-abominor to retract. "Does feeling ill disgust it?" I nod again. "I thought so. I can work with that. Kailey, I need you to focus on me. Look at me." His hands are soft as they grab my chin and turn my head toward his face. "Please know I love you. It's time we have a talk."

Focusing on his face, his abyss-like eyes enrapturing me with the deep secrets held within—deep, deep secrets that I need to know now, I say, "You have my attention," feeling a bit more stable.

"Where do you want me to begin?" he asks as I continue staring at him, saying nothing. "I'm just afraid too much too quickly might turn you into a beast, but you need to know things."

"*I'm already a beast*!"

He contemplates my words, most likely remembering the visual of me tossing that strange man-hungry brunette to god knows where. Ladimer then retorts, "You are not a beast, yet, even if you do make me extremely angry at times. When I look into those gorgeous eyes of yours, I see *it*, true, but I still see that twinkle of light which only you possess—that small candle burning as a beacon for troubled times, that source of warmth for the soul. You are still the Kailey I've loved for the past few decades, the Kailey that I'd give my life for." His soft hands are strong as they hold mine.

"But why? Even if one moment I'm the same stupid girl you've watched all this time, another I am a demon contemplating how to bury my claws in you—in one way or another."

His eyebrow rises briefly as my words slink into his ears. "Because when I look at you, I see *her*, too, and how similar your bold hearts are—were." Visions of my mother's smile bob through my head like apples in a bucket as he sits down next to me. "Your parents and I had a long history together, Kailey. They were two of my very *best* friends; they were always there for me, often watching my back as they dragged me many a nights from The Wicked

Whale, drunk beyond words, starting fights with anyone who doubted my abilities. I was so full of myself."

"*Was?*"

"You have no idea what I used to be, and the things I did that I will openly admit I am ashamed of. But your parents continued to love me, despite the stupid predicaments I got into, which ultimately dragged them in, too." He hesitates and I can feel he wants to tell me more, much more. "I loved your father like a brother, and your mother, well, I grew to love her differently."

"Oh," I say, realizing where this is heading. Memories of the last time I saw my father come flooding back to me and as clear as day I can envision the hatred in his eyes as he looked at Ladimer that doomful day my mother died.

"Your mother and I grew very close over time, for her care and belief in me transformed the man I once was, the very man who would inflict a skin disorder because of a mere awkward glance tossed in my direction. In time I grew to understand the good I could do for others, and that I needn't be so high on my horse; I'd be the same man she cared for on solid, even playing ground. Your father noticed our closeness and began making comments, jokingly at first. I played along, but in those moments that your mother and I shared, I knew that I wasn't being honest with anyone. I tried to keep my distance, especially nearer the time your brother was born. That was supposed to be a moment for the parents, and I needn't be around, causing your father strife during such a joyful time.

But without the comforts of your mother, I fell off the wagon and it was the stupidest mistake I've ever made. After several mugs of mead one night, I decided that it might be fun to walk the streets and randomly…turn people…purple."

"Turn them *purple*? That's horrible!" I say, imagining what I might do if I found myself purple.

"Oh, I thought it was a blast, especially because nobody knew what I was doing until they went home. I'd simply smile at them and shake their hand and tell them 'Good day.' Well, my last victim was a woman I found sleeping in an alley, who, in my mind, had also fallen prey to a few cups of mead. So as I giggled to myself, thinking how sly I was, I snuck up on her, and as I placed my hands on her shoulders, turning her purple, she suddenly took in the biggest breath imaginable—like someone who had been underwater for too long. She gasped for air, and as she focused her eyes, they fell on me, and by the look in them, she knew what I was—my capabilities. Those same eyes of hers suddenly grew very dark and the air around her started thickening, and that's when I saw the source of her 'nap': a broken bottle of poison at her side. Suddenly, a scream so full of pain and agony blasted from her mouth—no her soul—that I fell to the ground, holding my chest, for my heart felt like it was torn in two.

Your father and mother came running because they knew far too well that I was usually the reason for loud screaming that could be heard throughout the night, *in more ways than one*."

I roll my eyes at him.

"Your mother immediately fell to fawning over me, caressing my face and the like, for she never saw me in pain—hell, I never felt much pain, but I was going to discover a pain much worse than what I experienced that night." I begin to wonder if my mom is hovering near, hearing Ladimer's words.

"The woman was so distraught over coming back to her life—for I had unknowingly brought her back from the edge of her welcomed death—that she had to return the favor, in some way or another. Without saying a word, she walked over to your very-pregnant mother, laid her hand on your mother's belly and softly spoke a few words. She smiled at your mother, then at me, got up, and walked straight out of Meadow's Edge.

We weren't really sure what had just happened, but your father grew livid because I once again put your mother in danger.

The next day your mother gave birth to your brother, Stephen, and at that point we pretty much put those visions of that woman in the alley aside and simply basked in the joy of a newborn. He was absolutely adorable and so full of positive energy that I couldn't resist visiting often and spoiling him, as well as your mother, with goodies. I slipped her a few trinkets here and there, and her eyes would glow as she turned them over in her hands, watching them sparkle and shine with the light. But she would always hand them back, knowing it was best if she didn't accept them.

Your father was a great father, always showing off his very happy baby to everyone in town as he strolled around on his various errands, always making Stephen his number one priority. Your mother was the happiest I'd ever seen her, and her every thought fell solely on her new baby and overly-attentive husband, leaving nothing left for me. So once again I sank back into the darkness and watched this family that I considered my own grow and dance in the streets. It was so hard, but for the sake of your family's happiness, I suffered in the shadows.

As your brother grew, however, the happiness of your family wavered, because it was apparent that something was…wrong." Ladimer's eyes divert from my own as his gaze focuses on the trees around us.

"Wrong with *him*? Stephen?"

"Yeah. It all started around his first birthday. One night your mother came running to me, shaken up beyond all belief. When I followed, practically riding on her coattail to her house, I found your father sitting on the floor with your brother in his lap, and the family pet at their feet, dead and blanketed with blood. Your brother was also covered in blood, so I immediately checked for injury, but to my surprise, the only injury found was one to the pet—a ripped throat, specifically. I remember sitting there, watching this tiny little baby boy sticking his fingers in his mouth and sucking on the blood of the animal. We all decided to keep that moment to ourselves; it had to be an anomaly, something unexplainable and something not to be shared. Once again I was bound to your family. Thoughts of that woman in the alley came streaming back as the image of your brother replayed in my head.

As Stephen grew, we found that he seemed to have an insatiable need for meat. He was a very obedient child, but when it came to dinner, all rules flew out the window. The savagery in which he would attack a steak was beyond all belief."

"Hey, I like a good steak," I say nervously, trying to block the route Ladimer may be going with this conversation.

He shakes me off completely, too caught up in reliving his past. "Your mother tried the vegetarian route for a bit, but he grew extremely tiny and frail without meat and his hunger for it seemed to intensify nearest each birthday, turning this small child into a carnivorous monstrosity."

"Oh my god. Please don't tell me he's a cannibal…" I feel as though my increased pulse may force my blood to rush out my pores as I turn over Ladimer's words in my brain. Contemplation stirs deep within me as I sense sudo-abominor storing this information, and feeding on the repulsion it's provoking within me.

"Let me continue. There's more."

"It can't get any worse, right?" I laugh to myself as I know that it most likely did.

Ladimer continues. "We made sure as each birthday approached that Stephen was secluded, away from townspeople, with a full belly. Your parents almost went broke buying the butcher out each year, forcing your father to turn to some shady dealings to support his family. Your father's biggest monetary failure, however: an attempt to buy a parcel of land away from Meadow's Edge in a wooded area full of 'meat,' began his sharpest descent into murky waters. You poor mother couldn't work because she had to keep an eye on Stephen, constantly. I tried as best I could to keep your family above ground, but Stephen just grew so damn *hungry*, and as your dad dealt with the situation, he fell deeper into debt, forcing him to lose all the joy he once exhibited in close proximity to his family. I am also under the belief that this is when sudo-abominor somehow planted itself in your father." Strong emotions stir inside me as I think of how Devoten may have been pre-sudo-abominor: decent and likeable.

"But anyway, the situation grew so absurd that by Stephen's third birthday, we were so damn tired from attempting to cover up the 'eating' problem. I tried fixing him with my touch, but it seems that his affliction had nothing to do with his genetic makeup. It was strictly a magical condition—a curse.

All of Meadow's Edge's pets were turning up missing as Stephen would stay with your mother's neighborhood friends on occasion, and we felt things were going to get worse as he grew more independent. Your mother and I would spend so much time together taking care of Stephen and making sure his attention was always focused on something wholesome, and in our closeness, we shared…a moment. I wanted to ease her pain and we both knew my touch was able to do just that." Slowly, the particles that make up Ladimer's energy start vibrating, warning me that his thoughts are suddenly unstable.

As the muscles around his eyes strain and he remains silent while looking into my eyes, I see the slumping of his shoulders and the large swallow he makes. What he's implying suddenly hits me smack dab in the forehead. "No," I say, feeling queasy, "you and my *mother*?" I stand up quickly and he follows as I drill for blood with my gaze. "You took advantage of my mother!" I yell at him, and as reflexes are known to act on their own, so does my fist as it connects with his face, with both Quicksilver-style speed and sudo-abominor-style strength. His head quickly jabs to the right and as he turns back to me he wipes away the blood that has begun dripping from his mouth. He does nothing in retaliation, though.

"Damn," he says, wiping the blood on his pants, "you no longer punch like a girl, do you?" His jaw bones move left to right as he determines if I did any damage he may have to fix.

"Guess not," I reply, trying to ignore my throbbing knuckles.

He is talking again, shaking slightly as he takes my hands in his once again, and holding tightly against my will. "It didn't go as far as you think! We shared a kiss that I initiated, and I thought she cared the same for me, and believe me, I wanted it to go further, but your mother was still deeply committed to your father despite the distance growing between them. Their love was fading, but she still held on to the smallest hope that everything might turn around, and that her family would heal.

I was there for her, even after she made it clear that we were not going beyond that kiss. I was there when she needed someone most, especially when she became pregnant, again." The grip on my hands tightens as I try to wriggle away.

"Believe me, the intimate moments your mom shared with your father were few and far between, but as you know it takes one lucky moment to conceive. Your mother confided this in me, for I was her closest friend, and I just loved her so damn much. I did not take advantage. I simply filled the void." His tongue darts to catch a small trickle of blood as it oozes from his lip. "Your father was always in the picture, but always off sulking somewhere. He stuck around to witness your birth, and believe me, Kailey, he loved you, even still during the moment of your birth, when you were…revealed, for you were still part of your mother." He takes one step away from me after letting go of my hands.

"What? Why would there be any belief he might not *love* me?" I say as I take that one step closer again.

His hesitation and searching into my eyes makes me a bit nervous. "Kailey, you were born with blond hair—exceptionally bright blond hair." My eyes creep to his silken blond hair as sudo-abominor rises and rests on its haunches, quietly waiting, muscles prepared for the launch.

"When you were born, the shock I felt the moment I saw you was a mixture of disbelief and a bit of selfish satisfaction, but as you were passed out of the life pool, and landed in my arms, I knew instantly I had to try and stop any rumors before they began and…I kind of fudged with your DNA." My eyebrows rise practically to the top of my head. "I had to for the sake of your parents. This," he lifts a handful of my hair, "is how it should really look." My red hair suddenly turns blond in his hand and I rip it away from him, feeling it in my own hand. "It's all in the recessive genes, but in order for your mother to avoid all the secret whispers and righteous speeches, I had to do it." I'm still staring at my hair as he grabs my hand, forcing me to drop it. "I swore to your father that nothing ever happened between your mom and me, but your father never fully accepted the truth from my mouth. He stuck around for a bit after your birth and treated you as his own, but there was always a hidden doubt eating at him, and it ruined your mother. Then one day, again, around your brother's birthday, something happened that forced your father to leave your home for good. Something absolutely hideous."

The same memory of my father fleeing with Stephen in his arms comes spilling back, along with a new memory, one of red splotches on our wooden floor and a weeping brother standing over me.

"In the one brief moment that we left you alone with Stephen, he bit you."

His body is motionless, waiting for a reaction. "Kids bite, right?" I say, not wanting to hear anything worse than a simple bite.

"He bit off a piece of your ear. Well some…all of your ear." My hand immediately jumps to my right ear and I see the memory reeling through my mind as if I'm sitting dead center in front of a movie screen. The blood is everywhere as Ladimer scoops me up, grabbing my ear to reattach it, and stifling my pain as he works. My mother pounds on the front door as it slams shut, shutting both my father and brother out of our home for the rest of time.

"Despite the fact your brother was so young, I still saw a look of mature regret in his eyes, and knew at that moment that he would never have total control over his actions. Your father became a swirling mass of anger that night and with a violent explosion, he made a grave mistake." Ladimer's jaws clench at the memories. "In a fit of anger, he threw your mom to the floor, consequently breaking her wrist. I immediately stepped in and when I grabbed him, I felt *it* stirring. As I explored him, he knew what I was doing and allowed me to try and stifle that which was growing fast inside him, eating him up. It felt my presence and recognized a more powerful suitor, so it attempted to dislodge itself and burrow into me. I had to immediately send out an almost suicidal poison inside myself, forcing sudo-abominor to disengage. It did, but only retreated further into your father, further melding them together.

Your father took Stephen and himself away to protect all of you, and the day he stepped out, he left *behind* a certain lutheose ring your mother had given him as a token of her undying love and left *with a* bloodied, scabbed indentation where that ring used to reside." I know exactly which ring he's talking about: a ring made of a special Renhalan metal no longer produced, the very ring that lead to my father's demise, helping transform him into a key.

"Your mother sold the ring because she needed the cash and she did not want to hold on to something she knew was lost forever. Why she went back for it so many years later, well, I'm pretty sure—no, I *know*—karma was putting a divine plan in motion through you." My belly churns as I think of how everything eventually played out that fateful day. "Your father was not heard from for a long time after—not until your mother received this letter." His hand pulls a worn piece of paper from his pocket and he hands it to me. "I had heard rumors of him living a great distance away, with a son who was watched over by the local shaman. It was said that your father had the shaman create a bond similar to intangible chains to connect father and son together."

I read the letter, written in a beautifully creepy script:

*To feel sunshine beaming softly on your skin, to only feel it blister the surface;*

*To wallow in the aroma of a garden of roses, to only choke on the congestion;*

*To imagine love wrapped around your heart; to only experience the smother;*

*To know the peace from a loved one's existence; to only shatter at the thought of loss;*

*To know sudo-abominor is to discover hatred wrapped in a lovely package.*

I fold the paper back up neatly and pass it back to Ladimer. "'The chains are loose,'" I say, repeating Gunthreon's words from my mother, "because of what I did to my father. Karma strikes again." I cough as though tears are creeping down my throat. Sudo-abominor shifts all its weight to the rear, ready and willing to strike down any unsuspecting suitor.

Ladimer frowns as he closes the distance between us. "Because I loved your mother so dearly, I promised to watch over her baby girl as long as I still took in breath. It was easy in the beginning, but once your mom decided to come here to Abscondia, I promised myself I'd become invisible to the both of you, leaving your mother to a new beginning. I reached out to Gunthreon, my old friend, praying that he might watch over and help your mother, despite my disappearance from his life. He agreed to help, especially after finding out about sudo-abominor, and was there for your mother, constantly supporting her in any way she needed. Your mom might not have accepted any help, but with thanks to Gunthreon's persuasive ways, she did. She adjusted well and raised you to become a beautiful woman as I sat back and guarded—no," he shakes his head slowly and draws me in with his dark eyes, "watched…admired…and fucking loved with all my heart." The energy field around him aches like something I've never felt, making my insides stir and my own energy long to wind itself around his. "I've fought all these years against my growing feelings for you because I know karma all too well, and how I am a walking disaster waiting to happen. I never wanted to be close to anyone's heart ever again, *especially* someone in *your* family, for I was sure to end up destroying that which I deemed precious in any way. But you, Kailey, have proven to be irresistible." He steps within inches of me, his body warmth coaxing me to close the gap and revel in the comfort of the heat. "Any pain you endured in your life as I sat and watched made me want to sweep you up in my arms and hold you safe for eternity. I am not going to let you fall as deep as your father did."

"No, you love me because you loved her."

"Your soul is different. Everything about you draws me in: the way you roll your eyes as you bring up the right corner of your mouth, the way you carefully sip your tea and lick your lips afterwards, the way you fight for others, and the way your soul calls to mine for shelter. I won't lie…I need to be needed, too. You need me as I need you."

I look to meet his eyes and as the heat of his energy swells around him, his engaging eyes and delicious mouth look as though he desires to swallow me up whole. Suddenly, a sound in the distance has me practically jumping into his arms as a small black creatures with two tails scurries past us. Stephen's existence has me horribly frightened, but insanely curious. Then a horrible thought hits me. "When's Stephen's birthday, Ladimer? Is it soon?"

The lack of a reply answers my question and I shiver from head to toe. "Don't worry. He's not near. I'm sure he doesn't know how to find you here, at the moment at least. Do know, however, word travels fast, and well, with all your admirers, it may be sooner rather than later that he finds our location. I think we both know that he might be looking to make contact. But for the here and now, nobody, actually…is near," he whispers, the look in his eyes one of pure desire. His hands rise and reach toward my face and my desire for his touch on my skin distinguishes any anger, fear or doubts lingering, and instantly increases my want. I bask in the softness of his skin as his hands meet my cheeks and I lean into him, wanting to feel his even softer lips on mine. His hands wander lower, increasing my heart beat to an uncontrollable rhythm. The adrenaline surge seemingly giving an open path to sudo-abominor, sends my body forward, connecting my lips with his. A twinge in his energy reveals his surprise, but he gives in to my passion, kissing back with an equally needy drive, his hands moving even lower. His mouth is sweet and his energy even sweeter. The familiarity of the love felt between us welcomes me home as I then realize how addictive Ladimer's touch really is, for a giver's touch is beyond words, making you drop everything and dip into any and all emotions; it's tantalizing, but fulfilling and painfully pleasurable. I willfully surrender to the pull.

In spite of sudo-abominor drooling over the opportunity to strike, I work my hands under his shirt, running them over his flat stomach, reveling in the firm muscles beneath his soft skin. Then, as I force him to the ground and lie on top of him, knowing that my action of infidelity is wrong, but wanting him so badly, my hand moves to begin its journey beneath his belt. His pleasurable moan and slight grind against my hips sends my energy into a frenzy, even as sudo-abominor slinkily moves forth, forcing my unoccupied hand toward my monk's spade on my back. I try fighting it, but my eagerness to be as close to Ladimer as possible overtakes my common sense as I continue to kiss him down his neck. Moving slowly across my stomach, his hands force me to writhe slightly as I grasp the monk's spade firmly, bringing it off my back. He then whispers in my ear, "I'm so sorry. This is the only way." I look to meet his glossy eyes and know that I am about to experience karma's evil ways, and sudo-abominor was just too slow. An unbearable amount of energy from his touch suddenly burrows within my skin, directly affecting sudo-abominor's intentions. My eyes widen, my monk's spade falls, and a pain and sickness worthy of death forces me to fall off him and curl up in the fetal position.

Conner's energy comes rushing toward us with a sense of extreme urgency. "*What did you do to her*?" He suddenly rushes at a rising Ladimer who has put both his hands up in surrender clearly leaving an open path from Conner's fist to his face. He knew it was coming and was willing to take another punch for karma's sake, but as Conner's soulspeak spits out ugly and intolerable words, and he wrestles Ladimer to the ground with more pummels, Ladimer realizes that he's going to have to simmer the tornado that is Conner, down. They scramble, wrapped in Conner's anger which seems to be attempting to smother Ladimer. With one touch from Ladimer to the shoulder, Conner suddenly jumps off him, but continues with a stare-down worthy of undivided attention. Once again, Ladimer wipes blood from his face on to his pants. Conner turns to check on me and says angrily, "What is wrong with your hair?"

I still sit on the ground, sickened, and suddenly feel that I would much rather be dead than continue dealing with so many problems. I swallow the saliva that has pooled in my mouth, and just as my mouth opens to speak, everyone else comes rushing toward us.

Gunthreon speaks first. "What's this about?" he inquires as he looks from Conner's face to Ladimer's then to my hair. He looks thoroughly perplexed as he warbles, "What is wrong with your hair? Oh—," his eyes quickly turn to Ladimer.

"Yes, we had *the* conversation," Ladimer says quietly.

Conner soulspeaks, speaking of his need for clarity on what the hell is going on.

"My natural hair color," I say as Conner's widened eyes quickly dart to Ladimer's hair, "but he's changing it back." I stand and walk toward Ladimer as grief and heartbreak pelt him like a hailstorm. "Recessive red is more my color, right?" I say, my lips trembling. "Weakness of the soul is prevalent in my life right now."

With reluctance, Ladimer's hand rises to cup my head behind my ear, sweeping back my hair. "No, red is the color of fire, perseverance, and love. Remember those of us who have always admired your strength and will continue fighting that which threatens your safety. Seek your shelter when you need it." He then leans over and lays a tender kiss on my cheek which sends a pins-and-needles hotness surging through my veins.

*Yes, fighting even your own feelings for me.* I stifle a small sob which has crept up my throat as my hair changes back, and feel as though I am somewhat settled back in my own shoes as I finger my coarse hair. I look away from his steady gaze and walk toward Conner.

Conner's concern physically reaches out to me and I let it coddle me, feeling the instant sensation of comfort as my stomach stirs with sickness, but knowing that he senses something went on that shouldn't have, yet he doesn't ask. "You okay? You two aren't related, right?"

"We aren't related, Conner."

His strong arms tighten around me, his energy surging at our touch, creating the briefest of shocks—actually the briefest to date. "He tell you about your brother?" Not wanting to speak, I nod. "Kailey, know that as long as I breath, in my best attempt, I will not allow any further harm to *touch* you while I'm near," he says, glancing at Ladimer, with fierce eyes. "I would never take advantage of a soul as precious as yours." The soulspoken words are thick as they drape around my shoulders, almost protecting me from the ice cold heart of sudo-abominor.

Another promise of lasting protection on a soul which could easily extinguish the very breaths in which they speak of. *How naïve.*

# Chapter 13

## Acceptance

We wake after sleeping in our dune and Lupa feeds us all some sort of spicy—almost like gingerbread—nutty rosabread and applesauce made with starcka pearls that Madam Eve left inside our hut while we were gone. To my surprise, I don't eat as much of the starcka as I had done previously and think that perhaps my churning insides are to blame for the lessened need to gorge. I throw down my last piece of bread, drink my last sip of lemongrass tea, sigh, and look to Bu, who also has some food left on his plate (a rare occurrence). He shrugs his shoulders at me and Kioto looks longingly at his plate. I give her the last scoop of vet-approved dog food from Lupa's everything pack. She sniffs it, and then stares at it, as though she can telepathically persuade it to change it into a filet mignon.

I dress and instantly regret that I've packed so many black items of clothing, especially with sudo-abominor's special ability to get me heated up at the flip of a switch. There were several moments on the trip back to the dune, during our "supposed" sleeping hours, and this morning, where I had to really pull myself together and hold back my want to drop-kick my fellow travelers. I've noticed that my patience seems to be decreasing by the hour. My greatest fear is that soon I may be lost forever, and with my loss would come forth a monster so strong and unstoppable, I fear for the safety not just of my friends, but of both realms. I notice everyone watching me from the corner of their eyes, possibly afraid I may attack at any moment. It sickens me as I almost instantly move from one good thought to one of violence.

Jenna notices the constant shifts in me as she quickly avoids getting near me at my darkest moments; the ugliness of my aura is clearly visible and the sight must be menacing by the look on her face. She makes her move at precisely the same moment I sense my monster inside slumbering. "Kailey, I'm going to do some *exploring.* Got it?" I do. She wants to look for the equipment that I mentioned. We both walk outside the dune, sweat instantly appearing across our brows. A snake matching the sand begins slinking across the landscape, away from our dune. We both watch it move effortlessly and with an almost admirable gracefulness.

Turning my attention back to Jenna, I say, "Go for it." She begins walking away. "But Jenna…"

"Yeah?"

"Please be careful. If you get hurt, I don't know what might happen to me and my grip on sanity."

The last gets her freezing in her tracks, as if she doesn't know whether to take it as a compliment or a jab from a sarcastic monster. "I just want you to know how much I care about you. With the way things are progressing, I may never get that opportunity again." I kneel near her and lay my hand on her arm, then move to sit Indian-style next to her.

Her cute little woodsprite face examines my colors as she climbs into my lap. Her arms wrap around my belly as she snuggles into me. "You're still in there," she says, quiet and sad.

"It's a losing battle, though. I don't know how much longer I'll be able to hold it off. Jenna…"

"Yeah?" She moves her head to look at me.

My eyes fix on her face, drawing every bit of attention from her. "I need to ask something of you. Something extremely important. Something you cannot say no to."

"Sure. What?" Her energy field becomes nervous, shaking as she waits for my reply.

"If I go under… If I become too big of a threat…"

"Yeah?"

"You need to finish me off." I send out my feeler across the sand to make sure I'm not being overheard, but unfortunately it's sent sprawling up into the air, reflecting off the granules of sand, but not without creating a mass of swirling hot sand. Immediately I feel a bit of anger as sudo-abominor wakes, sensing vulnerability. *I won't tolerate vulnerability.* I shake my head at the thought. *Vulnerability keeps me human.* If Good Kailey is actually debating with sudo-abominor, the melding with Bad Kailey is accelerating. *This is bad.*

Jenna jumps off my lap, her face scrunches up as she looks around at my aura, then at the vortex I seemingly aggravated into action. "What? Why would you…*No*! I can't do that."

"I have nobody else that can do it," I whisper quietly, but with quicker speech, realizing the need to get this out before the beast stops me. "You know it has to be done. The probability of me doing substantial damage is too great, and the others around me, well, they wouldn't be able to handle the results, I think. You're stronger, emotionally."

She plops her butt on the ground and buries her puny little head in her hands. As the space between her fingers starts to shine and she looks up, I see her tiny tears dripping from her eyes. She wipes her face and says, "You saying I'm hard-hearted?"

"No, not at all. Your heart is as tender as one can be. It's just that we've had a shorter history together and—" She opens her mouth to talk and I interrupt. "Yes, I know love can exist in a second's time, but you really think Bu can survive having to do something of that nature? He'd probably spontaneously combust." Her body turns to look away. "Jenna, you know how many people and creatures I may hurt, even kill, right?" She nods. "Sudo-abominor hates everything. There's no sympathy. I'd clear a path with total destruction in this world, as well as Abscondia. I know it. I feel it." Suddenly, dozens of mini sand storms pop up, swirling and twirling themselves into mass hysteria.

Jenna's eyes widen as she exclaims "Fine. If I must!" to pacify me and my vortex minions. She pulls herself up, refusing to look me in the face. She knows the truth as well as I do.

"Good. Now go see what you can find," I request, patting her butt, forcing her to move forward.

She turns back to look at me and says, "I love you, Kailey."

I force a smile at her. "I know," I reply. "Now go." I don't tell her I love her, though every ounce of Good Kailey is fighting to shout it at her.

Her speed is amazing as I watch her run off, still wiping at tears that have begun falling, even as she takes one last peek at me before disappearing around a dune.

I look out into the distance, knowing my mess-of-a-brother is out there somewhere, perhaps even watching me this very second. It pains me that one moment I fear for my ears, the next, sudo-abominor dares him to make a move.

Walking into Luvia directly from Golden Dunes is nothing pleasant. One minute I'm sweating from the dueling suns' relentless blasts of heat ricocheting off the sand, next I'm completely saturated walking into a land whose air is as thick as molasses. Sir Cuche practically faints as he steps into Luvia, pulling on his beard as though his nostrils might expand, allowing him greater access to oxygen. He also tries loosening the collar of his robe as he slowly leads his grumblepig on a most impressive leash and harness that Bu threw together with minimal supplies.

"Uh huh. I told you to ditch the robes," crows Lupa, in a manner very condescendingly Sir Cuche-ish.

Once in Luvia, everyone stops, taking in deeper breaths than normal, attempting to adjust their lungs to the extreme moisture we're suddenly subjected to. Terro's conversation about irrigation and drought have me stumped. The boy must be insane. The atmosphere warns of storms with its gray skies, but in further examination, I can't find a cloud in the sky. It looks and feels as though we are about to be rained upon, but I know that without clouds it can't happen—at least that's true in Abscondia. We are, however, in Renhala, a land exhibiting many exceptions to the Abscondian laws of nature.

Poor Bu repeatedly wipes himself down with a yellow chamois that he keeps his golden wrench rolled up in, inside his fanny pack. One whiff from this rag sends Lupa into a gagging frenzy and one glance at the golden wrench sends Sir Cuche into silent coveting. Bu catches his gaze and Sir Cuche clears his throat, then covers the grumblepig's eyes and nose as Bu quickly packs up his tool using the sweaty and pungent chamois.

Kioto's tongue hangs so low from her mouth that I cringe and ask Lupa for assistance in helping her. Lupa pulls a water jug from her pack and we shower Kioto with it, then give her some to drink. She laps it up for what seems like minutes, and even though I feel a need to drop her back in Abscondia, I know damn well she'll somehow just follow me here. Looking up at me a bit more satisfied, but still hot and panting, she looks for a scratch behind her ears as she then lays down with a loud "humph."

I move to stand on the threshold of lands, one foot in Golden Dunes, one in Luvia, and admire the work of Neda and Velopa. I ponder how it's even possible that there is no slow melding process between lands, but extreme and almost knife-sharp differences between each, even at the boundary lines. It's like a poorly-spliced film.

"Absolutely awe-inspiring. Isn't it?" Conner, also saturated, stands beside me, but unlike Bu, Conner smells delicious. "Dunes, with no body of water nearby for hundreds of miles."

"Yeah, it seems I won't be needing a shower tonight," I say, pulling back my dripping hair. "It appears I've already been soaked." I move one step closer to him and point to the landscape. "It takes some pretty powerful magic to uphold this, don't you think?"

"Indeed. Look, even the sand stays on its side, for the most part." Looking down to the ground near us I only see light sprinklings of sand in Luvia, most likely the very sand that Jenna shook out of her kinky hair.

"You think that Neda and Velopa ever contemplate moving into Abscondia? Like, maybe, they want more lands to claim as their own?" I say, testing my thoughts.

"Where's this coming from?" he asks, curious as to my thought process.

I sigh and look toward the farmland, not far from us. "We saw what happened when Devoten unleashed creatures into Abscondia, right? What if another powerful creature threatened Abscondia? You think one of the Higher Ones would come in to intervene? Neda came in, once, but didn't stay long. What if one of them could be convinced of inhabiting Abscondia to keep a watch on the realm?" I can tell that Conner realizes I don't really need an answer; I'm mainly talking to myself.

"I know what you're thinking."

"I can't help but prepare for the possible future." *I need a backup plan.*

"We are going to fix you before the future you think you foresee comes to fruition."

Sudo-abominor grumbles inside of me, hearing Conner's comment. Its anger abruptly and turbulently flows through my veins, once again awakening Bad Kailey. "*Fix me*?"

His eyes widen, and Gunthreon, hearing my irritation, steps forward. "Let me talk to her," he says.

Conner pulls him aside and I hear in a quieted voice, "...almost schizophrenic at times. We have to do something."

My teeth grind loudly and then I growl. *I growl? I growled!*" I cup my hand to my mouth, then start coughing from the vibrational disturbance in my throat and look to Kioto who has her tail between her legs, then to Bu, who is trying to take shelter behind Gunthreon. Everyone's eyes are staring at me, for they are most likely fearful of my newfound talent of canine communication. "Holy shit! I really just did that, didn't I?"

"Yes, you did," Ladimer and Conner reply in unison, both keeping their distance.

Gunthreon shakes his head while looking at me, persuasively stating, "Kailey, hold on to yourself. That which is lurking inside is doing its best to intertwine with the fabric of who you are. Please put up your best fight, girl. We do not need a werewolf in the pack." His stare is intense, forcing me to focus on his words, but I don't feel his powers making any measurable difference in my feelings, currently.

I only nod, not wanting to go into details as to how fucking impossible it is to fight something that takes over my thoughts in the blink of an eye, plus the fact that his persuasion may no longer be effective over me in the near future, especially while sudo-abominor exists. I change the subject. "Where's Madam Eve and Elivon? They were supposed to meet us here." I begin walking toward the plants, everyone falling in behind me.

Looking across the rich farmland lined with perfect rows of what I am assuming are starcka plants, we all gape. The farmland seems to go on and on forever. Tall, white, approximately six-foot tall stalks with heavy, somewhat-drooping yellow pods litter the landscape.

Without even looking at Lupa, and by simply feeling her energy's excitement, I know she's in her glory. I turn to find her stroking the nearest plant, examining the striations in the paper-white leaves and smelling the pods. I catch Gunthreon's wandering eyes as she bends over examining the dirt along its roots and deadheading the pod-less branches. Slowly the plant starts increasing in size, in both height and girth. With a nod from me, Gunthreon sneaks in the quickest of butt pinches on Lupa. Totally surprised, she jumps just as an extra energy swell flashes around her and one pod opens, dropping four seeds onto the ground. Her excitement at both occurrences can be felt through her aura as she suddenly points east and exclaims, "I think they're over there. I heard talking." Feeling no other source of energy near, I continue watching her as everyone else looks in the direction she pointed. She quickly moves to pick up a seed and tosses it into her pack. We meet eyes and she impishly smiles at me.

"I don't think anyone is near, Lupa," says Gunthreon as he scopes the area. "Kailey, can you do us the favor?" Lupa then sneaks her own butt pinch on Gunthreon.

"Sure," I reply, lingering on Lupa's smiling face for a bit with knowing eyes before I send out my feeler. I close my eyes and reach out.

It's not long before I reach Madam Eve, but she's not with Elivon. She's with Terro, I think, who is very upset and is chock full of anxiety, making his energy field feel a bit different. I pull them both to me and they appear dazed before us, even Madam Eve's snakes.

She looks over her body and with one touch from her hand to the snakes, they start slithering again. The look on her face is one of pure anger. "I do *not* appreciate what you just did. That is clearly an invasion of privacy!"

Terro, on the other hand, is pumping his fist and jumping around. "Holy Neda! That was the coolest, ever! Do it again."

Still laughing from his enthusiasm, I speak to Madam Eve. "So sorry, but you signed the contract. We assume that our clients read the fine print first." Her jaw clenches and her snake dressing writhes about her body, angrily.

Suddenly spotting the starcka plant that Lupa was molesting, she redirects her attention. "How? Who?" She runs over to the plant and searches the ground, picking up the seeds. "Where's the fourth? *Where is it?!*" She's pawing at the ground like a dog searching for its buried bone. It's quite the scene seeing Ms. High Maintenance crawling around in the dirt, kicking up a fuss as the dirt embeds itself under her well-manicured nails. Her frantic rummaging stops as she looks up to Lupa. "Was this your work?"

Lupa's energy twitches with nervousness as she nods. "I couldn't help it. Sorry."

The laugh that leaves Madam Eve's mouth is loud and disturbs Lupa a bit. "You have no reason to be sorry, my dear. We've been having difficulties getting these plants to reach their potential, which is dropping their seeds." Her hand shakes the seeds she recovered as she looks up to the clear sky. "We can't use the seeds we force out for they die almost instantly." Madam Eve moves within Lupa's personal space and says, "Can we talk at a later time?" Just as I think she may kiss Lupa, Lupa holds up her hand, blocking Eve.

"Mother," Terro says with a warning.

"Sure, I'll chat with you later," Lupa states, "but respect a girl's space bubble, please. It was like you were gonna kiss me or something." Sir Cuche and I snicker to ourselves.

"Lupa!" Gunthreon squawks, chuckling a bit.

Lupa's stern face has Madam Eve taking a step back. "Of course, my *sweet.*" Her last words flow off her tongue in almost a hiss. I can't help but feel a slight pang of jealously that I am not the only one that Madam Eve wants to plant her lips on.

Madam Eve eventually loosens her eye grip on Lupa and turns to us. "Did you enjoy your pearls this morning?" The smile across her face is innocent as her eyes speak otherwise.

I speak up first. "We did enjoy them…well at least what we finished. Thanks so much for the treat."

"What? You didn't *finish* them?" She turns to Bu, who she is clearly assuming ate all his. He simply shrugs his shoulders. Madam Eve's snakes start nipping at the air, in a manner similar to angry Chihuahuas—something totally odd for a snake to be doing.

I add, without really thinking, "Yeah, they tasted a bit different, I think. Kinda gritty. Maybe just a bad batch? Or perhaps it's just all our nerves."

"*No!* We do not have *bad batches*!" Madam Eve is walking around in circles, thinking something awful, for her snakes are slithering with something like cocaine-induced speed. It's like she flipped her crazy switch.

Lupa steps forward. "You've said it yourself; your plants are not behaving as normal. There must be something going on with your crops." Ladimer takes a step toward a non-Lupa-molested plant and pinches the tip of the plant. I'm the only one noticing as he does so because everyone is attempting to calm down a panic-strewn Madam Eve. He suddenly looks straight at me with a look of contemplation on his face as he cocks his head to the side and crouches down further, feeling a pod closer to the root.

*I must divert attention.* "Terro, everything okay? I sensed you were a little wound up a bit ago," I say as he carefully watches Ladimer's every move. I see that Madam Eve now has her full attention on me and her son, exactly what I wanted.

"Yes, Kailey. I am fine," Terro responds, now turning to me. "Thanks for asking. At least someone cares about my emotional health these days." His glare in his mother's direction appears as though he's trying to tunnel right through her, perhaps it's the only way to touch her heart, or maybe he's just acting like a normal angst-riddled teenager.

Facing us, Madam Eve says, "Kailey, what is said between me and my son is private. We have normal parent-child issues. Something *you* wouldn't know about. Am I right?" Very slowly she turns and give *me* the same glare Terro bore into her seconds ago.

She approaches me to stand inches from my feet as I suck in a breath. "It seems that you are taking your sweet-ass time even making decisions on a mate, let alone a decision on being responsible for another human being," she says very quietly, but not without emotion. She's attempting to strike a fragile chord. "Lucky for you your only choices are both stupid enough to stick around like pets," she says, her "s" harmonizing with the hisses of her snakes.

Looking to both Conner and Ladimer, she finally breaks the chord in two. I push her several steps back and one of her snakes reaches out quickly, lunging at me, but I'm quicker. The small amount of hostility I feel toward Madam Eve suddenly quadruples as my monk's spade burns on my back. I whip it off and hold it in front of me, taking steps toward her as she stands firmly. "Do it," she insists, a grin lingering on her face. "You're such a tough-ass, aren't you, Kailey, the karmelean? Do you always threaten your high-paying clients?" With my anger taking over, I lunge at her, taking her down with the pole of my monk's spade. I hold it firmly against her body, pinning her down. Her snakes wriggle and hiss underneath my weight, and a few slink around my wrists, but they don't squeeze with much force as I think that this surely should provoke an attack. "You would just love to finish me off right now, wouldn't you? I *felt* that in you." A snake, small and skinny, but particularly long, lingers near my ear. Through clenched teeth she proclaims, "You destroy this deal, and I will destroy *you.*" I increase my pressure on her as sudo-abominor dares me to slice her head off. The baby snake comes nearer. "It only needs one thought from me," she says, looking at the snake.

Suddenly wanting it away from me, I attempt to move, but sudo-abominor evidently feels no threat, for its ego suddenly storms forth, speaking through my mouth and bringing me an inch closer to her. I can't seem to stop it.

"How? What powers could you possibly use to destroy *me*?" I laugh a bit crazy-like. "All I see is a money-hungry, insidious bitch-of-a-woman who hides behind a wall of reptiles. What are you hiding, Madam Eve? Whatever it is, it is surely nothing impressive. Velopa wasted its efforts on you." After a brief look of surprise on her face, and a moment of hurt in her aura, her beautiful white teeth begin dazzling through her grin as my feeler slinks forward, attempting to feel and grab something, but there's nothing that feels substantial enough to grasp. "You as so much look at me the wrong way henceforth, I will disembowel you quicker than a lightning flash."

Her grin lessons, but her eyes still say she knows something more than I do. "I pity you right now," she says.

"*What*?" I reply, drunk from the power I have over her, and squeezing down on her full force, currently hating everything about her, especially her brazen will to struggle against me. She has no idea what sudo-abominor and I are capable of.

"I recognize all too well a woman struggling to keep her head above water, and you, Kailey, have britches full of boulders. You're going to sink fast, my dear, and are doing whatever you can to take your last beautiful breaths, despite the liquid filling your lungs." I then realize that my feeler, totally barraged by sudo-abominor, was too late in sensing that which drew near. The disbelief of an innocent soul washes over me as Terro stands directly over us, watching me tear into his mother. The hurt in his eyes as he looks at me in my current state of insanity douses even sudo-abominor's feverish rage. Instantly feeling a blow to my heart as he takes a small step toward me, his pitchfork revealed and ready to strike directly into his beloved "superhero," I cringe. *Great way to hide, sudo-abominor.*

In a voice a bit higher than normal (as a male on the verge of adolescence might sound), while holding back tears, Terro prattles, "We just want my sister back."

Bu lifts me off Madam Eve as Conner soulspeaks to her, ensuring that these actions of mine won't happen again, being as uncalled for as they were. Ladimer then pulls her aside and asks if she's okay as he wipes away a tear now running down her cheek. He puts his arm around her as Terro comes up to her other side. She kisses Ladimer on his cheek, a sweet and thankful sort of peck, but it's enough to get me fired up again. She then steps aside, looking directly at me and takes an unbelievably long intake of air, a breath if you will—a breath to mock me. "Make sure your other 'pet,'" her eyes on Bu and not Kioto, "doesn't trample my precious plants."

Bu pets my hair voraciously, trying to calm me—as well as himself—down as Madam Eve gives me one quick smile, that one small snake of hers moving close near Ladimer's ear. "Kailey must stop attacking people."

"Yes, I know, Bu. Thanks for the words of advice," I remark, cockily.

"Kailey welcome." He then lifts me with one arm, hugging me tightly into his side. "Where Jenna?" In my hastily-made decision to assault Madam Eve, I forgot about Jenna. She should definitely be back by now. He puts me down and I look to him, not saying a word. "Checking equipment?" His words are another reminder that Bu is smarter than many others—Madam Eve included—would think. I simply nod and he does the same, looking out to the dunes beyond Luvia. "Jenna fast. Give her a bit more time."

Suddenly, a loud tinkering noise travels through the air to our ears. Gunthreon and the rest are well ahead of us, but he turns and waves us forward. Throngs of creatures dressed in harvesting gear start filing down the rows of starcka plants as Bu and I work our way forward to catch up to the others. They are similar to Elivon: dry skin, painfully thirsty energy fields swallowing up any good in their lives, devoid of hope, most of them exhibiting some form of deformity or another. There are shortened limbs, extra small or extra-large craniums, hunched backs, and crooked eyes to name a few. I notice one worker that has stopped dead in his tracks and is staring at me: Gurgl. He continues staring and I pretend not to notice him as I reach out my feeler in his direction, but upon reaching his somewhat sticky, fly paper-like energy, it forces me to quickly withdraw. He then disappears among the starcka plants.

Glancing around at the workers, still looking for Gurgl, I notice a few female workers hold small babies in sacks draped around their babies, and it is these very workers that actually feel a bit *different.*

As Bu and I approach one of them, she pulls back, covering and pulling her baby close to her breasts, and defending herself with what appears to be a broken pair of pruning shears. My feeler reaches to her, letting her know that we are no threat to her or her child since my monster is resting from its display of showmanship against Madam Eve.

The mother's tension eases as I extend my hand toward her hidden treasure held closely to her heart. Slowly I pull back the material and see inside her sack the most precious child; its skin flakey, its energy warm and innocent, its body devoid of any deformities. "Your baby is absolutely captivating," I say, laying a gentle kiss on its forehead. The baby's mouth begins sucking motions immediately upon contact, feeling the moistness of my energy. Bu puts his finger near the baby's mouth and mother giggles the most precious of laughs, bringing serenity to my soul as a stir of an energy so inviting and comforting whirls around us, making the mystery of the "difference" in this woman's energy now clear: navi. My senses are clear enough to recognize it, and in my recognition, a small ache throbs in my heart as I think of Amber, a small hope springing forth that perhaps navi exists in her life, too.

Mother stops giggling and looks out toward where Madam Eve was but has since entered a tall, white marble, and gold-bedazzled building. "Thank you, sweet ones." She leans down and begins pulling and tugging at thorny weeds near the base of a starcka plant, becoming entirely engrossed in her project, but stopping to break off what she keeps attempting to cut with the shears. Bu stops her, makes a simple adjustment with a pair of his pliers to her shears, then hands them back and watches as she begins cutting with a huge grin on her face.

Bu and I leave her, walking toward the large white building which looms above the crops, looking especially bright from the contrast against such gray skies. Without paying attention to the ground I'm walking on, I suddenly trip over something very low.

As I stumble to the ground, I notice a few gravestones that are situated neatly in a row, here, smack-dab in Madam Eve's starcka fields. There are three: one tall and oval shaped, and two flat rectangular stones, each with a different flower delicately positioned in a circle atop the inscriptions. My eyes settle on one of the flat markers: a very small, cream-colored marble stone with the words SWEET BABY ANGEL delicately embossed upon it. There's a single long-stemmed pink and purple flower circling ANGEL.

"Hmm, odd place for a gravesite," I whisper, looking at Bu.

"Starcka is important to her. These are important, too," he replies.

"Let's go," I tell him, grabbing his hand and guiding him toward Madam Eve's home. Several workers are washing down the outside marble walls, polishing the gold doorknobs and fence finials, as well as working on shingles on the many high-pitched roof peaks. "I can only imagine what's inside, and," I say to Bu, "the heyday that a certain ugly grumblepig is experiencing." Bu giggles.

We step through her doorway expecting luxuries beyond belief, but my jaw still drops at the extravagance that Madam Eve envelops herself in daily. Two staff immediately rush forward and start wiping Bu's and my feet. "No dirt in my house!" Madam Eve's voice travels from beyond the entrance. Bu giggles as the workers continue to wipe his feet, evidently tickling them in the process.

My eyes moves from one crystal object to the next and from one solid gold statue to another. The starcka trade has indeed provided Madam Eve with many profound luxuries. I hear the grumblepig snorting and snuffing loudly, causing Sir Cuche to snort and snuff, himself, most likely from the task of keeping the restless grumblepig from gobbling up all of Madam Eve's furnishings. Her voice is echoing to us and I hear her shouting something about re-polishing the gold.

We find all the others in a stairwell wide enough to fit six grebles, side-by-side. Sir Cuche is pulling on the grumblepig's leash, but appears to be losing the battle.

I turn to Ladimer and ask, "Can you do something about that maybe?"

"And ruin all the fun?" he laughs as Sir Cuche falls on the floor, losing his grip on the leash. All Madam Eve's nearby workers begin chasing after it, and falling as they do their best at lunging on the surprisingly fast animal. My frown toward Ladimer is enough for him to stop laughing and instead make a move toward the varmint.

Once captured, with a small brush of Ladimer's hand, the grumblepig is suddenly complacent, only swallowing one big swallow, most likely pushing something further down to its fat belly.

With narrowed eyes, Madam Eve says toward us, "Follow me to Flora's room, please. Maybe you can find something to get you moving on this contract so I can get Elivon's stupid shipment of byproduct glue ready for his mummified followers." She begins hurriedly walking up the stairs as we all follow, quick-toed after her. I note the aggravation stirring within her energy as it slowly evaporates and is replaced with determination as she effortlessly continues gliding up the stairs. A loud panting reaches my ears as I turn to find Lupa struggling to make the hundredth stair. "Almost there, dear Lupa," calls Madam Eve from the top.

Suddenly, bursts of screaming resound from the main entrance. "*How dare you*! *Ahhhh*!" The thirst that bursts forth and reaches my feeler is strong and I immediately know it's Elivon, and he has Jenna.

"*Kailey*!" Jenna screams from beyond the walls. The effort she is using to scream suddenly drains similar to a battery on its life's end. I can't help but grab at the unseen Elivon. Once I touch him, his energy begins thrashing about like a hooked fish while Quicksilver has me at Elivon's throat in godly speed. Bu then follows steps behind. One look at Jenna's dry and shriveled body lying on the marble floor doesn't bring any sympathy at the sight of Elivon's pinky tip in her mouth. In a fit of insane anger that I can no longer hold back, I start pulling, and pulling hard, ripping pieces of Elivon's aura like fabric swatches.

His scream is one to cause nightmares as I continue, nobody stopping me until Madam Eve comes charging, knocking me off balance. As my head hits the marble floor, I still hear Elivon screaming with mixed emotions of both anger and apologies. Blood flows from my head across Madam Eve's highly-polished and most-likely-sanitized floor as sudo-abominor fights to get me to my feet, but to no avail. Darkness welcomes me.

# Chapter 14

# Ambiguity

The wonderfully intoxicating smell of lilacs wakes me. Feeling a bit dizzy, but otherwise fine, my eyes open to find myself in a comfortable, squishy bed covered with sweet-scented sheets. Pillows surround me, and a few support my head, specifically. My hand rises to my noggin and I notice dried wads of blood in my hair, then look down to blood stains spotting my shirt. Jenna is asleep next to me looking healthy, even moreso than normal. Ladimer's energy lingers on her skin and my worry for her dissipates as I brush her hair from her forehead. I'm assuming Elivon's fingertip is also reattached.

My ever-watchful companion, Kioto, jumps up from the bedside and glides her tongue over my hand as I stir. She rises on her back legs and places her front paws on my chest, forcing a brief blast of air from lungs. As I sit up and cover Jenna, I take in the view of the heavily-adorned bedroom. Recognizing it as a young girl's room, I assume it's Flora's; there's plenty of normal, eighteen-year-old items, not one white marble or gold statue is to be found here, but items that she feels represents *her* character, and make *her* who she is.

My feet find some stable ground and I rise slowly, allowing my bearings to adjust and my head to clear. I walk around, touching items, hoping to soak up an energy remnants left about. Across her vanity I find small vials of rouge and perfumes of such invigorating scents that I can't help but dab a spot on my wrist. She's got good taste. Scarves slouch over her vanity finials, and I run my finger over the many fabrics, as well as brush them against my cheek.

Opening a tiny silver box, I find that Flora is a fan of dried jambleberries and I laugh to myself at the defiance she must exhibit on a weekly basis. Thoughts of Amber suddenly invade my mind as I recall her many tokes as a teenager near the dumpsters located behind our first job of working at Burrito Burgers. She only let me try it once though, saying that I was the one to keep a clear head and a clear conscience—that I was the smart one. The fact that the one time I tried it made me nauseous confirmed her plan was a good one, in both our minds. Letting me sleep it off in a storage area, she basically worked both our shifts that day. A faint smile forms on my lips as I think that good memories still loiter in my brain hidden from sudo-abominor.

Watercolor and oil paintings of colorful sunrises, as well as some disturbing, gothic, pencil-etched scenes canvas Flora's walls. I can't help but smile at the ambiguity of her character, the same as mine was at seventeen, and unbelievably, how I feel again since sudo-abominor.

There's a particular painting of sand dunes and its inhabitants that I find curious and work my way over to examine it closely. From afar it seems all the beings are fully represented in their deformities, but as I move my face within a few inches of the paper, I see that each character has a small red heart painted on their chests and their extra limbs are actually vegetables and flowers. The work is remarkable and I find myself running my hand over the faces, feeling the texture of the canvas and its blobs of long-dried paint.

Across her shelves are some stuffed animals, again polar-opposites; some are unbelievably adorable, while others scare the shit out of me, especially the evil clown-like ballerina puppet with its bloody hands and mouth. I can't help but cover it with a scarf. I close my eyes to feel for energies and again I get nothing. "Flora, you're eighteen. Surely you spend time here," I whisper to myself.

"She's very talented—my daughter," Madam Eve's melancholy voice says, startling me. Kioto barks a bark expressing her annoyance, for she too was surprised by Madam Eve. Kioto's interest is then perked by Madam Eve's snakes and she moves closer to them, wagging her tail as the snakes hiss at her. She playfully tries to poke them with her nose and then nips at them. Madam Eve ignores Kioto's lunges and continues talking to me. "She definitely doesn't get that from her mother." Her smile is sad as she stares at a watercolor representing a hauntingly gorgeous thunderstorm; instead of rain, the clouds seem to be dropping small skulls. "Kailey, I know we have our differences, but I need you to know that I love my children with all my heart. Please accept my apology for my earlier actions. I don't want you thinking we are enemies. I want you thinking we are just two very powerful and persistent women doing what it takes to survive. I'll admit that I was probably acting a bit foolish, something that Elivon brings to my attention often."

Calling Kioto to my heel, my shoulders slump from my own regret for my actions and I look to meet her eyes. "You've lost your daughter. That has to be very hard on your heart. I am also sorry—sorry for my lack of sympathy."

"It's so hard without her here. When I think of what could have happened to her, it makes me insane, and makes me…difficult. I know this. And poor Elivon. He's being neglected, and what kind of a mate does that make me? Especially at a time like this."

I rather not start a conversation regarding mates after our earlier go-about since I know sudo-abominor might start something vicious again between us. "Um, speaking of Elivon, what happened with Jenna?" I nod my head in Jenna's direction, her body looking extremely small against the fortified wall of gigantic pillows around her.

Suddenly, I feel the very soul I speak of approaching the door. "Nevermind," I quickly add, "perhaps he can speak for himself." On cue, he enters, and as I see him standing in the doorway, sudo-abominor makes its presence known by making my heart pound loud enough inside my head to almost knock Evil Ballerina from the shelf. "Elivon," I say, acknowledging his presence, and noticing the new weakness in his aura's energy. Kioto walks to Elivon and then suddenly stands on her hind legs, placing her front paws on his shoulders.

He pats her head once, then says, "Get off of me!" It's clear to me he's angry by the noticeable attempt of his energy to create sporadic turbulent swirls surrounding him. "I understand you have a mission here, and I understand that gives you permission to dig for clues, but *you*," he says, pointing a finger at me, "must understand you *do not* have free reign of the dunes. Stop sending your *minions*!"

Locking eyes with Madam Eve, I notice her brow furrows. "You must cooperate, Elivon," she says, pleadingly, "I—we—need Flora back. Certainly Kailey and her crew don't mean to cause problems by doing a bit of detective work. Right, Kailey?" Her eyes ask me to be cooperative.

"We are as eager as you to uncover all truths," I say, looking directly into Elivon's eyes.

Madam Eve takes a few steps to close the distance between us and she lays a lingering kiss on the side of my mouth, once again catching me off guard. The snakes move about her body slowly, twisting and hissing, peculiarly sensual. Her breath is hot on my ear as I hear: "Please play nice with Elivon. He may be thirsty, but he's easily quenched." With a squeeze to my arms, she then says louder, "Feel free to continue looking. We'll leave you alone now. Elivon, your glue is ready, anyway. I want it moved as soon as possible, and you are going to give me extra nutrients this time for the starcka."

A wave of her hand has an aggravated-looking Elivon close behind her as she walks out the door, but I grab his arm before he leaves, and then let go quickly, the dry heat bursting from his body is like angry, mini sun flares. "You best not be playing with fire," I warn him, attempting to refrain sudo-abominor from shredding his already frail energy field. "The UFOE might be surprised at what they find hidden in Golden Dunes."

His body moves slightly toward me and I feel the heat of my spade traveling through my shirt, forcing my hand to move toward it, to be ready for a needed response. "A little money goes a *long* way," he drawls quietly, "and in my opinion…I think word of a thriving sudo-abominor would capture *much* attention. Don't you agree?"

I'm speechless as my hand drops.

The distance between us lessens and he brushes his hand against my cheek; it's like sandpaper sloughing off a layer of varnish, and painfully disturbing. "I fear you, Kailey, but it's best you know that I find you equally desirable. I like strong woman—admire them. Just don't push on the boundary fences, though. Your friend," he looks at Jenna who is feigning sleep for I sense her well-bottled anxiety, "was an accident, I admit, but was surprisingly a small shot of something most fabulous—something quite…tasty." He smacks his lips, but it sounds more like a ticking noise. "It was even worth the momentary loss," he adds, looking at his perfect once-again-whole finger. His glossy eyes rise to meet mine. "And I'm sure you would taste extraordinary, if I got a bigger taste."

Jenna begins stirring and making fake and loud waking noises as I see her peeking at me with one eye. I know she sees my energy colors and is attempting to divert my attention, somehow. Elivon takes one quick glance at her, smiles politely at me and says, "I have to go *barter* with Madam Eve now," as he shuts the door and leaves.

"Oh…My…Neda!" Jenna sits up straight with the right side of her head flat as a pancake, but her hands work quickly to rearrange her hair back to bird nest form. "He drained me! That totally sucked! No pun intended."

I walk toward the bed, doing my best to concentrate on something positive as I sit down next her. Imagining sitting, drinking a relaxing cup of tea with my mother brings my mind to a clearer place and helps me fight sudo-abominor's want to chase down Elivon and cut his leg off this time. I bring my hand up to rub Jenna's back and distribute some of my good feelings directly to the field around her. "You feeling okay now?" I ask.

"Yes. Thanks. I see what you're doing." The smile she gives me touches both her ears and I lay a small kiss on her forehead. "I'm wondering how Elivon knows about your *condition*." Her tiny face then hardens as well as her energy field as she says, "You know it really did suck when he drained my fluids, and ewww—his finger in my mouth," her fingers moving to brush off her tongue, removing any leftover taste. "But, his aura was so disrupted after he did it."

"What actually happened earlier?"

Her faces scrunches up tightly. "You want a second-by-second account of the pain I endured?"

"Just give me the summary, then. You find anything?"

"Besides a fingertip in my mouth?"

"Yes, *please*." I pause, then say, "Well, maybe that part, too. It taste like beef jerky?"

"*No*!"

I laugh. "Nevermind, give me the 4-1-1." She folds her arms and pouts, giving me an expression that I am perhaps talking in tongues. "*What…did…you…find*?!"

"Okay! First off, I didn't find the equipment you spoke of. There's so many tunnels! I did, however, happen to hear a strange conversation between Elivon and Gurgl—you know that one with the really *loongg* arm?" As she exaggerates her words, she pantomimes how long she thinks his arm is. *It's not* that *long.*

"What was said?"

"That Gurgl guy evidently thinks you have a nice butt." I inhale, almost choking on my own spit. "Watch out, 'cause he may grab it all the way from the dunes." I quickly smash her face with a small pillow. "Stop! You want the 5-1-1 or no?"

"It's 4—Oh nevermind, continue without any more details regarding my ass."

"Well, they did a lot of murmuring of words which I couldn't quite understand. I heard words like hidro-jim and arpiems?" Her eyes widen in response to the change of expression on my face. "Then," she says as she scoots closer, wanting to share a deep secret with me, "Elivon said this, word-for-word: 'She will surely regret her actions.' I'm kind of scared, Kailey."

Feeling particularly disturbed, I grumble, "This is messed up. I'm almost thinking we should cancel this contract." I stand and look around the room, my eyes settling on a tabletop, wooden-framed watercolor of Terro with his arm wrapped tightly around an almost exact version of him, the only difference being the slightly longer hair. Flora. I think of his bright and cheerful youthful energy, which then sadly leads to the image of his disappointed face hovering over me. And then…my thoughts turn to Amber and her innocent baby—a baby that no matter how much anger I house in regards to Amber, deserves to live a happy and destruction-free life.

Terro and Flora's matching set of gorgeous smiles warrants my attention, so I pick up the picture and then turn to smile toward Jenna, realizing I can't stop this contract now.

"I got it." I hold up the frame and gobble up the vibrations.

Jenna, Kioto, and I make our way down the hallway of the common rooms, and I can't help but be drawn to the faint whisper of a broken heart from behind a particular closed door at the end of the hallway. "Go ahead. I'll catch up. Take Kioto with you, please," I ask of Jenna.

As I continue down the hallway, taking an unusually long look at a massive room, mid-hallway, that could pass as an Abscondian bathroom—with a working shower and all—my feeler can no longer put off visitng the aching soul sitting melancholy in his room, stinging from the disappearance of someone near and dear to his heart. I knock lightly, then open the door and peek in. Terro is sitting on the floor, and spotting me, he immediately turns flustered. "Oh… Hey, Kailey." He puts down a sketch he was looking at, and I recognize its artist. It's a picture of a red-headed skull with rainbows shooting out of the eye sockets.

"Can I come in?"

He jumps up quickly as I enter without waiting for an answer and shoves the picture under his bed. Moving across the room quickly, he fumbles as he pushes a bunch of objects—one being a small clay model with red hair, similar to my own—off a desk, into his drawer. Bending down, he also grabs a flyer off the floor—a flyer which I recognize as one made by Jenna months ago when I was on a mission and needed help locating a small amount of lutheose. "Sorry, I never really expected you—a woman—in my room." His eyes scan the room quickly for any more souvenirs, of me, I'm assuming. He finds a miniature monk's spade and quickly moves to pick it up. I blush, which only encourages him, because I sense his energy suddenly change and become bolder, a typical characteristic I've noticed in men after a woman exhibits the tiniest bit of embarrassment.

"No worries, Terro. Don't clean on my behalf. You should see my place." His eyebrow rises and a small smile begins forming on his mouth. As I blush even more, I quickly add, "Not that you should be in my apartment—I mean, you know, it's messy, too…like here." *God. He's eighteen for god's sake.* His attention on me makes me feel girlish and I do my best to focus on my goal by diverting his thoughts to my progress in their case. "You might be happy to know that I felt something." From the explosion of warmth that suddenly emanates from his body and the biggest grin imaginable spread across his face, you'd think I asked him to hop in the sack. I realize how he is totally misconstruing my comments. "Uh." I hold up the frame from his sister's room.

"Did you find her?" he asks with a jolt.

"I didn't look yet, actually. Was going to let your mom know first before I soulsearched."

His smile quickly turns to a frown as he takes the frame from my hands. "Isn't she good?" He's admiring the craftsmanship of the picture, tracing a finger over his sister's face.

"Most definitely. I saw her artwork and it's top notch stuff. She should sell it. Does she?"

"No, she has…other *responsibilities* and doesn't have much time for herself. She ends up creating her work when everyone else is sleeping."

"You two are barely adults. You should have some time for yourselves—time to do all sorts of things. Elivon and your mother works you guys hard. Am I right?" I'm gently pushing for some clues of any sort.

He straightens up his shoulders and stands a bit taller, attempting to thwart my opinion of his "barely-adult" stature. "Elivon's fine, and my mother doesn't work *me* as much. You know, Kailey, you are not *that* much older than us and you seem to," he says while moving uncomfortably close—a this-shouldn't-have-my-heart-thumping-this-fast close—to me, "have more responsibilities than most much-older individuals. Am I right?" I take a step back but he only takes that one step closer. "Perhaps you need to be convinced that males of my age are capable of many tasks at once."

He bumps up against me as I lean on a small table, knocking off a pile of clothes. In the heated moment, my hidden beast suddenly steps forth, taking my increased heart rhythms as a sign I'm being threatened. I grasp his shirt and his eyes widen at precisely the same time I notice his "feelings" for me. "Terro, believe me, you don't want to go there." Pushing him off of me harder than I should, I watch as his expression transforms into one of confusion.

"Sorry, I just couldn't control myself. How stupid of me—you know, Conner and all." He then rubs his chest. "You're strong, aren't you?" Looking at me as though I sprouted horns, he apologizes again.

My sudden laugh adds insult to injury as he turns a bit angry. "Don't worry about it. I won't tell anyone, especially Conner. Just don't be so aggressive with the girls. Got it?" He nods, still looking at me oddly. "Just be the gentle soul you're meant to be. Girls like that." His toothy smile returns and he pulls himself up a bit taller. "Let's go downstairs and let your mom know the good news." I take the frame from him and head out the door.

Everyone is sitting in a large formal dining room around a long, rectangular table graced with one very large vase of deep purple flowers I have never seen. From each wide petal's tip hangs a strand of silver, silky webbing, and of course Lupa's eyes keep darting to examine them. There are also several plates of delectable goodies situated around the table: chocolate-dipped fruits, crepe-like pancakes smothered in a golden honey syrup, and other fancy and time-consuming desserts, but everyone's plate is empty, except Bu's. His is piled a mile high. His belly is covered with hundreds of crumbs and his face has brown liquid—most likely hot chocolate—smeared around his mouth. I notice a setting with nobody seated before it, next to Conner. The plate consists of one scone and a steaming hot cup of tea. I sigh.

I hear Jenna talking low, telling Madam Eve the benefits of walkie-talkies.

Conner and Ladimer both rise from their seats, but my eyes settle only on Madam Eve's. I feel Terro's arm wrap around my waist as we walk toward the table and Conner's eyebrow rises as Ladimer bites his own lip, stifling a laugh.

I nod my head at Madam Eve and the tension in her shoulders releases as she realizes I found something worthwhile. She reaches over and squeezes Elivon's hand while his eyes reveal nothing; they are momentarily barren. His energy field seems to be repairing itself from my ravaging, which in turn just makes him seem simply tired.

Everybody sits as I stand, focusing on the picture in my hand. Closing my eyes and skimming the surface for energy, I pick up the small vibrational pulses that once belonged to Flora. Then thrusting out with all my might, I inhale as my feeler's reach travels far and swift. Something calls to me and within a second's time, I am standing inside a room deep within a dune, with wooden desks situated in straight lines, all vibrating with leftover energy. I do not even have time to explore, because suddenly, without even trying to travel, I am back in Terro's room, staring at the exposed portion of the skull sketch under his bed. Unsatisfied, I push out again, searching, but knowing that most likely Golden Dunes' sand will prove a hindrance if Flora is anywhere located near that location.

"No," escapes my mouth as I then reappear back in the dining room. I notice Madam Eve has risen from her seat and is nervously fidgeting her hands. I close my eyes and once again find myself in the empty school. Frustrated, and knowing that my search might alternate between both places, I plop my butt on one of the desks, allowing my eyes to scan the room, with its many props, charts, and glass jars of ugly and nameless floating objects. I look up and spot a small ventilation duct which is undoubtedly the way my feeler found its way past the reflective sand outside. *Thanks be to karma, for there has to be a reason I'm here.*

A huge chart pinned across one wall seems to be a chart of the elements; oxygen, hydrogen, and nitrogen are circled with a bright oily paste. I continue about, examining the many odd and surprisingly intriguing tools and contraptions lining shelf upon shelf and notice that nothing is beyond what should exist in Renhala. There are chemical-tainted gels and liquids that make me "Gah" and groan, but still nothing that screams "suspicious."

As I decide it's time to give Madam Eve the bad news, and a second before I travel, a weak vibration from a small metal jar tickles my feeler. I walk toward the jar placed on top of the teacher's desk and instantly know that Elivon was recently holding this jar. Then almost instantaneously, I recognize tiny vibrations of him everywhere in the class and realize this is his classroom.

I open the small jar and find inside, small and crudely-shaped balls of something chalky. My nose sniffs it, and reveals nothing, so I take a piece and run it across the stone chalkboard, but it almost instantly crumbles into nothing. My finger then rises to my mouth and as my tongue briefly touches the residual powder, I grimace at the bitterness of it, but notice it's slightly sweet. Placing the tin back on the desk, I turn my gaze to the surface of Elivon's desk. As I dig around, I find a folder covered in colorful hearts, rainbows, and dancing zombies, as well as trace clues as to who else had their hands on it, that very soul that can end this godforsaken contract if found. *Elivon is Flora's instructor.* Opening it, I find only a well-preserved dried up starcka leaf and a handwritten-in-gold-ink note reading:

*I love you more than life itself,*

*Mom*

"Huh," I grunt to myself. In a last attempt to find Flora, I reach out my feeler, but it keeps retracting, finding nothing but this room, so I angrily throw the folder back on the desk, knocking a plain, non-rainbow littered folder to the floor and watch as stomach-churning, heart-stopping sketches tumble out—sketches that Bu might drool over, and something most definitely illegal by the UFEO's standards, but possibly something of great leverage, especially the dried, brownish-burgundy blood drops splattered across them.

# Chapter 15

## Loss

My arrival heightens everyone's anxiety, freezing everyone in place. Shaking my head at Madam Eve, I watch as she sits back down on her seat, burying her face in her hands. "She's gone," she cries as Elivon places a hand on her shoulder. "*Gone*!" she suddenly screams and disregards his hand by running out of the dining room. Elivon quickly rises, but Terro holds him back, offering to follow his mother. Bu's eyes start dripping brilliantly bright tears, but he wipes them away quickly.

"I'm so sorry, Elivon," I state toward him, waiting for a response—for any slight change in his field—as everyone else sits around the table, silent.

His face is solemn and his energy remains weak. "I know you've done your best. We appreciate your attempts. I'll make sure you get paid for your time."

Everyone rises and I watch as Lupa collects her everything pack, sneaking in a piece of the silver webbing from the flowers centered on the table. Jenna grabs a biscuit off a plate as Conner offers his hand so that she may climb up onto his shoulder. Ladimer remains seated, staring at me.

For dramatic flair, I then add, "Oh, Elivon," capturing full attention of his eyes, "I'm not done here, yet. In fact, I am fully committed to this contract and its completion." The clenching of his jawbone gives me the response I was looking for. "Oh, and I have something important to show you." I reach my hand inside the elastic of my black pants to pull out the sketches, when suddenly there is a resounding ***BOOM BOOM BOOM*** on the front door of Madam Eve's palace. Workers begin scrambling and shouting strange babblings as they run to the door after picking up small and shiny things off tables and counters and out of drawers along the way.

Several new energies enter the threshold and walk toward us with quick, wide strides. My monk's spade begins warming on my back as everyone else reaches for their own weapons. The door to the dining room opens fast and several individuals dressed in black uniforms enter with the workers trailing, offering them several gold and silver objects. The uniformed officers brush them off as they focus on the armed bunch in front of them: my motley crew and I.

The largest, most-muscled guard in front says, "Please, ladies and gentlemen and…*creatures*," the latter toward Bu, "no need for weapons. Remember, we are here to protect you." The letters UFEO are roughly embroidered into his chest. I also sense a few lingering energy presences loitering outside, out of our view.

Jenna's eyes practically pop out of her head as she screams, "Gah! I didn't do it!" and runs behind Bu, dropping her cell phone, her arm quickly darting out to pick it up and shove it under her shirt.

The head officer blows her off and states, "I am Officer Bayle. We are here for our monthly check and will be out of your hair in no time, if…of course we find nothing that needs to be confiscated and further *examined*," he says in Jenna's direction. "Cooperation is *recommended*."

One of his followers grabs a small silver bracelet from one of Madam Eve's workers and shoves it into his pocket. It seems I am frozen in time as I stand, paper sketches held out before me as they slowly become unfolded and openly viewable. The instant change in Elivon's energy field as he now sees what I'm holding is enough proof that he is guilty of something, and something big.

"My, my. What do you have there?" asks Officer Bayle as he steps toward me with his big heavy boots.

I smile and look toward Elivon. "Elivon, here," I gesture in his direction, "seems to be quite interested in some rather illegal-looking items. Don't you agree, Officer Bayle?" He takes the paper from me and examines the sketches carefully.

"Hmm," he mumbles, looking at Elivon. "These are definitely something of interest," he states, shoving the plans in his pocket. Elivon continues standing in place and I notice a slight shift in his stance as he locks eyes with Officer Bayle. "You're coming with us," Officer Bayle snaps as I smile, but as his hand lands on *my* arm, my secret monster reacts.

Twirling around, snatching my arm away from him, I create a barrier between us with my monk's spade. "Those aren't mine. They're his!" Both my weapon and my instantly-boiling blood make me feel as though they are singeing me both inside and out. Bad Kailey quickly makes her way to just below the surface as my imagination conjures wonderful imagery of me slicing both Officer Bayle and Elivon in half with one swing—a quick answer to my current situation.

Elivon's shoulders loosen up a bit and he says, "Kailey, why must you cause problems when you're being paid to fix them? I suggest you cooperate with Officer Bayle. He really is a nice guy."

All officers step forth as my friends then form a wall between them, and me and Officer Bayle. "Please, miss, put down your weapon." Officer Bayle's hands are suddenly holding a short, but deadly looking trident-shaped weapon which looks sharp enough to easily skewer me. "Just come with us and we'll discuss the matter, peacefully." My friends continue standing their ground, waiting for action. The sad part is that they are probably worried more about *my* actions than the UFEO's. I'm the erratic one these days.

Bu starts unzipping his fanny pack while Officer Bayle's posse watch him nervously.

I look to Gunthreon as a last plea for help as I hold back the demon in my body which is chomping at the bit. It won't take much before it breaks through what it is bound by: my sheer will.

He reads my face as Lupa stands by his side, her small spade in hand. "I suggest that we discuss the matter *here*, Officer Bayle *and friends*," Gunthreon says.

Officer Bayle's expression changes as his brain registers Gunthreon's request and he slowly places his weapon back where it was originally hidden. "Okay. I agree to discuss the matter here, because…as Elivon said…I am a nice guy. You get a second chance, so make it worth your while." I can see that he has a duality in his energy that's disturbing: straight-laced rule junkie on one side and calculatingly deadly and perverse sadist on the other. I don't even need sudo-abominor's help to hate this guy.

We stare at each other, both of us sketching detailed defensive and offensive moves in our heads, similar to football diagrams. I'm wondering if our plans crosshatch just as he says, "Violation of any regulations established in the UFEO's main bylaws *usually* results in immediate jail sentence, but we can, however, be influenced—as so stated by the rules—to take into account all pleadings on *extreme* circumstances. Are you agreeing to the statement that your case is *extreme*?" My eyes wander to Conner just as Madam Eve enters the room, looking surprised for a brief few seconds, but as her eyes lock on Officer Bayle's, a crooked smile forms on her mouth. A mirrored image then appears on Officer Bayle's. "Madam Eve," he says while he nods his head toward her, respectfully, "pleasure seeing you. You look lovely today."

"Thank you, Officer Bayle. Is it that time, already? I could have sworn you were just here a few weeks ago?" Her hands begin adjusting her luscious locks of hair behind her back, revealing her full figure—all dangerously snaky in its entirety. He does his best to not let his eyes wander, but the sadist in him is practically doing backflips.

"It is actually time for an inspection already," he says, his smile downright eerie, "but this time, we may have a problem."

Her smile instantly fades. "It appears your guests here have intentions to violate some rules of ours, in a *big* way."

"Surely there must be a mistake," she says, dragging out her S's in that sexy way she does naturally, and never leaving Officer Bayle's eyes.

Officer Bayle replies, "No mistake, Eve. We were just about to discuss the matter."

"Oh, *come on*!" I blurt, my nerves sizzling. Terro grabs his mother's hand and pulls her to a far corner of the room.

"Kailey—" Gunthreon starts, but I intervene.

"*We don't have time for these games*!" I spit out, my face turning cherry red with anger. "If you just go on over to Golden Dunes and check out the large equipment they are storing, you'll stop wasting our time—our time that can be used to search for a lost daughter, which is far more precious than some *bullying, holier-than-thou group of stealing thieves' time*!"

"Uh-oh," yelps Jenna from wherever she's hidden.

Officer Bayle's weapon makes its re-entry as I dare him to make a move, with his swirling mass of angry energy. I'm ready for whatever he's got.

Sir Cuche holds out his rather large pocket satchel toward Officer Bayle. "Please, we are not here to cause such disruptions. Take this. Take it all and we'll leave without further mention of what went on here."

Officer Bayle turns, sticks his trident into the satchel, slowly cutting it open, allowing the bagged jewels to drop to the ground with small thumps. "Step away from me, or this *purse* will not be the only thing I…slit…open."

Bu, golden wrench in hand, takes a step toward them, honorably ready to defend his friend. Officer Bayle then turns his weapon quickly on Bu. "You think *your kind* scares *me*?" A dastardly wicked laugh escapes his lips. "You're nothing but a huge mass of stupid." I grip my monk's spade with bone-breaking strength, pleading with myself to keep my anger under control. I begin shaking from the amount of energy it's taking to withhold my want for carnage and desecration of the demon standing before me.

Conner, noticing my struggle, can't help but step forward, soulspeaking toward the officers: "My friend and I," he states while slowly arcing his arm and motioning toward everyone except me, "mean you no harm. Do you really want to fight a karmelean—a direct link to Neda and Velopa?" All officers, except Officer Bayle, begin fingering the trinkets in their pockets and begin shuffling their feet. The officer who took the silver bangle hands it back to Madam Eve's staff.

"Oh, I believe you soulspeaker, but let's just say I'm willing to take my chance with the karmelean," says Officer Bayle, taking it as a challenge rather than a warning, for his foot steps one tiny millimeter forward in my direction—just enough for me to notice and react.

As my monk's spade swings toward Officer Bayle' trident, he quickly ducks and stabs at my feet, but my Quicksilver jump is too fast. His eyebrows rise as a gigantic smile crosses his mouth. We exchange blows, but continually seem to be matched in our fighting prowess despite my speed, for somehow he moves as quickly as I do.

Blades swing, weapons pummel and curses fly throughout the room as I hear Gunthreon attempting to yell over the fighting, but it's too noisy and he resorts to some stellar martial arts that I notice out of the corner of my eye. Lupa watches him in admiration as she throws her own punches and stabs with her small spade.

I then feel the mass outside move in our direction. "*Reinforcements are coming*!" I yell as loud as possible as I lock eyes with Elivon. He then turns and attempts to run to where the officers entered but I grab his energy, stopping him from moving any further. He fights and tries to pull away, but I hold fast until

Officer Bayle throws me to the ground, his small trident piercing the skin on my shoulder, forcing me to groan as he buries it deeper and deeper into my body. Elivon, now free from my grasp, moves, but stops right before he is out of eyeshot and stares at me for a brief moment before he runs past an entering deathman—which is always a surefire guarantee to intensify the moment, for someone's about to die. It stands off to the side, simply watching the entertainment as another extremely large greble and three additional officers enter the chaos and begin fighting my friends. I hear Madam Eve call after Elivon, but she is sidetracked as I hear her yelp.

I hear quick footsteps enter the room from the direction in which Madam Eve entered, and the sudden scream of "*Mother*!" has me turning my head slightly. I see Terro run toward the officer holding Madam Eve.

Officer Bayle, whose back is to the deathman, simultaneously turns his trident and pushes down harder with all his weight, actually pinning me to the ground and forcing me to turn back in his direction. Sudo-abominor becomes so insanely distraught that the pain I should be feeling disappears, only to be replaced with hate—a hate so powerful I want to literally pull off Officer Bayle's face with my teeth, like my brother might do. He grinds against me as he notices by my facial expression that I don't mind the pain. "You should be screaming, my dear. It makes things much more pleasurable, you know."

I speak normally, as though there is no weapon slicing my arteries and cutting through my muscle tissue. "Wonder who that deathman is here for." His eyes widen and he can't help but turn slightly, opening a small entryway for me. I knee him in the groin and as he stumbles backward a few feet, he conveniently lands on Ladimer's blade. My hand pulls out the trident still stuck in my shoulder and I throw it to the ground and cover my gaping shoulder wound with my hand.

"Go ahead, scream. I want to feel the *pleasure*." I say to Officer Bayle.

Ladimer quickly pulls out the blade and allows Officer Bayle to slump to the ground before his feet. Ladimer holds me back from slicing off the injured officer's head and then administers a brief spurt of sickness through my body, forcing sudo-abominor to retreat. He whispers sternly, "Kailey, listen to me. It will be your choice. I can either heal him and we suffer the consequences if caught, or we can leave him be, as is. No death by your hands." We look to Officer Bayle, who is immobile, but still breathing, occasionally scrunching up his face from surges of pain. Blood trickles out of his mouth as he stares at Ladimer's hand which has moved to my shoulder, reattaching muscle tissue to muscle tissue and artery end to artery end. "Just know I am behind you in your decision, for I know you'll choose what's best." He stands before me, his hand still caressing me as we stare into each other's eyes as those around us continue fighting. His power courses through my body and my own power reacts as it mingles with his, bonding us for a brief moment, and creating a small extra energy around us. My breath stops short as he also recognizes that which flows between us and suddenly around us.

He pulls his hand away quickly as Bu and the greble Bu's been battling suddenly trounce upon our space. Ladimer touches the larger greble for a brief second and it falls to the ground, looking as though it's asleep. Bu says, "Thank you," as he wipes off the blood from his golden wrench. "Kailey okay?"

I look to my shoulder which now only contains one small, teeny-tiny scar. "Yes, Bu." I look around us and decide there and then I must do something. Closing my eyes and using the last of the energy from Ladimer, I pull out all the stops, grabbing each enemy, gathering their energies into a bundle. In hoping that I may receive outside help in my moment of need, I focus on the gods which created Renhala, and as I concentrate, thinking of the majestic unicorn I once encountered, I instead, repeatedly feel Velopa's presence, not Neda's. Quickly I grasp the bundle and do exactly what I did to the female that Ladimer had "contacted": shove it as far away as possible, maybe even into the very hands of Velopa, the Stern.

Without the fighting, all I hear is the heavy breathing of my friends and the occasional gasp escaping their mouths as they wince in pain from their many injuries. Ladimer runs about, carefully handling each of them, using all his power to make them whole again; he heals a cut on Jenna's face, closes up a gash on Sir Cuche's arm, and then gets shafted as he tries helping Conner, who is bleeding from his leg.

As I examine each of them, my eyes notice that the deathman is not where it was standing last. Then, a scream as loud as a siren penetrates my eardrums as I look to see the deathman standing above Terro. "*No. Get away from him*!" Madam Eve screams as she punches the deathman, her snakes darting their possibly poisonous tongues, and the longest snake attempting to strangle the deathman.

It continues standing above Terro as I run to him, sliding along the bloody marble floor. As I scramble to be next to him, I notice he is still alive, but barely, for his energy is as faint as a dawn fog fighting to keep its existence as the morning sun breaks the horizon—its normally sweet, caramel-like feel gone.

"Terro," I say, softly above him as I call Ladimer over with my arm.

Terro's hazy eyes suddenly focus on me, as a delicate smile forms on his mouth. He whispers, "Kailey, thanks for caring. You are so…" He begins choking as blood oozes out from his chest, totally covering the front of his shirt with a stream of crimson, but finishes with, "dedicated." His arm reaches up and squeezes mine as he holds on, wanting to tell me something else. I move a bit closer as he then whispers, "But please don't let it cast a shadow on that which thrives on light." I am moved by the words of mature insight as I look deep into his eyes—almost searching the soul beneath—when I notice a difference in his energy, an almost mellowness I didn't notice before, like an acceptance of approaching death. But with the eyes—the windows to true intention— I see through them years of hardship, and an exhaustion of both body and soul, that which was sucked dry.

Ladimer stands above us, assessing the situation, and then bends over, trying to lay his hands on Terro, when the deathman holds him back, unexpectedly, shaking its head at him. Ladimer tries to push and shove, and throws spurts of power, but the deathman is apparently impervious to his attempts. Stunned, Ladimer kneels, then sits back, giving Madam Eve a look of apology, for he knows that the deathman is here to complete a mission, one that entails taking the soul of her child.

Lupa reaches for Madam Eve and bops each of her snakes on their heads until Madam Eve melts into her comforting arms, releasing the deathman from her snakes' grips. "Neda will embrace him with open arms, Eve. He was a beauty."

As the deathman kneels over Terro, I lay one gentle kiss on his forehead, simultaneously transferring a bit of calming energy for his last moments in this life. "You will forever have a place in my heart, Terro. See you on the other side, my dangerously handsome friend."

"Handsome," he remarks, his voice extremely weak. A corner of his mouth lifts up, and he chokes out one loud laugh, revealing another sweet dimple I hadn't noticed before.

The deathman begins its maestro-ish movements above him as Terro's gaze turns to look directly at his mother. Madam Eve, who has gained her composure, kneels as her snakes move about her body slowly, almost solemnly.

Terro gently tugs on her sleeve to pull her down even closer and begins whispering in her ear, his breath rustling thin strands of her hair around her face. As Terro continues pushing out his last words, her expression suddenly changes; her eyes widen and she pulls away from him, exhibiting a gaze of such consternation that I try to move closer to hear what Terro might say next. She begins shaking her head back and forth, back and forth, as she watches Terro's gaze turn to look at something beyond us all in this space and time.

As Terro's eyes close, the deathman begins its call for what it came to acquire: a wonderfully shiny, sparkling, rainbow-kissed orb residing inside the teen. It grabs the orb, swallowing it with one quick gulp and then lays a single hand on Madam Eve as she stares, still wide-eyed in shock, at its hideous inside-out face. It withdraws the hand and proceeds to leave out the door it entered as she stands and stares at everything around her: the beautiful, but now bloodied opulence of a queen—a queen that has lost all of her most valued possessions.

The sound that escapes Madam Eve's mouth is one I'll never forget.

# Chapter 16

## Indignation

After finding ourselves totally devoid of energy—not even enough to change out of our bloody and ripped clothing—after arguing with Madam Eve to let us move Terro's body for her, we sit around in our designated dune, looking at each others' dismal and exhausted faces. I recall Madam Eve's insistence that we leave her alone as she dealt with Terro's death and the preparation and burial of his body before Luvia's full moon. Our guilt that we did nothing for her wavers around us.

Conner is first to break the silence as he sits on his bed. "I've never felt so disparate in my life as I do now." His voice turns quickly to soulspeak as he mumbles, "Who is one to trust? How can we continue?" as he looks at his blood-splattered shirt, then slowly turns his gaze to each of us.

"We can't go home now, if that's what you are thinking," I say, "because we are going to find Flora for Madam Eve and…Terro. Elivon is up to no good and I won't let him succeed. We have a mission."

"Well your *mission* is going to cost us more lives—someone sitting in this very room, no doubt. Did you forget Gunthreon's trip to the beyond, already?" I look to Gunthreon and he reflexively feels where the hole in his head once existed.

"And your explosions are far too consequential in regards to threatening our well-being. How much are you willing to risk for your own satisfaction, Kailey?" Locking eyes with him, I don't reply, but reach out invisibly toward him instead and grasp onto his energy in an attempt to coax him back on my side. He recognizes what I'm doing and shakes his head. "When will you realize that cooperation by those close to you shouldn't be forced, no matter what you see as the end goal?" I withdraw and sit, feeling a bit disgusted as I recall Terro's last words to me about casting shadows.

Ladimer begins his own conversation. "You know, Elivon may not be the only danger we're dealing with."

"What are you thinking, my friend?" asks Gunthreon, sitting next to Lupa, who is suddenly digging through her everything pack.

"Those crops of Madam Eve's, well they're not exactly on the healthy food list."

"What did you find?" Gunthreon asks as Lupa holds out her hand with the stolen starcka seed sitting in her palm. Ladimer reaches over, grabs it and examines the tiny, inconspicuous kernel.

"This simple little grain is by far one of the most complex things I've ever seen."

Jenna, curious, asks to see the seed and Ladimer tosses it to her.

Ladimer then adds, "It's also poison."

Jenna immediately squeaks, dropping the seed to the floor. Bu sprints over and walks on it, squishing it into smithereens.

"All her customers are slowly being poisoned," Ladimer says, "and those poor people of Golden Dunes have been eating mass quantities for who knows how long."

Images of the deformities of Golden Dunes flash inside my head. "Oh my god. They're addicted to it," I respond, sadly, "and literally drowning in it—inside *and* out. Their food, their homes…"

"It's a narcotic," Ladimer announces, "which feeds on a high level of nitrogen."

Bu, with a suddenly excited energy, adds, "The equipment!"

Everyone besides Jenna and I looks confused.

"What equipment, Bu?" Ladimer asks while watching as Jenna tries to pretend she instantaneously fell asleep, snoring in a too-exaggerated manner.

Bu looks to me, hesitating on any further release of secretive information. "Ummm…"

"Kailey?" Gunthreon knows I'm involved.

"Elivon is hiding something in those dunes," I reveal. "Bu found some equipment and we've been trying to figure out exactly what it is. Those papers Officer Bayle took were the blueprints." Gunthreon begins scowling at me because I've withheld vital information.

Bu, once again excited, blurts, "The equipment that Bu saw…" He looks to me for approval, so I nod. "Was surrounded by barrels of liquid nitrogen."

"Bu, you are amazing," I remark lovingly.

Sir Cuche, looking worried, gets his grumblepig to lie down on his straw bed and then adds, "Why the hell do they need liquid nitrogen? Kailey, what did the schematic look like?"

"You might as well ask me to speak Japanese, Sir Cuche."

Gunthreon, matching Sir Cuche's uneasy expression, says, "Ladimer, think that maybe you could do some exploring…as one of their own?"

"Great minds think alike," he replies, and in a flash there is a creature standing where Ladimer once was, looking all rough-skinned and decrepit, but a bit comical for his left eye is much bigger than the right and his tongue is partially sticking out of his mouth. He's dressed in Ladimer's clothes.

Jenna starts laughing in an overly-tired manner and seemingly can't stop as she begins rolling on the ground. Bu joins in, his whole gigantic body shaking from the giggles he's trying to keep bottled up. Lupa puts a purple flower behind Ladimer's ear—a play to help lighten the mood further.

Conner, definitely perturbed, suddenly blurts out, "How can you guys act this way with what's going on? Elivon is planning to blow up Renhala and you're all mocking and joking like a bunch of morons."

"Conner," says Lupa, exhausted, but he's up and out the door without hesitation. It instantly darkens our moods, once again covering us in a blanket of distressed uncertainty, awakening my own dark persona, and increasing my desire to hunt Elivon down and force him to drink his liquid nitrogen.

"Let him go, Lupa. He's not taking things well," Gunthreon says. "Kailey, I agree with continuing this mission. We have to make sure we leave without any loose ends, for loose ends easily unravel. We don't want others tripping on the mess." Lupa frowns as she plucks the flower from Ladimer's ear, crushing it and throwing it toward the grumblepig as a snack.

Ladimer heads toward the door to leave but Gunthreon stops him. "This is more your color," he suddenly jokes, planting a starcka leaf and pod behind Ladimer's ear. Gunthreon and Lupa share a smirk as I notice the wondrous spark of the energy I'm learning to respect: navi. I smile at Lupa as I draw a circle in the air around them and she smiles back, soon realizing what I mean by the charades. Her arms suddenly wrap around Gunthreon and she lays her head on his shoulder, snuggling into him.

Watching their actions toward each other and bathing in the gift that is navi, I decide that despite the menacing feeling I have that things might get worse before they get better, I know that through this whole journey, beautiful and positive results are coming of it and sudo-abominor can kiss my ass.

# Chapter 17

## Frustration

"Well just don't eat any food that Madam Eve gives you," Gunthreon says to Bu and Sir Cuche, a look of worry crossing Bu's face. "Lupa has enough for us in her pack, so don't worry. You won't starve."

"But Bu eats…"

"I know you are in need of much more, Bu—your huge muscles and all," Lupa says, drawing a smile from Bu. "So don't worry yourself. Here." She hands him a gigantasaur of a yellow gourd which I've tasted before—butter in texture, but honeydew in taste. "Isn't that kind your favorite?"

Bu breaks the gourd in half with one attempt—undoubtedly exhibiting his *huge* muscles—and grins as the guts spill onto his chest. "Jenna want some? Kailey? Sir Cuche," he says as he offers small pieces to us. As he is busy offering his goods, Lupa sprinkles some of her lilac powder on his back (the one she uses when we haven't had showers in some time).

"No thanks, Bu," I answer as Lupa playfully sneaks over to me, indiscreetly sprinkling powder on my head and shoulders. I thankfully spread it over my skin and in my armpits.

She then says to me, "I think full bellies will help us sleep better. Kailey, take a bit of the gourd." I reluctantly take a small chunk and gobble it up, almost instantly feeling sleepy. Sir Cuche does the same.

Jenna quickly snatches a larger piece than Bu offers and shoves it into her mouth as un-daintily as possible. Kioto comes near, sniffing as Bu puts a piece on the ground for her. The grumblepig slowly walks toward it, also sniffing toward the gourd, but Kioto's growl has the pig turning right back around as it resorts to eating Sir Cuche's straw bed, even as he lays on it. Sir Cuche lazily swats at it, but falls asleep after once glance at his own naked ring finger.

As I slink into my bed, I say aloud, "I feel so bad for those poor people of Golden Dunes. You know, though, I found a baby that was perfectly healthy with no deformities, so perhaps the starcka is losing is potency?"

Gunthreon shakes his head in reply. "Unfortunately, that's something we just can't assume. We have to do something, but first we must sleep."

"What about Ladimer and Conner?" I say, groggily closing my eyes.

Lupa answers softly, "Don't worry about them. Just go to sleep."

As I drift into needed sleep, I feel a caress of my hair and a slight, cool chill runs down my body. "Watch over them, Mom." I say as saliva pools—very lady-like—in the corner of my mouth.

The dream starts again; my mother sways to a melody playing only in her head as she smiles sweetly at me this time and I embrace the warmth that fills my body. I feel the rays of her happiness dancing in sync with the movement of her hips. Back and forth, slow then fast they move as she moves closer to me, then winks a wink reminiscent of silent understanding. As we share our brief moment, I notice the slight change in the curve of her mouth as she looks beyond me.

She slows her dance, her happiness dissipating into the air around us as she motions to take a ring off her finger. Her hand works slowly, twisting and turning the ring, and then once loosened, she pulls it off completely. Rising, her hand then holds it out as if presenting it to me, so I walk toward her, meeting her eyes, and I reach for the ring—the ring that was once my father's. But as I am about to grasp it, my hand travels right through her hand as a ghost's might. I try and try again, despite knowing deep in my heart I'll never again feel her skin or feel her heart beating against my own during a mother's embrace. As I am still standing, wallowing in the pain of loss, it is then I notice she is not looking at me, but through me, at something—or perhaps *someone*—else. Quicker than I can turn, I notice that a body has synced up with mine and stands over me—no inside me—as though we are one. A man's hand reaches out from me and caresses my mother's face as she buries her cheek into the welcomed palm. This hand then moves to pick up the ring she is offering, and as I feel an overwhelming weariness through my body and hold my breath in the moment, a small skinny snake moves across my foot. I try kicking at it as it begins crawling up my mother's leg, but as an apparition might do, I touch nothing, therefore creating no hindrance whatsoever as it continues its path up my mother's body.

I step out from the body that stood in mine and as I turn to face what I think is my father, I find not Devoten, but Elivon's scaly face. Immediately a burning sensation so intense flows through my veins and hate spills over and through me. It solidifies the apparition that I was, creating a solid presence that can now reach out and strangle Elivon. I willfully grab and as I enjoy watching his body struggle to intake the tiniest of breaths, my mother begins shaking her head rather violently at me, just as the snake wraps around her neck.

In my last dreaming moment, I slowly turn back to find that the neck I am squeezing the life from is now not Elivon's, but is Conner's. In horror, I immediately release and sit up, awake, in my straw bed, feeling as though I am swimming and struggling against currents of abhorrence and repulsion.

My friends, whom I have awakened with my loud gasps, look to me from their beds as I struggle with my internal dilemma: How do I hold onto the image of my mother's serene face for hope's sake, but also satisfy the urge to destroy Elivon and bathe in his blood? *I can't.*

Sudo-abominor is far too strong as I find myself brushing past my friends—my subconscious recognizing but not acknowledging both Conner and Ladimer—with my monk's spade.

"Kailey, don't—" is all I hear as I quickly and haphazardly soulsearch in randomness in the wee hours of the morning, falling on anything that brings displeasure: my ex-best friend's old office; the wedding hall in which I lost my mother, still displaying its worn carpet, bleached in the very spot where her blood spilled; my first apartment where my blood flowed at the hand of a Renhala assassin; and lastly the tip of a golden dune, hot from the morning suns' fury.

"*Elivon*!" I scream, tired, but soon fired up from sudo-abominor's need for an outlet to its hate. "I am going to find you, you bastard." I blast out my feeler, time and time again, bouncing from hill to hill, kicking up the sand and wind around me. Knowing that I am only being sent on a wild goose chase since I'm only reflecting my spotlight to the skies, and even back to myself, I continue. I repeatedly scream for Elivon, and in my sudden and sporadic soulsearches, find myself outside a window of Madam Eve's, on a very peak of her roof. Not worried about falling to my death and thinking that perhaps karma has her hands in constantly diverting my personal monster, I look through the glass and find Madam Eve searching frantically through Terro's room. As she throws around wooden boxes, and whips his red-headed clay figure against the wall shattering it, her eyes fall on something sticking out from underneath Terro's thin blanket. She pulls back the blanket, and in trying to see what she sees, I find myself grappling the wooden frame of the window with my fingernails.

After some time of waiting for her to stop staring and reveal the hidden good, she eventually lifts a raggedy, stuffed pink dog.

She eventually picks it up and smells it, then weeping a bit, she decides to storm off to another location. I move with Quicksilver speed to another peak of the roof and find Madam Eve now inside Flora's room, where she has begun pulling out handmade purses one-by-one, and searching the various pockets. She huffs and storms through the small space looking like a wrathful woman—one dangerous and on a warpath. She screams a single word: "*Why*?!"

Suddenly, she stops in her tracks as she spots what appears to be a roughly-crafted, indiscrete box, partially exposed and hanging out of askew Evil Ballerina. Walking toward the puppet, she looks hopeful. She picks it up and withdraws the box, dropping the puppet, and then holds the box tightly for what seems an eternity.

I sense her small amount of anxiety begin swirling at a deadly RPM, transforming into a frenzy as she opens the box. A small piece of the chalk-like substance I found in Elivon's classroom soon appears between Madam Eve's fingers and a strange expression of curiosity crosses her face at precisely the same time my foot slips on the slated roof. As my speed down the roof accelerates and I frantically try to secure my footing as I slide down, balancing as if on a skateboard, I only end up tripping clumsily over an unruly shingle and begin my flight over the edge to my probable death.

As my arms wave and grasp at the nothingness of the air around me, I see a young man running toward the very spot where I may hit the ground, his eyes open wide as his red cape flaps around him. Awestruck, I hear the words "Kailey, travel *now*!" suddenly echo loudly through my head like a boom of lightning as I notice that gravity seems to lessen its pull, but I'm still falling quickly enough to cause some serious damage once I hit ground. While freefalling, I forcefully redirect my thoughts to Elivon while mid-air and close my eyes, recalling his face from my dream and the intense emotion I felt as I watched him. I also, unknowingly, grasp the energy below.

In a moment's time, just as my body should impact the ground, I hit something with much less force and realize I've fallen lightly on sand—hot sand—and *he* is lying directly beside me. We both freeze, staring into each other's face, but then quickly stand up, my stance more warrior-like.

I take several calculated steps away and place my hand on my spade, wary of the creature standing in front of me. I can't help but stare at his face, though, for his blue eyes, his perfect nose, and even his hair color, is exactly my mother's. "You look just like her," I say, caught up in sudden emotion. "Stephen?" My eyes water a bit, as the thought sinks in that he's here, right in front of me now: my missing big brother—a piece of my life's puzzle.

He nods. "Yes. And you look just like *him*, Kailey."

Grasping my weapon a bit more firmly, and ignoring my want to grab and embrace him in a hug meant for my mother, I say, boldly, "You're following me, aren't you?" He nods again. "Why? Why come to me this way? Showing up in my apartment like that? Are you stupid? Kioto could have attacked you, maybe bit off your—" I freeze mid-sentence, feeling as though if I speak the words, they may suddenly turn him into a meat-frenzied zombie.

He nods—a man of few words, it seems. "I…I don't have anyone else."

"He's gone, really gone, isn't he?" I say, quietly, waiting for a nod.

"I think so. I'm free, aren't I? 'The chains are loose,' as they say. I have a feeling you may know much more information on the matter, as well as Amber's disappearance." As he speaks, his jaw clenches slightly, and a bit of a twitch appears under his right eye.

"You knew *her*?!" The heat that begins searing my veins works up sudo-abominor, instantly. "You knew that *bitch*?"

"Amber was actually very kind to me, as well as Devoten."

"Amber is not kind to anyone. *That stiletto-wearing bitch was the very soul that began my ruin!* I trusted her despite her problems, and did so much for her, and she practically smothered my sanity…like one of her boyfriends in her breasts!" Stephen's expression changes to one of interest and amusement as he listens to my anger-induced, but albeit colorful prose. "*Amber doesn't deserve an ounce of worry wasted over her*!"

"What about the baby, our half-sibling? What does *it* deserve?" he asks, in much more of a steady tone than mine, but displaying a suddenly violent eye twitch.

"Who do you think you are stepping into my life now and talking all this stupidity?" I ramble, knowing it's not really stupid talk. I'm just angry. My emotions take a nosedive as the thoughts of an innocent child in turmoil run rampant through my brain. Switching gears, I reply, "Enough Amber talk. You've saved my life twice now, so I must thank you." His face dances and acts with the signs of an underlying internal struggle.

Looking directly into my eyes, he replies, "That meeple deserved its death, and as you were falling off that roof I only directed you in thought—that's my power. I believe that you slowing down mid-air, well, you must thank someone else entirely for that."

A furrow appears in my brow, and as I look into a male version of my mother's face, I suddenly realize who it was that helped with my gravity issue.

"Does she visit you, too?"

He doesn't answer my question, only says, "Here, I want to give you this." After his hand reaches in his pocket, it pulls out a small yellow frog. "It was yours when you were little." I slowly move toward him and then quickly grasp the frog. I don't remember it, but realize that this is an important gesture, for his energy is plastered over the item in layers. "Sorry."

A sadness in my body begins to vibrate to match his when I suddenly notice the toes of his right foot burrowing into the sand and his hands suddenly clenching into fists as a bit of blood escapes the corner of his mouth. I take one more step back from him, and in a blink of an eye, his sadness is gone and replacing it is a hunger like no other I've experienced.

As his eyes look up slowly to meet mine, I see it: the monster Ladimer depicted him as. "Stephen!" I exclaim as I also ask, "Your birthday?" He suddenly throws his cape over his head and the words "Don't follow!" scream through my head. He then disappears.

I stand, torn between following my flesh-eating brother and staying put. Satisfied that I didn't get killed, but frustrated I'm even in this predicament, I force myself to focus on my original goal, so with Quicksilver speed, I jump from dune to dune, frustrated beyond words, leaving my brother to Neda-knows-what.

"Goddamn! Ahhh!" I am so upset that I start stomping childishly on a dune and with one hard swoop of my monk's spade, I hit the sand with enough strength to break through to the guts of the dune. I fall hard and hit the floor with such velocity I hear a bone crunch under my weight as I land on my arm. My lungs empty all their air with a sound much like a whoosh of a basketball through a hoop.

As I look up to my surroundings and take in the deepest breath possible at the moment, I discover I am not the only one inside this particular dune; I sense other, sorrow-riddled energies in such pain my heart aches without even laying eyes on them. I turn behind me, and there before me stands Elivon and a green-hooded figure, standing close to one another, looking as though a very passionate conversation between the two has been oddly interrupted by a woman falling from the heavens.

Trying to ignore the intense pain from my arm, my eyes focus on the green-hooded figure, and as I stare at the face, my confusion slowly transforms to bewilderment because it is then that I think I may finally have some closure to Madam Eve's case, because it can't be *him* standing there, alive and well before me with tears dripping down his face. I squint my eyes and question aloud, "Flora?" but before I receive a response, my leg is pulled out from underneath me, and as I turn to avoid falling on my most-likely broken arm, I see, low to the ground, Gurgl's smiling face. His long arm has reached out and his hand has wrapped around my ankle. My head hits the ground and my vision blurs as I sense sudden movement around me.

# Chapter 18

## Sensation

Burning. I feel burning. My face. My arms. I sit up and have to brace myself with both arms—forcing me to instantly cringe—as my vertigo lessens. Scrunching my face in pain, I sense the telltale sensation of a horrible sunburn, and as I lay my hand on my forehead, I look up through the hole in the ceiling to the two fading, but still mocking, suns which I imagine laughing at the fair-skinned redhead who didn't wear her SPF this fine morning. In observing their position, I can tell that I have been knocked out from some time.

Sitting up carefully, I notice there was a pillow under my head—an actual, fucking, pillow. "Huh."

A quick sweep of the area—the old fashioned and normal way using eyeballs—tells me I'm alone, so I slowly stand up, still holding the pillow and arching my back like a hunchback, until I can straighten up without feeling woozy. In examining the area around me, I find there are various paths—extremely dark and creepy paths—leading out of this room, paths I'm not excited about exploring. "Hmm." Not knowing which to take, I shoot out my feeler just in case it works, but it shoots right back at me, almost knocking me over. I could travel back to my friends, but since I'm here and I spotted Elivon and Flora together, I have to venture into the dune caverns, even if it terrifies me by conjuring images of giant spiders, meeples, and rotting chained-up corpses. I even think I hear a snake hissing in one of the many tunnels, echoing loudly off the walls and creating a sense of *many* snakes.

As monsters run through my thoughts, I suddenly have an idea. Even though I know I shouldn't, I know I need to purposefully rile up sudo-abominor; it's the only way to summon the needed courage to travel down one of the paths. I stand, still slightly woozy, and begin focusing on my broken appendage and the fact that Elivon and Gurgl didn't do anything for me while I was passed out with a possible concussion or maybe even an exploded aneurysm *they* forced to erupt. I look at the sandy pillow in my hand and whip it at the wall. "A fucking pillow? A dirty, smelly, ugly pillow!" A sand beetle conveniently crawls across the pillow as I toss profanities, hoping to speed up the process.

However, a moment before I begin my journey into my dark, mental territory to conjure the beast, I see a small thing resembling a faint reflection of light on the wall. With my concentration broke, I look around and see absolutely nothing worthy of casting a reflection—no glass, no metal, no *anything.* I look again to make sure it wasn't simply a figment of my brain aneurysm and as I wave my hand in front of the light, it darts to position itself a few inches away, not wavering at all in appearance. *Like a playful fairy.* Suddenly, childhood memories of my mother reading me passages of *Peter Pan* begin flooding back as I recall my incessant whining that I just *had* to meet Tinkerbell; she *had* to live in one of my many fairy houses that I built, with their tediously-glued-on Q-tips, toothpicks, nail files, and tampons—anything within reach, inside my mom's bathroom. So what they probably would have collapsed and smothered dear Tinkerbell; I made it with Tinkerbell's tinkering soul in mind while my mother bathed, watched, and laughed so hard she almost choked.

I move closer and cup my hand over the light which mysteriously does not appear on the back of my hand like a normal reflection, but stays beneath it. Slowly it escapes my hand and starts moving across the wall, down one of the paths. I instinctively follow, totally enthralled by this tiny bit of impossible light, and let my good memories flow. "Oh Mom. I miss you so much."

For hundreds of feet, feeling inspired beyond belief, I move my legs slowly down the path as I feel against the wall with my good arm, staying close to the traveling light. Unfortunately, the sweet and sentiment-infused adventure doesn't last long as a loud suctioning noise captures my attention. The beginning of a loud slurping noise approaches from further down the path and I freeze in place as something suddenly grabs a hold of my leg, somehow, and then secures itself like a succubus. Shaking my leg, but feeling the motion is worthless, and realizing I can't swing my monk's spade without slicing off my leg, I resort to grabbing the surprisingly wet thing with my hands and begin pulling on it as my hands slip and slide over its ooze-covered body. A slight burning sensation begins crawling from my palms up to my elbow as a fast-working poison leeches my circulatory system.

With no budging whatsoever from the creature, I find that it has something like a tongue wrapped around my leg. Moaning in pain, I continue unwrapping as more slurping noises reach my ears.

Succeeding in finally dislodging it and whipping it against the wall, it sends out a shrill scream sending a shiver of coldness burrowing into my bones. Scared beyond belief, I scamper down the path, pulling my monk's spade off my back and hoping more creatures don't follow, but as I gain speed, I trip over a large bump in the hardened sand floor. Falling hard as I contort my body in an odd way to avoid falling on my broken arm, I sit, wincing, feeling desolate and frustrated—no pissed—and then recognize a certain friendly personality in my "schizophrenic"-self wake with vengeance. *It's about time.*

Gathering my strength quickly, and suddenly feeling as though nothing can stop me, I begin running down the path with no regards to the squishy and slurping creatures I step on, the strange noises of whispered warnings from various side paths, or the slimy goop that drips down the walls and off the ceiling. *I am indestructible.*

The endless paths continue to vein out like a labyrinth beneath the dunes and I realize that I totally underestimated the amount of livable space underneath the dunes. As I feel myself traveling deep enough into the ground to reach Renhala's core, a small amount of light finally shows ahead, and I speed up faster, hoping that maybe once I emerge I can surprise whomever or whatever is beyond.

Feeling no pain, I reach a large entryway and with my monk's spade held tightly in my hand, I thrust myself into the flickering light. I'm ready to fight to the death, ready to mutilate Elivon—to thrash anything in my way, but *so* not ready for this…

# Chapter 19

# Satisfaction

"What. The. Hell." Stupified, I stand motionless and fixated on the rows and rows of long rectangular tables that fill the huge expanse of a room I've entered, with each table's end containing what appears to be a large candle-heated hotpot, and various vials of liquid and glass containers full of multi-colored powders. Also seated at each table is approximately twenty equidistantly-arranged, energy-vibrating wooden chairs, and one large and hinged metal box labelled **Stock 3** located dead-center. But what really captures my attention are the hundreds of liquid nitrogen tanks stacked hundreds of feet high, surrounding the room, looking like tin soldiers creating a barrier of possible disaster. Loud rumbling and motor noises traveling from another room beyond this one echo off the tanks, creating an ominous tune, completing the chilling and foreboding experience. I notice sudo-abominor has taken a backseat, once again. I add confusion to the list of things that it chooses not to deal with.

Placing my monk's spade back on my back as my hands become numb, I walk to the nearest table and open one of the metal boxes, and find inside hundreds of white pills piled neatly on top of one another. Courageously running one over my tongue, I recognize it as the very substance I found in Elivon's classroom, and most likely found by Madam Eve in Flora's room.

Curious, I venture slowly toward the room located next door, and as I peek around the corner to make sure I am alone, I see the source of rumbling and stare at the huge tumbler rotating slowly on its axis. Knowing the sand walls around me will most likely provide hindrance for a search by my feeler, but feeling an extreme need to pull in my most technically-savvy friend, I walk around the room, searching for something to spark an idea. As I near the machine, I notice a flexible accordion-style pipe extending upwards. *Ventilation.* Remembering Elivon's classroom and my success in sending the feeler out and beyond the sand, I think if I blast it high enough, it may be possible to travel horizontally and drop down directly on my goal.

Concentrating on who I want, and imagining him standing before me, I then focus on the end of the tube and thrust. A bit slower than normal, but definitely successful, I grasp and pull forth, just as I hear approaching footsteps. Bu, arriving with a huge watermelon-looking fruit or vegetable in his hands, and red juice splattered around his mouth, drops it as his mouth opens wide at the gigantic tumbler roaring next to him.

"Change in plans. Elivon wants Stock 3 finished and ready by nightfall," we hear as the nearing footsteps stop within feet of the doorway to this room.

Whispering to Bu, I say, "Shit. We have to go." I attempt to grab his arm with my useless appendage, but he ignores me, instead inching closer to the tumbler's controls. "Bu!" I say through clenched teeth. "No!"

"But…but," is all that escapes his mouth as I travel, dragging him against his will, with me.

We appear outside our dune just as all the others are exiting. The suns are almost at the horizon, but the heat still remains.

"*Kailey*!" Lupa yells as we startle her with our sudden appearance. "Where did you go? Why would you do that, running off and worrying us all!" Kioto begins jumping on me and licking my face as I open my mouth to speak, but Lupa's not going to listen. "Don't do that again! We need to stay together and not go running off all willy-nilly. Understand?" she rants, suddenly scanning my red, sunburned face, then my arms. "What happened to you?"

"I was just being me, I guess," I answer, trying to hold down Kioto. "On another note, I found Elivon's secret lab." I wince from a sudden and throbbing pain emanating from my arm thanks to Kioto's sandpaper tongue's attention. I notice that blisters have begun sprouting where the poison from the tunnel creatures has seeped in.

Ladimer moves quickly toward me and lays his hand on my shoulders. "Broken arm? What have you been up to?" His magic travels through my body and I practically sink into his arms as my body starts recovering from its injuries. "And poison from something nasty, I see. Was the 'adventure' worth it?" he asks, with a slight lift of the eyebrow. He leans in close to my ear and breathes the words, "You're awfully lucky I like you," as I smile an almost drunken smile because I feel *that* damn good as he continues caressing, despite the fact I feel completely healed.

"Bu and I found something dangerous. I know it."

Bu's feet start shuffling, nervously. "Kailey, Bu needs to see it again."

Looking extremely worried, Sir Cuche and Jenna step closer to us. "Kailey, you look so tired," Jenna says. "No more of these adventures on your own, please. We are in this contract together."

"Speaking of contracts, I found Flora, and…" I say, watching Gunthreon's energy swiftly change. I decide to keep Stephen to myself.

"And what? Where?" Gunthreon pries, eager to know.

"I surprised both Flora and Elivon by literally breaking in on their party—through the roof, actually. Gurgl was there, too." Jenna mumbles something about falling on my ass and Gurgl comforting me.

"Actually, I landed on my arm. They were mighty upset. I am assuming they got word of Terro's death."

Gunthreon's mood changes to one of contemplation. "You know, he was like a father to Terro. He has not yet paid his respects, as well as Flora," he says toward me.

Images of cemetery gravesites pop into my head as if planted. "Yes! Thank Neda we have someone with brains in this group," I say as Ladimer quickly lifts his hands from my body, pulling a moan of frustration from me.

"Tonight, when the moon is over Luvia," Gunthreon says, "we will put an end to this."

Conner stands apart from us all, appearing in my feeler's eye as melancholy and lonely, and all behind a thin wall of energy which he is using to barrier himself off from me. He looks elsewhere as I reach out to him, trying to persuade a bit of happiness or even frustration to grow—anything but the loneliness. He brings his hand above his eyes to shield them, and in looking out over the dunes and straining, evidently seeing something of interest, his energy flips. "We've got a guest," he claims as he quickly drops his hand, and then changing his tone to one of surprise, says, "Well, I'll be."

We all look and Sir Cuche is the first to reply as the figure becomes distinguishable. "Why is *he* here?" he cries, picking up the grumblepig and running back inside our dune.

I begin running to the best of my ability through the sand as our visitor struggles and ultimately falls on his big belly as the creature on his shoulder climbs near his head. He rolls over on his back, spitting out sand. "Hoolie Hal!" I exclaim as I notice that the lack of energy around him tells me clearly that a slight case of dehydration has sucked him dry.

Lupa runs up next to me, pulls out a water satchel from her everything pack, and pours water into his mouth as I lift his head. Choking on it, he coughs violently, but a bit dramatically. "It's warm!" he yells with a scratchy voice.

"Shut up and drink it," Lupa retorts, "or I'll pull out the thermos of hot tea."

My face rises to meet hers at the mention of tea. "What kind?" I ask, disregarding Hoolie Hal for the moment.

"Ehh! Who cares!" Hoolie Hal blurts out.

"Orange, with a hint of lemongrass."

"Ooh, sounds delightful," I return.

"I'm dying!" yells Hoolie Hal as his eyes suddenly close, his head lolling to the side.

"You are not dying," I reply, almost laughing as Bringling shuffles in close to me. I feed him from the water satchel and *he* doesn't complain. "What on Earth are you doing here, anyway? Who is watching the hoolies?"

He stops feigning unconsciousness as his eyes open and stare at me. "I let them go," he replies in a serious tone as Conner comes up beside us.

"What?" Lupa and I say in unison.

"Yesterday."

"Why?" Conner asks in an almost knowing manner, kneeling as Bringling walks to him. Picking him up and examining a very deep but healing gash in Bringling's hide, Conner begins petting him slowly as Bringling's eyes avoid contact with mine—something Conner clearly notes to himself as he turns away from us, heading back to the others.

Hoolie Hal starts coughing as he sits up, watching with a hawk's eye as Conner heads away with the hoolie comfortably perched on his shoulder. "I've got a story if you've got a place for me to stay," he says, his stare never wavering from Conner.

"If you don't expect anything lavish, we have a deal," I say, extending my hand. "Just don't expect a bath or shower. Oh, and don't eat anything given to you, except by Lupa." He warily shakes my hand, looking as though maybe the deal's not worth it.

We all stare—Bu most intensely—as Hoolie Hal inhales an endless amount of goodies from Lupa's pack. "You done yet?" I say, trying to hide my annoyance, but evidently not well enough, for Lupa shoots me a look charged with daggers as I feel inside her everything pack for something else to eat. Bu nods at my comment, as though agreeing Hoolie Hal should indeed be finished.

My hand finds a small tin in Lupa's pack and I pull it out to examine the ivy etching on the lid. While she's not looking I open it and two dried jambleberries fall out. I squeak as I cover them with my foot and admire Lupa and her free spirit.

"He must restore his energy. Right?" Lupa coos, looking at me oddly and patting Hoolie Hal on the back.

Noises from Sir Cuche suddenly pull our attention in his direction as he buries his grumblepig beneath several layers of pillows. I pick up the berries and shove them in my pocket while sneaking the tin back in Lupa's pack.

"I'm not backing out of the deal, Sir Cuche, so stop smothering that poor creature," Hoolie Hal laughs.

Sir Cuche stops and begins fidgeting with his robe instead as his eyes wander to Hoolie Hal's right hand, specifically his ring finger—the very finger now wearing Sir Cuche's ruby wedding band. He humphs and holds back a comment most likely about the fact that Hoolie Hal isn't even married. "The grumblepig has lost his ability to search for gold, anyway," he says. "Ladimer took it away. The pig is worthless." Sir Cuche, making quick eye contact with me, swiftly switches his attention to Bringling, who is occasionally grabbing a bite to eat from Hoolie Hal, then sharing half with Kioto. I let her be happy and allow the table food.

"Done now?" I say toward Hoolie Hal, ignoring Lupa's glare.

He wipes his face with a napkin and sighs loudly. "Fine," he replies. "I'm surely not going to enjoy any peace and quiet with this bunch," he pouts toward Bringling as he hands the creature his last scrap. "Might as well tell the story. So, after a long hard day of bookkeeping two days ago, I decided to reward myself with a day of play with my hoolies. So," he says, popping five huge chunks of melon into his mouth, "yesterday, early in the morning, I decided we were going to play hide-and-seek, where I hide various things and they sniff them out…" He starts fading off his conversation as Conner moves closer to him, almost standing directly in front of him. "They like it!"

"Training thieves," Conner remarks, sarcastically.

"Do you want to hear the story or not? I can easily pack us up and leave, right now, and not even tell you where *she* comes in!" Hoolie Hall growls as he points to me.

"Me?"

Conner whispers an "Of course…" after hearing that I have something to do with Hoolie Hal's story.

Lupa hands Hoolie Hal a giant chunk of hazelnut chocolate-iced sweetbread, patting him once on the back.

His eyes smile as he turns to Conner. "Can I continue without interruption?"

"Yes!" I blurt, frowning with my eyes toward Conner.

Ladimer sits to the side, making no comments, snacking on some nuts as he watches all of us: his own personal drama theater. He chews loudly, however, and as we all gawk at him, he rolls his eyes. "Continue, Hoolie Hal. Please. I have a feeling this is going to get very interesting."

As Hoolie Hal's mouth wraps around the bread, savoring all the gooey goodness, he slowly starts mumbling through the crumbs. "Yeah, so me and the hoolies were having a good 'ole time playing—Bringling here is the best," he says, scratching the creature behind its ear, "when all of a sudden during feeding time, bodies just start falling from the sky. Bodies! They were landing on the enclosures, totally pulling the whole things down to the ground and opening huge holes for the hoolies to…" his eyes move again to Conner.

"Escape," says Conner, filling the word in for him.

"I could have stopped them all, easily." Hoolie Hal turns to Lupa, saying, "I *allowed* them to go." She rubs his back slowly, nodding, prodding the chocolate-faced monkey to go on.

"Ok, enough about the damn hoolies! What's with the bodies?" I shout, getting suddenly fired up at the mere mention of falling bodies.

"Grebles and UFOE officers! Some were dead, a few others were not—they fled—but there was this one that kept moaning something. I moved close to him and that's when I heard what he was really mumbling." Waiting for me to pry the words from his mouth, he takes another bite of his messy bread.

My hand moves to my spade as Gunthreon approaches me, saying, "Relax, my dear. Let him talk."

Hoolie Hal gives in and says, "He kept mumbling: 'Kailey…Kailey," and he was holding something very tightly in his hand."

"Bayle!" exclaims Jenna. My breathing becomes quicker and shallow.

"He eventually stopped talking—and breathing—and that's when Bringling crawled over his body and took this from him." He hands a piece of paper to Bringling. "Well, he could only pry half. A death grip is mighty powerful, you know." Elivon's blood-splattered sketch is handed to me by the hoolie, half of it missing.

Bu jumps up quicker than a fox, snatching it from me. His eyes roll over it, carefully.

"Bu?" I say, hoping for a final answer in the mystery that is Elivon's creation, an end to the questions. My eyes intense, my brain anticipating news, and my breath held, I wait on the edge of sanity.

"Bu needs to see the machine again. This," he holds it up, "could be many things."

A quick scream escapes my mouth and I suddenly feel like my whole being is on fire, like the Kailey I have been holding on to so tightly is slowly being burned alive. She's screaming inside as her soul is smothered, as her shell-of-a-body is being slashed and burned, allowing room for new growth to appear through the ashes—the growth of something inflammable, adaptable, and stronger.

Gunthreon stands up the same time I do, saying, "Kailey, you need to—"

I whirl around toward him, my weapon out before me. Everyone tightens up, procuring stances to enable quick movement, especially Conner. Even Sir Cuche has his hands in his robe on his hidden knife—his tiny stupid knife. Lupa's moving slower than a sloth as she heads near her love, Gunthreon. *That's a fucking joke*! I keep a close eye on Ladimer—my biggest threat—as he sits still, watching, like he always does. I yell at him, "Go ahead and make your move, mighty 'giver.'"

Kioto growls a loud noise of warning at me, but I growl back *as an alpha.*

Jenna bravely steps forth, making slow (but valuable in her mind) steps toward me with her blade behind her back. She's watching my body for movement, but cannot take her eyes off my aura. I can only imagine the horror that is hovering above and around me. I'm not threatened by her, so I laugh, causing her to shed a small, tiny and glowing tear. "Kailey, please. This isn't you."

A rumbling deep in my chest—another, but different growl—tickles my insides and I laugh again, louder. "Please what, woodsprite? Yes, this *is* me. This is the me that you were all hoping to *fix*. Don't think that because I *loved* you I'm sparing you any pain if you come in my way. I *remember* our deal—both deals," I say, looking directly at Conner, but moving my monk's spade within inches of Jenna's face. "You think I'd really allow you to destroy me? No. I've decided that it might be much more fun if I coerced you into *thinking* you could destroy me, *believing* that sweet, kind, weak Kailey is still buried inside. That girl is actually gone." Bringling shrinks into Hoolie Hal's arms, shielding himself from my possible energy wrath.

Feeling the need to express its strength, sudo-abominor blasts out my feeler in the small area, much too strong, forcing it to ricochet off the sand walls, causing everyone to stumble, including myself.

Ladimer seizes the opportunity, moving with such quick and unanticipated speed, that I don't have enough time to bring up my spade to do some serious damage. He knocks me down, and holds me with both hands, sending a sickness throughout my body that would send the average Joe into a coma. I fight hard, and as I do, I send out a blast of energy, slamming open the door to outside, allowing my feeler to run rampant among the sand dunes. As the wind outside picks up with enough ferocity to shake the dune, sand starts blasting through the door, pelting everyone like shrapnel.

Ladimer lets go of me in an attempt to shield his face as the sand tries burrowing into his nose, ears and eyes.

As I gleefully squeal while everyone screams, but still feel as though I might vomit from the sickness flowing through me, I realize I'm unable to protect even myself from the sand. *I have to escape it.* In thinking it best to avoid any of my vortexes, I travel to Luvia, hoping that Gunthreon's plan comes to fruition so I can deal with Elivon in my own special way. Landing in the middle of Madam Eve's starcka fields, I stretch out my arms and take in the lovely scenery illuminated by the Luvia moon: wilted pod plants all brown and crunchy from lack of rain (despite the high humidity) look like sad, ugly little bulbous-headed aliens.

I scan the area thinking that perhaps my brother is slinking around somewhere, munching on some crispy Golden Dunes flesh or gnawing on a femur. It brings a smile to my face as I think that maybe, just maybe, he could be a part of my new "team." He would most definitely scare the shit out of my foe. Laughing, but knowing he's nowhere close to be able to make him an offer, and not wanting to waste any needed energy on grasping and bringing him forth, I begin walking toward Madam Eve's secret little gravesite. Within minutes I know that she is also on her way to the same destination.

My feet become lighter, moving through the plants quietly as I determine what my best approach should be. Weeping soon drifts to my ears as I lessen the distance between us, as she begins mumbling to herself, "Stupid move. Why? *Why*? What did I do? Where is he?" Slowly I move in, forcing my breath to become almost nothing. I feed off the anguish as it flows from her broken soul, filling me up with power. "Go on as planned, Eve," she says, pulling herself together. "You need—" She instantly stops at the precise moment I crack a dead starcka plant in half as I move it to the side. Something very low to the ground starts heading in my direction from her location. I freeze and listen to the characteristics of the approaching creature. It's small, and very light, and quick. *A snake.*

I watch along the ground carefully, but not seeing it I start swiping through the dead stalks and leaves that make up the mulch throughout the fields. *Nothing.* The movement stops and I decide better now than never to make my move. I begin a more rapid movement, covering the last fifteen feet between us in heartbeat thanks to my ungodly speed. Just as I break through the plants to the gravesite, I see her, standing solemn and broken, but smiling.

We lock eyes. "Are you waiting for him, as well?" I remark. She doesn't talk, but continues to smile a smile that does not light up her face, but only exaggerates the fact she knows something—

something I don't. "What's with you and the cat and the canary act?" I pull my weapon in front of me, pointing it directly at her. She doesn't budge and it annoys me, tremendously. "Maybe you need to open your mouth and let me see the feathers."

"I must go on," she declares as her head slowly turns toward the new, freshly dug grave by her feet. I follow her movement, also looking down, and as I move in toward the marking stone with slow steps, I notice the starcka stalk and pod carefully placed in a circle around the name on the stone. As I stare at it, trying to focus in the darkness, and not fully interpreting what is going on, confusion once again stymies sudo-amobinor's intentions—at the very unfortunate moment that I am pulled to the ground by the relentless snake I forgot was stalking me, the very one that buries its secret fangs in me.

"They fooled you, too," she whispers as another poison courses through my veins, paralyzing my extremities, as well as my mouth. She grabs my legs and begins pulling me away as my eyes finally read the beautiful gravestone script commemorating the dead buried beneath, the script naming that which I may stop seeking: "Flora."

Madam Eve proceeds to drag me to her home, purposefully hitting each and every mound of dirt and protruding rock along the way.

# Chapter 20

## Determination

"You didn't complete the contract, Kailey. You didn't save her. You let her die before our very eyes. Ladimer could have gotten past the deathman. I know it. He would have *for you."* She's tying me up in a chair in her dingy basement, with its dilapidated walls which are allowing nameless roots to vine in through the cracks. Her hands tug hard, securing each and every knot, ignoring me entirely as I notice the corner of my mouth is able to move.

I'm running through scenes in my head, trying to decipher what the hell has happened and why, but I'm coming up with no answers as Madam Eve repeatedly catches my skin insider her knots. I can feel the pain, now, but still cannot move my arms or legs. My concentration is blurred as I try to gather the energy needed to travel, but find that I cannot do that either.

"Uhhh..!" I mumble, and finally catch her attention. "Stop."

"Wearing off already? That's fine, we can always give you another dose without killing you," she explains as her snakes move about slowly, looking as though they are patiently waiting for the go-ahead to bite, "because I need something from you first." Her face moves close, her lips above mine as I struggle to move *anything* but my mouth, but I can't, no matter how hard I fight the poison. "I need a…*determination* replenishment, if you will. I need to re-focus and come up with a whole new plan now, thanks to you." Her lips touch mine and I close my eyes, waiting for the pain—for something—but she only pulls back, empathy bleeding from her eyes as she stares at me. "I'm sorry, but I must do what I must to survive. I will never go back to what I was."

She continues talking to herself more than me as I suddenly sense energy vibrations moving quickly toward the house, and as I interpret them, a small amount of hope refurbishes sudo-abominor's brashness. My mouth is finally free and in my desperation to keep her focused on me and not those approaching, I slowly choose my words as I talk to her. "It's not my fault Flora and her brother decided to pull one over on you," I grumble. "There must be good reason for your own family to betray you with such elaborate plans."

Her jaw immediately clenches as she holds her knife to my throat. *Yep, that did it.* Her empathy toward me shuts off immediately as she shouts angrily, "*I gave them everything—the finest* of everything." Her eyes suddenly widen and her snakes wriggle about, aimlessly. "It was Elivon! He made them do it. *That son-of-a-bitch*! See what happens when you actually trust someone…when you show them your vulnerability…when you open your *heart*?"

Sudo-abominor really wants to stir her up, and I must buy time while my friends hurry. "In my opinion, it wasn't your heart you opened…" escapes my mouth without much thinking as her backhand connects with my face.

She laughs. "It's that," she growls as she points at me, "that I want from you. You don't know how to usefully direct that 'grit' you possess. You know what? I thought you, out of all people might understand my plight—my fight—to build myself whole again after tragedy. I guess I was wrong. You're not much of a woman after all, are you? You're just a little girl with a big weapon, possessing a certain something that I will soon uncover…and own, myself." Stroking her snakes lovingly, she pays careful attention to touch each and every snake as they take turns slipping toward her fingers and looking up at her with their eyes, which in closer examination, seem to exhibit human affection. *What has Velopa done to her?*

Once the energies are near, and noise reaches our ears, a belief of rescue arises inside me and I notice that Madam Eve is not reacting accordingly, instead she is smiling her evil smile again.

Suddenly, as the doors burst open, the realization sets in that I am not going to be rescued after all. None of us are going to be rescued, for all my friends, tied up and gagged, are being dragged in, one-by-one and carelessly dropped to the floor by various staff members of Madam Eve. As my friends' limbs lie motionless, I know they all have a current of matching poison flowing through their bodies.

Bu is the only exception. I occasionally see small movements from his fingers, but every time Madam Eve looks at him, he stops. His massive size would most definitely take much more poison to subdue, and he smartly played along, most likely waiting for the perfect opportunity to take action. *That's my Bu.*

Lupa and Gunthreon are placed in chairs, side-by-side, and Ladimer and Conner are left on the ground at opposite ends of the room, with Ladimer nearest Bu. Hoolie Hal is also left on the ground next to Sir Cuche who pleads with his eyes to not inflict any harm on his grumblepig as it is brought in last and left near Ladimer's body. Jenna, Bringling, and a muzzled Kioto are all in cages, barely big enough for each of them.

"Make yourselves comfortable, my friends," Madam Eve says hospitably toward her refrained guests as she motions for most of her workers to leave. She stops one of them and whispers quietly to him, "Elivon and Terro?" The worker shakes his head as Madam Eve's snakes begin moving violently around her body. Dismissed, the worker looks at me out of the corner of his eye. "Well, well," Madam Eve says as she looks at each of us. "How about some party games tonight? I'm gonna see what you all are made of." She walks about with a small pouch in her hands, examining each of her bound guests and then decides to stop above Lupa. Her hand digs into her pouch and pulls out a long-needled syringe of some kind. A stream of green liquid squirts out the tip as she tests for air.

Leaning down over Lupa as Gunthreon's eyes widen, she sticks the needle into Lupa's arm, pushing the liquid into her bloodstream. Lupa's hand begins moving and Madam Eve smiles as she watches the struggle that ensues as Lupa's fingers attempt to thrash about, trying to reach something, anything. Madam Eve then works her way over to Gunthreon, paying close attention to his face as she kneels over him, transferring one of her small snakes to his body. Slowly it moves over him, heading toward his head, and as it nears his ear, Gunthreon's eyes open wide and his breathing speeds up as his energy begins flailing wildly. The snake then reaches its destination and slowly enters the orifice that is his ear. As his eyes open as wide as possible, I feel as though he's attempting to scream *through* them.

Then he suddenly stops as his eyes stare forward, at nothing. I know he's not dead, because his energy still exists, as still as it has become. "Gunthreon, can you hear me?" Madam Eve asks sweetly over him. Her eyes then move about as she notices small movements from my friends. "Ugh. That's ok. We'll fix that soon," she says with a smile.

"Yes, Eve," Gunthreon replies in a robotic fashion, his mouth now working.

"Good," she brags, happy with herself. "Are you willing to do as I ask?"

"Yes, Eve," he says, again in the same un-Gunthreon voice.

"Ok. Hmm," she ponders, thinking of a good request. She stands up, looking around her basement and heads toward one of the particularly long roots scaling her basement wall. She tugs at the end, disconnecting its grasp from the wall, but keeping it intact and says to Gunthreon, "I ask that you please have Lupa here show off her mad skills." Carefully placing the root in Lupa's hand, Madam Eve then steps away. Lupa drops it, but Madam Eve picks it back up, placing it again in Lupa's hand and holding her hand shut.

Gunthreon, following orders, says, "Lupa, use that root to ensnare." The root quickly grows, becoming longer and thicker as it sits in Lupa's palm, still held closed by Madam Eve. The root slowly begins moving up Madam Eve's leg.

"Eh, eh," Madam Eve mumbles, as though scolding a child. "Gunthreon, direct it away from me, please."

"Lupa, you shall not ensnare Madam Eve. Please redirect the roots to others." The root begins growing small branches that then begin extending toward all my friends, then winding up their bodies and cocooning them inside, tightly. A small, bright tear falls from Lupa's eye.

Madam Eve lets go of Lupa's hand as she then claps, excitedly. She walks toward her table and picks up a small, potted, wilted starcka plant and frowns at it as she takes strides back to Lupa. Immediately after placing the small stalk in Lupa's hand, the plant sprouts up, looking healthy and renewed as it drops four seeds onto the dirt floor. "Oh, Lupa. Thank you."

"Gunthreon, stop!" I shout as Madam Eve laughs.

"Oh, honey, my snakes listen only to me."

"You are such a bitch," I say, hoping to stir up her emotions again so her concentration can slip, but she ignores me. I close my eyes, hoping the poison dissipated enough to allow me to travel, but I find I cannot do anything except read energy right now—I cannot manipulate it.

Madam Eve travels over to Ladimer, and as she walks I notice that Bu's right hand, which has worked its way from the roots, is slowly unzipping his fanny pack of tools. I speak to her, quickly. "Whatever you are planning is not going to work, Eve. You know that, don't you? Karma will definitely have her say."

Her actions are quick as she spins around with her knife bared and walks wide-gaited toward me. "I have fed enough of my blood and tears into karma's bank to have a savings for the life I deserve. Don't you threaten me with your righteousness—you who has committed enough sins in your contracts to have a one-way ticket to Velopa's hands." Her attention then turns to Conner as he begins loudly struggling inside his root covering. "You are indeed beautiful," she says as she runs her fingers through his hair, "and we might produce some lovely offspring, but unfortunately, you are actually useless to me. Soulspeak? Truth? I need that like I need a slit jugular. Gunthreon?"

"Yes, Eve."

"Ask him what he has of value to me."

Gunthreon then says, "Conner, give Madam Eve something of value to her."

Conner's hand begins moving near his pants pocket as Madam Eve cuts away a small amount of roots near the location. She reaches in and carefully pulls out Conner's clay udoa, and as she rattles it, her expression changes to one of intrigue. "Not what I was expecting, but something, I guess." Her hand rises slowly to a point far above Conner.

I sense what she's going to do and I fight through sudo-abominor's hate, screaming: "*Eve, don't—*" but she continues with her movement, changing the direction downward and fast, ending in a quick slam upon Conner's head, breaking the udoa wide open and spilling both Conner's blood and his hidden treasure from his treasured friend. Seemingly excited and with childlike pleasure, she picks the valuable up and examines the gold and diamond ring that was locked inside. She then makes a small movement, directing a snake off her body and onto Conner. It begins wrapping itself around his neck and squeezes.

As my concentration becomes clearer through my growing anger, I feel my monster surface entirely as two warm bodies are sensed approaching. They move quickly and the determination spewing from their bodies is enough to feed Madam Eve for a lifetime. Rushing through the doors, surprising Madam Eve as she tightens her grip on the ring, the two force her to wield her knife.

"*Eve*!" yells Elivon as he slows his speed, taking in what is happening throughout the room. "What have you done?" He stands perfectly still, now looking into her face, asking for a logical explanation as the snake around Conner's throat relaxes its hold.

"*No*! What have *you* done? *Both of you*!" she cries, her eyes landing on Terro's face just as a deathman enters behind him. It turns and walks to a wall and stands among the roots, becoming a figural elephant in the room.

"Mom."

"Don't you *mom* me! You are officially no longer under my protection, Terro. You killed your sister: your flesh and blood—your exact twin, playing your stupid games. Now I must do this," she says, pointing at all of us. "You know I will do what it takes to survive. I mustn't let them stop me."

Terro trembles as he gathers the courage to talk. "*I* was not the one who killed Flora. Go ahead and try to push the blame on someone else like you've done your whole life. It's always been someone else's fault, hasn't it?" Quickly his anxiety turns to anger. "Neda forbid *you* take responsibility for *your* actions and what *your* actions have done to others—your actions like forcing Flora, day after day, to expend all her life force on calling the rain needed for your *precious* plants, your actions like killing all those unborn babies inside the wombs touched by your *fucking* plants! How many do you want to kill for sake of a comfortable lifestyle?"

Elivon begins inching forward as Madam Eve is blasted with Terro's harsh words. Angry with Elivon's presence, sudo-abominor sits and watches, hungrily. Just as he reaches his last foot of distance between them, and Madam Eve suddenly realizes his proximity, she tightens up her muscles, but allows him to take the final step and to reach in, not with an attack on her, but with a tight embrace, one vibrating of a love so deep it shakes both their energies.

She hangs on tightly, cherishing the affection from her mate as her snakes continue to slither about her body, avoiding his touch. Sudo-abominor is absolutely disgusted at the act as it sizzles my body from the inside out.

While they are still embracing, Elivon pulls back a bit and asks her, "Will you let me help you? Will you work with me toward a new start? One without starcka? We can fix things, Eve. We can do this, together. I've got big plans." He goes back in, squeezing her tight.

Upon cringing slightly at the words "trust me," Madam Eve, who had begun shaking her head, says, "You don't know what trust is, Elivon." Knowing this may be her response, and downhearted hearing it, he steps away from her, pleading with his eyes.

Sudo-abominor screams through me at Elivon as I realize I can now move my legs a bit. "*You are never going to have the chance, either of you!* Big plans, Elivon? How hypocritical you all are, when you have your own plans to destroy…to kill… That storage unit you have set up is enough to blow several lands to Abscondia."

Elivon's head turns to me, slowly. "Kailey, you must forgive us for all that has happened. You have all been led astray and were allowed to run in circles too long."

Madam Eve interrupts with, "Apologies will get you nowhere, fast. You are so weak, my dear—always have been." She shakes her head as she turns her attention to Conner again. "Let's see how far your apologies and your 'science' will get you when people realize what I did and what you *allowed* to happen. They are going to want blood—my blood. Will you defend me then?" Looking down at Conner, she adds, "You want a new start? We do it my way. I'm the one blessed by Velopa." The green snake around Conner's neck starts squeezing again, and hard as the lack of oxygen turns Conner's face purple.

"Eve, *stop this*!" Elivon retorts, but she continues standing above Conner. Elivon approaches her, and as he nears—to all our surprise—his now knife-possessing hand rises to strike, gaining enough speed to bury the blade deep in her back. The deathman watches and then takes a few steps forward in their direction.

At the very moment Elivon brings his knife up as far as his arm will allow, a large and camouflaged brown snake hiding amongst the roots breaks away from the wall and lands directly on him, bringing him down fast.

Watching Eve, I catch her closing her eyes as a look of regret passes across her face as all of her snakes leave her body, exit Gunthreon, and begin attacking Elivon, biting and debilitating him for the last time as he screams her name with an agony not only representative of physical pain, but also of a broken heart. Lupa and Jenna begin whimpering as Elivon soon lies lifeless, eyes open, his energy silent.

"*No!*" Terro screams, moving toward Elivon as Madam Eve glares directly in his face. "*He was helping them!* His pills…they were working. No, Mom," he cries as he bends down, closing Elivon's eyes with his young hands. I recall an image of the boxes of pills I discovered and now realize they were a drug developed to help the Golden Dunes inhabitants and all those who became dependent on her shipment of starcka, perhaps break them from their addiction.

Madam Eve wails, "He was working—helping—to *destroy me. That's* what he was doing! He hated my prosperity. He was always jealous."

"No, believe it or not, he…and Flora…loved you with all their hearts despite your wicked ways," Terro says as Madam Eve tries her hardest to stay bold despite her want to curl up beside Elivon. Without her snakes, her energy is open and vulnerable as it stirs. "We've been working for years…his machinery…his work." The pain that Terro is trying to cut through to speak his mind is thick, thick as steel. Sobbing, he begins speaking louder at her. "He succeeded in making a machine that turns our sand into cement—no need for your stupid starcka byproduct! Golden Dunes no longer needs your plants. Our plan could have worked… You would have been free to start anew, to focus on your *family*. But now…you have none left."

Bu suddenly squeaks and instantly stops as Madam Eve turns to the sound. His excitement at the revelation of the machinery's true purpose is hard to contain—a purpose based solely on the need and want to help people, not destroy.

"And once your plants were dead, Elivon and Flora planned on harvesting your favorite flower in those fields—the hartflower." Madam Eve begins wavering and wobbling as she inhales the information. "But his genius is now gone from this realm and all because of your black-hole of a heart." The deathman begins working over Elivon's body despite the snakes and I can't help but feel anguish.

"Terro," Madam Eve says softly as she walks toward him, but he closes off his energy and takes a step back from her. Her snakes slowly start slithering back to her, climbing up her body and creating a fortified wall, one that has shielded her for decades.

"It is not *you* that is disowning *me*, it is I who are forever stepping away from you, my own mother. I will continue Elivon's work and without any help from you, for you will never again step foot in Golden Dunes. Oh, and forget your starcka. We've been slowly killing your fields with gountum oil. Flora's 'absence' just sped up the destruction plan." Madam Eve's muscles in her jaw clench and unclench as she begins swimming in the deception invading her mind.

Bu is suddenly working at the roots around him, as well as those around Ladimer, while Madam Eve is preoccupied with her son. She screams as Terro turns and runs out the door for help, forever turning his back on his heartless mother. She whirls around, angrily, suddenly focusing on me. "You are done. I am no longer wasting my precious time. It's just me again." Her footsteps are quick as she moves within inches of me. "That which is hidden in you is now mine."

"Believe me, you don't want it. You can't handle it. I'd say Elivon wasn't the weak one here," I say, sudo-abominor working her up for a chance to be free. Her long green, skinny snake suddenly weeds its way out from her mass of snakes and slinks toward my ear. "Don't do this. *You'll regret it*!" The snake touches my ear, and in desperation, sudo-abominor screams and growls, "Consider yourself dead." She reveals her smile, looking like Evil Ballerina as the snake burrows inside my ear, forcing my eardrum to burst, ripping the inside of my head apart. As I scream, sudo-abominor working up a frenzy, my head turns to Ladimer, who has his hand free. I also feel Conner's energy wake after the knockout. They both begin working frantically at the rest of the roots snaked around their bodies.

The familiar feel of someone inside my head surfaces as I hear "Kailey." I smile, knowing he is near and for the fact that sudo-abominor is now blocking the pain that I should be feeling.

With his hands now free, Ladimer reaches over to the grumblepig and touches it briefly, reawakening its insatiable appetite. The pig suddenly squeals, but Madam Eve, who is concentrating on her snake that is somehow wrestling sudo-abominor, isn't aware of the pig's movement. Violently, my head shakes back and forth, forcing a scream from inside that is both my own, and something hideously barbarian, and also shaking loose the frangleberries in my pocket.

Madam Eve sees them fall and bends to pick them up, her eyes softening as she most likely remembers her daughter's tendencies. "Let's see what these stupid berries did for you," she says, popping them into her mouth and chewing. "Tangy."

As she continues chewing, and I am feeling the most like a monster, the fire inside me suddenly dies and a feeling of total exhaustion emerges as my blood spills from my ear. Pain rips through me as she says, "That's it," her attention back on the snake in my head, "almost there." Her grin widens as she sees her snake beginning to withdraw. As more of its body is revealed, however, her expression changes, for the snake is now black. Its tail leaves and then slowly the reptile climbs onto her, slithering toward her ear as she attempts to slap and tug. Her fight is useless and the snake penetrates her ear at precisely the same moment the grumblepig jumps on her, trying to eat the gold on her finger. Stumbling toward the middle of the room as the snake disappears, Madam Eve begins shaking like an epileptic seizure has taken over her bodily functions.

As we watch in awe, the twitching slows as all her snakes turn the same black and a deep, hearty, maniacal laugh escapes her mouth—one that frightens me, but does not work up the anger of sudo-abominor in my soul; it's now hosted by someone entirely capable of destroying Renhala: a scornful Madam Eve.

Reacting to the threat, I close my eyes and focus on reaching when *he* answers by suddenly bounding into the room as a totally oblivious Madam Eve aims her knife at my heart and then lunges. Stephen glides in quickly as her knife pierces my skin, beginning its burrowing into my body slightly right of my heart. Feeling his presence, she turns toward him and asks, "What god are you?" His confusion hovers around him as he looks around the room, trying to interpret what has occurred and why she would ask him such a question. "Stupid berries," she prattles as she then turns back to me, turning her back on the silent god as she begins turning her blade in my chest.

Stephen moves closer, glaring at me over her shoulder, asking me for permission to do what one should not. Conner stands up beyond him, his face angry. With what's left of my energy, I answer Stephen with a simple, "Happy Birthday, Bro," as he goes in for the kill, burying his teeth deep in her neck, her eyes widening with surprise and terror.

Slowly beginning to fade, I attempt to stay conscious to watch as she struggles to reach behind her as he drains her of all blood, and then begins eating her skin and bones, all the while biting the heads off of the snakes. That last thing I see is a faint image of a blood-splattered snake, dead on the floor. As my eyes close, Madam Eve's piercing scream echoes in my head as healing hands grab my body and a sedative energy begins flowing through my veins. Somewhere, I hear my mother's words: "You're free, Kailey. Rest." Comfort.

# Chapter 21

## Transposition

"Beautiful again," I hear from a soft voice next to me as someone strokes my hair.

"Mom." I say as my eyes open slowly. Jenna is sitting next to me with her legs crossed and her chin resting on her left hand. "Oh."

"Good morning," she whispers to me.

Kioto stands on her hind legs, then lays her front paws on my chest—my chest that is now closed and fully healed. She begins licking my mouth, cheeks and eyes as I feel near my ear for blood. Next to me lies the sketch of Elivon's cement mixer.

"What happened? Where am I? Good morning? Why do I always pass out for so long?" I ask, avoiding Kioto's tongue as I speak. As my body pulls up in a small cot, I take a full three-sixty view of the small room in which we are sitting. The cot, one small table, and a large oil painting of Flora's—no doubt—are the only items in the room. I hear loud noises beyond the sand walls. Looking down at the sketch I run my finger over the blood stains.

"You use a lot of energy in your daily life, Kailey. Everything's okay now. We are in Golden Dunes, deep in the tunnels—Elivon's storage area, precisely. This is a resting room for staff." I then recognize the sound of the giant tumbler spinning on its axis. The genuine and loving smile Jenna gives me as she examines my aura bring instant joy to my heart, knowing my monster has been exorcised. It warms me up knowing that I am me, and only me, once again. I can't help but wail in my pillow, something I haven't done in a year, and something that feels utterly right and oh-so-wonderful.

"Kailey! What's wrong?"

I look at Jenna's little face and say, "I'm fine," and begin wiping my tears. "It's just that…I forgot how much I *truly* loved you, and how deep you're rooted in my heart."

Her little arms wrap around my chest for a brief hug before she then asks, "Can you get up? Come see everyone!" She bounds off the cot and waits for me by the door. I follow, and as we walk through a few tunnels, I hear many voices and feel many strange energies ahead of us, and then slow my speed as my anxiety heightens. "It's totally okay. Keep following me."

I look behind us for tunnel creatures, and not feeling or hearing anything slurp-ey, continue to follow Jenna right into the large, nitrogen tank-lined room. Once inside, all of the Golden Dunes inhabitants seated at the tables stand up in ovation and clap loudly, even cheering a bit. Overwhelmed by the motion, I blush and meet eyes with Ladimer, who is standing against a wall, and whose smile instantly heats up my insides. Another figure begins moving toward me and as I look beyond the people of Golden Dunes, I see it is Gurgl. He stops before me, and as we look into each other's eyes, he suddenly does his best bow while grabbing my hand and kissing it.

"Umm, thanks," I say.

Terro then steps forward, walking up to Gurgl and patting him on the shoulder. "Gurgl here wanted to do that for so long." He and Gurgl exchange brotherly smiles. "He thanks you from the bottom of his heart. He can't tell you, because, well, thanks to my mother, he was born without a tongue." Gurgl's embarrassment shows on his face, so I bend down near him and give him the tightest hug possible, and then throw in a kiss on the cheek for good measure. The immediate response of his vibrating energy says that I made his day. Basking in the glory of his energy and feeling generous—and wanting to make his year instead—I turn my body slightly, grab his hand, and let him pinch my rear end. A rumbling noise comes from his throat as he turns and walks briskly back to his table, his friends patting him on the back.

I hand the sketch to Terro and ask, "What's with the blood?"

"That's Flora's," he answers, sadly. After a moment he pulls himself together and brightens up, smiling. "She didn't know what she was doing with some connections and cut herself good on wire clippers. She was like that: always wanting to help, no matter what it entailed. She lived to satisfy people."

It's then Bu's turn to rush at me, hugging me as his excitement churns around him. "Kailey! Kailey! Bu is gonna stay and work on the machinery!"

Apologizing to Terro with my eyes, I then say to Bu, "Oh. Really?" Bu recognizes my sadness and suddenly frowns. "Oh, ignore me, Bu. That is absolutely fabulous!" I try to seem excited for him.

"Just until Terro finds a good enough energy source to spark the tumbler into overdrive." I look to the canisters of liquid nitrogen as he then replies, "The nitrogen is needed for the cement. It's not worth wasting for the spark, no matter how big it may be."

Terro nods in agreement, looking a bit baffled at the predicament as the rest of my friends enter the room, looking exhausted, but relieved. I notice, however, that Conner won't meet eyes with me. Sir Cuche and Hoolie Hal are quietly chatting respectfully toward each other.

"We'll figure it out, soon, I hope," Terro says. "Kailey, I do owe you the biggest apology. We knew things might get dangerous, but did not expect deaths to come of it. Really." His eyes well up as thoughts of his family surface an emotion so full of sadness it pains me.

"Terro, I'm so sorry you have lost all your family: your mom, Elivon…Flora. I know Flora was practically your other half, for your energies were so similar. Your own mother didn't know—"

"My own mother. . ."

"It is I who needs to apologize," I say.

He then interrupts me with his hand. "Elivon, Flora, and I have been working on our tumbler and pills for the past two years, and when we finally thought it best for Flora to stop feeding the fields, we had to fake her disappearance and begin trading places. We started this hellish plan, and for the sake of the health of all those here and elsewhere, we had to keep going. I had no idea that my mom would call on you all." His teeth suddenly shine at me. "I do have to say, however, that I was most excited when I found out—you know, being a fan and all," he says as I feel his sweet, caramel energy moving toward me. Suddenly its journey stops.

"What?" I ask, noticing his mood change.

"The whole black snake, scary thing. What was that? It's like you…like you had two of you inside you this whole time: one the Kailey I've heard such heroic stories about, and one a very dark and sinister being." I stand perfectly still and silent as I slowly look to Gunthreon. "If you can't tell me, that's fine. It's gone, isn't it? Oh, and that guy who ate…" A sensation of disgust begins swirling around his body.

Images of the day I became cursed with sudo-abominor begin reeling through my head as I remember how quickly the evil force passed from my father's body into my own as he died. My eyes widen. "Oh my god, Gunthreon. Is *it* gone?"

Disappointed-like, he shakes his head and looks to Ladimer, who answers, "We don't know. Jenna here doesn't see it, but well, some of Madam Eve's snakes slithered off. Stephen took off as well. There was no stopping him, without losing a finger or two—or an arm perhaps."

"Ech," mumbles Lupa as she shakes her head, trying to shake the image in her mind as she hugs Gunthreon. As he hugs her back, a spark between them grabs my attention as I feel it grow, and grow, as does the most wonderful idea.

The giant tumbler still rolls, but begins slowing down, and with a downtrodden look from Terro, I know my idea is worth a try. "Everyone, grab hands. *NOW!*" As everyone mumbles and looks to one another, I suddenly yell. "Just do it! Gunthreon and Lupa, you two stay in contact. Conner!" He looks up at me as I wave him over. "Hold my hand," I say, extending my hand to him. His hand rises, reluctantly, and I quickly grab his, waiting for our usual spark, when nothing happens.

His eyes, devoid of emotion, say everything as he drops his hand. "You let him eat her," he sputters quietly.

"I had to!"

"You saw—knew—I was free," he remarks, louder in soulspeak.

"I had to," I say with less emotion. Ladimer approaches and in knowing I must continue with my idea, here and now, I extend my hand to him, instead. His hand is warm and as we touch, I feel it—the exact thing I need. Closing my eyes and ignoring the conflict with Conner, I let Ladimer's touch guide me into the emotional territory needed to make this work. With everyone grabbing onto one another, and focusing on the energy of each and every soul with me, I reach out to Neda.

Far and wide I travel, and as I approach the field of fruitful trees, I know the energy as it waits for me. Breathing deeply, I grab it with all my strength and bring it forth as navi continues to stream from Gunthreon to Lupa to Jenna, Bu and on and on. As our energies begin burning brightly and I see everyone's astounded faces at the sensations traveling around and through them, my feeler rounds up the resultant energy, bundles it up and throws it with one toss toward the tumbler. Sparks bursting from the room, we all hear the sound of rolling speeding up. Bu breaks from the circle and runs toward it, Terro on his heels.

"*Yes!*" Terro yells as I also break free and move quick enough to see him high-five Bu, who doesn't realize his own strength as Terro yelps and grabs his own hand, shaking it as the stinging dissipates. He's smiling ear to ear as he leaves Bu and walks over to me quickly, hugging me, then sneaking in his own ass pinch. Jumping, but returning his smile, I shake my finger at him.

Bu continues to examine the machine and its many gauges as he reads some sort of meter then looks up toward the ventilation system which is shaking form something unseen. I see the gears working inside his head as Terro walks toward him. "The wind outside is strong," Bu states.

"Must be the vortexes. It's the season for the strong winds," Terro answers.

"Harness it," Bu comments as Terro's eyes widen, the gears in his own head churning to match Bu's rhythm. "Kailey, maybe you could give us a boost with the sand?" I nod.

Terro suddenly slaps Bu on the back as our friends join us. "You are pure genius, Bu. You know…with Elivon gone, we are minus one science teacher."

Bu's head quickly turns toward Gunthreon, and without even thinking, he nods toward Bu. Excitedly, Bu picks both me and Terro up, squeezing us fiercely. Terro imitates Lupa's "ech," as he inhales Bu's delightful stench as his face smooshes against Bu's chest. I laugh wholeheartedly as I lean into Bu, eating up his glorious excitement.

# Chapter 22

## Farewell

After numerous goodbyes to the many Golden Dunes inhabitants, we pack up our belongings and stand outside the dune, watching a handful of vortexes across the dunes as they whip and whirl a bit more from an extra blast of energy I send out across the sand. Bu hugs me long and hard as he says quietly to me, "Bu love Kailey so much. Even when you were the ugly monster," navi lingering between us.

"And I love you, too. I'll come visit you when I can. Okay?" Show them all your brilliance, Bu." He nods, then turns toward Gunthreon, a great sadness wrapping around his heart.

"I'll be sure to check on you, also. Don't think you're escaping my watchful eye," Gunthreon says as he gets the goodbye squeeze from Bu.

Bu then trounces away hurriedly toward the school as Hoolie Hal and Sir Cuche (who is actually out of his robes and is now wearing a pair of shorts and a white tee-shirt) make their way over to me. "Well, I think this is where we also say our goodbye for now," whimpers Sir Cuche as his energy wavers to match his voice. Clearing his throat, he then adds, "I've—we've—decided to do some traveling through Renhala and maybe look for some more grumblepigs to adopt." Instantly Conner's eyebrow rises as he looks to Hoolie Hal.

"*It was all his idea*!" yells Hoolie Hal as he points to Sir Cuche.

I help by adding, "We believe you, Hoolie Hal, for I know that Sir Cuche may have ulterior motives?"

"We'll let karma decide whether it leads me to her," he says to me, knowing that I know his love for his wife will never die. I hug them each goodbye and then watch as they both walk away, each helping the other from falling down as they drag their feet through the sand. Sir Cuche suddenly stops yards ahead, turns, and yells, "*You will find the rest of your payment in Abscondia*!" They then turn and continue into the distance.

Gunthreon and Lupa stand, holding each other's hand and then tightly grab me, enveloping me in their loving energy. "You guys are amazing," I say, looking into their faces. "You stood with me that whole time, even when I—" My voice shakes at the memories. "I was a nightmare, and you could have walked away, but you didn't."

"Your mother left a legacy inside you that couldn't—can't—be ignored, no matter how bleak the future may look. Kailey, you will always be magnificent, and one doesn't have to be an energy reader to see it. I will forever be here for you," Gunthreon confides, still holding Lupa's hand. Whispering for my ears only, he says, "Thanks for the learning experience." Then, a bit louder for Lupa's ears, he chortles, shaking her hand in his, "I gotta show this little woman what I really got."

Lupa, smiling, but wiping away tears, says, "Tomorrow at Gunthreon's I'm fixing cherry chicken and rhubarb-jellied biscuits. You gonna come?"

"I'll bring the tea," I respond. Then, in a blink of an eye, they travel back to Abscondia.

Ladimer and Jenna still stand a bit away, petting Kioto, as Conner trudges over to me.

"I wish things hadn't happened like this," he admits, again not meeting my eyes, his energy flip-flopping between heartbreak and anger.

"Me too."

"I'm assuming that you'll travel back with them," he hisses, looking toward Jenna and Ladimer. An intense flash of pain appears and disappears as he looks, specifically, at Ladimer.

"We can all go—" I start, but he immediately shakes his head.

"No, I want to stay civil."

I bring my hand to his. "Please know that I am forever grateful for what you've done for me this past year. It was so hard with…my mom gone and all. Please don't shut me out after what has happened, please. I still need you."

"You need me," he says, a brief laugh escaping his perfect lips as his hand separates from mine. "Have *I* no needs?"

"Of course you do. It's just that—"

He shakes his head again as he speaks in that beautiful language that is soulspeak. "Two magnets that are drawn to each other can also deflect, given a situation where one turns its back."

"Conner…" I begin in an effort to rid this situation of angst, but end abruptly.

"Please. Let's not fool ourselves into thinking that there is no certain tension between us now. We will walk our separate ways and if our paths cross again, sobeit. Karma's got us all on a leash anyway," he remarks a bit too sarcastically. "I've done what I can for you. I just feel that…well, you're capable of something entirely more, but without me. I'm not one to play childish games."

"What does *that* mean?"

"Take it how you must," he says. We share a moment looking into each other's eyes, and just at the moment I think he may take it all back, he gives me a brief, awkward hug, then is gone. I shiver at the odd feeling of his energy as it slowly blends with the air around me.

Confused from the sudden anomaly that is Conner, and feeling extremely worn out from his problems with me, I turn to Jenna and Ladimer.

Ladimer puts out his arms for me and I fall into them, wanting to hide myself away for the next year. "Let's get you home," he coos softly in my ear. "You need some relaxation and 'you' time.

# Chapter 23

## Satisfaction

"Wow! What a ride," Jenna hoots while jumping on my couch then playing keep away with a rubber ring toy of Kioto's. Kioto eventually just huffs after Jenna doesn't give it up and then walks about the apartment, hunting for a treat she hid last time we were home.

Ladimer walks into my kitchen and puts a kettle on the stovetop, then pulls out a few cups, honey, and creamer. "Let's get something warm and comforting in you," he says, peeking around the corner with a sly smirk on his face.

I blush and suddenly Jenna is standing at my feet, staring at me. The smile she gives me makes me swat at her, but she's quick. "Well, you two have some 'talking' to do, I'm sure, so I'm gonna go visit Evan at work. Maybe you can show up later…if you have time." I nod and she yells to the kitchen, "Bye, Lad!"

"Bye, pipsqueak," he hollers back.

"Kailey, make sure you rest, please? You need it. I can see an abrupt stop to your aura, up here," she says, pointing above her head. "It's in defense, shielding you. You need *sleep.*"

"Ok, Mom." We both smile at the word and she then disappears out the door.

As I walk to the kitchen to help Ladimer, I notice an envelope on the dining room table with my name written on it. "What's this?" I ask, a bit afraid of opening the envelope which has something of considerable weight in it. With curiosity winning, I peek inside while Ladimer watches over my shoulder. Then, ripping it open, I pull out a note and read:

*Forever indebted to you, for you've showed me what money cannot buy.*

*Forever thankful to you, for you gave a small bit of yourself to help a lost soul.*
*Forever out of the silly robes, and*
*Forever your friend, Sir Cuche*
*P.S. Please take care of the house, for it's now yours, but with one stipulation: YOU have the parlor wall fixed.*

I then empty out the envelope and watch as a single key and a giant ruby fall out. "Oh. My. God," I whisper, picking up the faceted ruby and holding it up, allowing it to glisten from a touch of sunlight.

Ladimer holds out his hand in front of me as he stands closely behind me. I feel his energy and in my best attempt to ignore the arousal I'm feeling, and the bit of excitement I'm feeling about owning a house and a giant ruby, I try to empty the ruby into his hand without touching him. Unfortunately, he grabs my hand instead of the ruby, and as an enormous amount of a giver's energy suddenly flows over me, I cannot help but turn to him and look into his totally-engulfing eyes. I swallow, and feeling a heat similar to a riled sudo-abominor, but entirely passion-induced, I say, shakily, "Ladimer, I don't care about each of our histories. Both you and I owe nobody. Don't deny me and I won't deny you. All I can say is that we're both fucked up—maybe me moreso than you, however."

With a laugh, and as his hand pulls the hair away from my face, he graces my skin with an energy full of lustful wants and needs. "You let your brother eat someone and I watched with an unhealthy eagerness." His smile grows bigger as he then adds, "But that doesn't mean we can't be healthily happy with each other." He lessens the small amount of space between us as I lick my lips. "I want this, and I'm willing to give it a chance. You want it too. I know this," he confesses, running his hand around my back, pulling me in closer. "No more denial," he whispers and then closes the gap while bringing his lips to mine. Kissing him back as his fingers touch my skin, a new sensation brightens my senses, coursing through me and directly onto him. Melding our energies as we continue to exchange the kiss, the renewal between us exhausts any inhibitions as I eagerly undress him and he does the same to me.

Standing fully naked before him, his hands and fingers travel everywhere over my body, with each touch sending a vibration worthy of fainting over through my entirety. I embrace the emotion and as my love for him—as well as the abilities he possesses—forces me to react with a healthy aggression, I pull him into me as we move to the floor and revel in the navi between us. His kisses travel down my neck and over my stomach until I feel I may die here and now, forever satisfied from a lover's touch.

As the journey between us continues and his energy flows through my blood, an expression of pure relief passes his face as though a chain which had been binding him was cut, allowing him to sample that which he had been forever watching and longing to experience. Lying next to him, and feeling both a happiness and a bit of sadness over what we've been through, I cannot help but whisper in his ear, "No more chains."

"Oh, I wouldn't say *that*…" he plays, suddenly exhibiting the smirk that I've learned to be wary of, but now entirely loving as he pulls my arms above my head.

With a newfound playful energy between the two of us, and a fun game of keep away, the next hours are spent taking time away for us, nobody else. After an especially fun romp between us, Ladimer pulls something out of his pants pocket and hides it between his hands. "Well, it's not a *house*, but it's something I still hope you love. I got this for you," he remarks, placing a gorgeous copper cuff into my hands, one very similar to those he was admiring in the Golden Dunes marketplace.

I wrap it around my wrist and admire the workmanship as I run my fingers off its precious stones and small clumps of hardened sand held in place by extensions of copper. There is also one petrified hartflower riveted dead-center. "I love it," I say, hugging him tightly.

As night approaches, and after a totally satisfying cup of tea, my apartment doorbell suddenly buzzes, surprising us both. I move to the doorbell and speak through the speaker: "Who's there?" laughing as Ladimer steals my ruby, putting it in his pocket and holding Kioto's rubber ring toy above his head like a halo. Nobody answers from below, so I open my door to check downstairs and find my neighbor, Karen, who is totally reeking of alcohol, passed out in the hallway. I shake her a bit trying to wake her, but she just moans and then tries hugging me.

Ladimer approaches from behind and begins laughing quietly as he moves to stand over her, then suggests that maybe he should change back into the small boy she once fostered. Shaking my head at him, he refrains, but instead raises his hand to touch her. Once his hand comes in contact with her forehead she turns purple. "How about this, instead?"

"Damn, Ladimer!" I giggle and slap him on the arm as we then both wander downstairs to answer the door. Seeing nobody standing outside it, I begin turning the doorknob, suddenly feeling very suspicious of the energy outside the door. I contemplate the feel of it, knowing it's just a trace and that whom it belongs to is not going to be found on my doorstep. I swing the door open as Ladimer comes up beside me. As I stand, staring at the small being sitting on the stoop before me, I shake my head. "No..."

Ladimer bends down and puts his arms out to the small girl, who smiles and falls into his embrace. After a small touch to her skin, he comments, "Kailey, your family is growing by the day."

"*Aw, hell no!*"

"Sorry, but hell yes. Say hello to yet another sibling," he says, taking a piece of paper out of the small child's hands, opening it, then handing it to me.

Inside are only four words written in Amber's handwriting:

HER NAME IS DENA

"She named her after my *mother*?! How could she even think about disgracing… I can't do this. *What the hell? Why? Where is she?*" I jabber, sending out my feeler but finding nothing except my own confusion.

"Let's hope *she* doesn't like flesh," he says, playing peek-a-boo with the child.

I stand still, staring at the beautiful head of blonde hair and the fair skin similar to my father's. Entirely flabbergasted, I can only grunt: "Karma is *such* a bitch."

# Acknowledgements

Oh the feels… I don't even know how to begin thanking those lovely souls who have supported me throughout this journey. With every step I took, some beautiful shining light was always guiding me; I was never alone (excuse me while I wipe some tears).

Big thanks to my bodacious beta readers: Lolita Verroen, Lori Parker, Jennifer Hayes, Kari Trotsky, Anthony Mryc, Bethanne Wilson, and Lynne Paul. Your feedback and encouragement kept me on track and inspired me to be my best!

Cover designers Claudia @ Phatpuppy Art and Ashley @ The Bookish Brunette also deserve props. Without them, that awesome cover would never have been born and I would have been stuck with a lame-o cheesy snake instead of the bad-ass snake you see now.

Hugs to my editors, Elizabeth DelPo and Jerry Eberle. You guys rock in red-inking those damn pesky dangling modifiers.

Thanks to all the readers turned fans. Your words of love for my current books and encouragement for future books really sums up why I keep writing. Yes I love writing—it makes my heart happy—but when someone else appreciates your work and makes the effort to let you know how they feel, well, it makes all those hours, days, weeks, months of an introvert's life worth it.

Hugs to you all…

www.ingramcontent.com/pod-product-compliance
Lightning Source LLC
Chambersburg PA
CBHW030619310726
48979CB00003B/789

*9780988281554*